*The Tig*

# The Tiger Roars

**KENNETH ANDERSON**

Rupa & Co

This reprint in Rupa Paperback 2001
Third impression 2007

Published by
*Rupa . Co*
7/16, Ansari Road, Daryaganj,
New Delhi 110 002

*Sales Centres:*

Allahabad Bangalooru Chandigarh
Chennai Hyderabad Jaipur Kathmandu
Kolkata Mumbai Pune

ISBN 81-7167-468-2

Typeset Copyright © Rupa & Co. 2001

Typeset in ClassicalGaramond by
Nikita Overseas Pvt Ltd,
1410 Chiranjiv Tower,
43 Nehru Place,
New Delhi 110 019

Printed in India by
Gopsons Papers Ltd.
A-14 Sector 60
Noida 201 301

# Contents

Introduction                                              *vii*

The Novice of Manchi ✓                                      1

The Lame Horror of Peddacheruvu ✓                          42

The Queer Side of Things ✓                                 84

The Dumb Man-Eater of Talavadi ✓                          129

The Killer of the Wynaad ✓                                172

The Man-Hater of Talainovu ✓                              202

Sher Khan and the Bettamugalam Man-Eater ✓                236

# Contents

# *Introduction*

PREFACES ARE NOT POPULAR AND ARE SELDOM READ. AFTER ALL, A reader buys a book for what he can get out of it by way of entertainment, excitement or knowledge, as the case may be, and no explanation by the author will increase or diminish these. But before I embark on a few more tales of my adventures in the jungles of southern India, I merely wish to make a plea for their preservation, that their wild life and their beauty may survive, not only for their own sake, but that future generations may enjoy them as I have done. Time is already short.

It is the duty of the government of India, of every government in every state of India, of every sportsman who visits her forests—indeed, it is the duty of every Indian—to make a supreme effort to save the country's wild creatures from extinction.

Game and bird sanctuaries have been formed, it is true. But this is not nearly enough. Rules are printed that cannot be enforced. For one thing, the forest guards and watches are not paid enough. For another, corruption is rife.

INTRODUCTION

In the state of Mysore as a whole, and also in the district of Salem belonging to Madras state, tigers and panthers are now almost extinct, wiped out by the villagers who use a poison supplied to them almost free of charge by the local governments as an insecticide to protect their crops. This poison they smear on the flesh of the kills made by tigers and panthers. These animals invariably return, eat the doctored meat and die within a few yards. So do the jackals, hyaenas, vultures and crows that follow them.

Deer continue to be slaughtered in hundreds every summer by the poachers who wait for them with muskets over the water holes to which they must come to drink. A few rupees, or a piece of the carcase here and there, silence the officials who are paid by the governments to protect the lives of these animals.

So death stalks the wild creatures of India. Extinction, particularly in South India, will surely and certainly follow unless the governments of the various states and the people themselves wake up to the fact very soon and become realistic. It is almost too late already.

I hope that you will enjoy reading these stories a fraction as much as I have enjoyed writing them, for in doing so I have been carried back to the forest life—not only to memories of bygone days but to its enchanting sights, its myriad exotic smells, its medley of sounds, its joys and its sorrows, the exuberance of life there and its tragedy.

# One

## *The Novice of Manchi*

THE NARROW TRAIL WOUND IN AND OUT BETWEEN CLUMPS OF GIANT bamboo that rose on every side, the tall graceful fronds arching like huge bouquets of elegant, feathery blooms. It was the time when the bamboo tree was seeding, when each length of cane was crowded at its tip with tufts consisting of thousands of tiny seeds. These seeds look like ripe grains of wheat but are smaller; yet the weight of thousands of them was enough to bend each frond low to the earth, creaking and groaning under its burden as it moved with the gentle breezes passing along the jungle aisles.

The seeds fell in showers, carpeting the earth and the narrow *path* with a thick layer that mostly decayed, but here and there showed signs of sprouting into tiny darkgreen seedlings. This carpet felt like sawdust and had a springy consistency: it deadened the sound of anything moving over it, and of the killer that now stalked from bamboo clump to

1

bamboo clump in search of a meal. Overhead, thousands of parakeets screeched as they hung by their feet, head downwards above the twisting trail, pecking the seeds with their razor-sharp curved beaks, deftly severing the husk from the kernel, which they crushed to a fine powder before swallowing. They were small compared with other members of the parrot family, being about twice the size of the domesticated budgerigar, but they were of many hues, ranging from emerald green to peacock blue, some with pale yellow wing-feathers and heads of rose pink or deep purple, and others of a uniform green, ringed around the neck with a narrow collar of red and black.

A lone traveller, walking cautiously along the jungle trail, did not heed the parakeets nor the thousands of other birds, including wild pigeons and doves, that fed on the seeds of the bamboos. He gazed intently ahead and glanced furtively to either side, slowing down and even halting now and then to study a particularly dense clump of bamboo before drawing level with it. His sharp, restless eyes tried to penetrate the thick growth to see if anything was hidden there. His ears, too, were alert for sounds far different from and far more arresting than the raucous, strident screech of the parakeets. The sounds he was listening for, and dreading to hear, were the sharp crack of a bamboo branch being broken, or the deep rumble of contented feeding, or the swishing sweep of ponderous feet brushing through the carpet of seeds and decaying leaves.

The man was afraid of meeting a wild elephant or a herd of them, for there were many in this area, especially at this time of the year. But his hearing was not attuned to the approach of the killer, who first sensed and then saw him. The killer made no sound whatever, unlike the screaming, fluttering birds above or the ponderous elephants beneath, engrossed in their search for vegetable food. This killer was by no means harmless, nor was he a vegetarian. He dealt death swiftly and surely and he was at this moment very hungry indeed.

The man was a poojaree, a member of an aboriginal jungle tribe that inhabits the forests of the Salem district in southern India, and the trail he was following was the footpath that led through the forest from the hamlet of Aiyur, southwards for about ten miles to the still smaller hamlet of Manchi, nestling on the slopes of a great range of hills. The *path* ran down a valley, as also did a rocky stream, the two crossing and recrossing frequently, and sometimes running parallel to each other, while the hills towered on both sides, to east and west, in an unbroken chain of jungle. The narrow *path* was visible now and again, but disappeared as suddenly beneath the tall, bending, swaying bamboos as they moved to the gentle currents of the forest breeze.

Fine webs, almost invisible, frequently caught and tickled the face of the poojaree whose attention was wholly concentrated on the possible presence of the elephants. He brushed them off angrily with both hands, much to the annoyance of the large, long-legged, yellow-and-black-and-red spiders, six inches and more across, whose webs extended from tree to tree, secured by gossamer-like threads that were unbelievably strong, supporting a central area of a web eight or ten feet in diameter and of an intricate, finely-woven pattern. The dew had condensed on these webs and drops of moisture glistened in the sunlight that filtered through the bamboo fronds. All was still, all was peaceful, except for the din of the feeding birds.

Keera, the poojaree, passed a dense clump of bamboo after making certain no elephant sheltered behind, but failed to see the killer in its black and rusty coat that crouched low to the earth and stared at him with malevolent, unblinking eyes.

3

The man heard a coughing roar twice: 'Aa-arrgh! Aa-arrgh!' Then the tiger charged.

Keera whirled around as a great shape with widely-extended jaws engulfed him. The poojaree screamed but once: 'Aiyoooo-oo-oo!' He screamed no more. The birds that had ceased chattering for the moment, when the tragedy was enacted, started to screech again and from the side of the pathway came the crunch and crack of bones as the tiger began his meal.

Away on the hillside a troop of langur-monkeys had been feeding joyously, their cries of 'Whoomp! Whoomp, Whoomp!' echoing across the narrow valley. Then the sharp hearing of the langur-watchman caught the distant sound of the tiger's roars and the fainter, futile, agonized human scream. He knew that the tiger had made his kill and the hoarse, guttural, langur alarm-cry issued from his lips as he stood on his hind legs high up on a branch to discover if possible in which direction the killer was moving.

'Ha-aah! Harr! Harr!' called the watchman, over and over again. The langurs ceased playing and scampered in terror, to huddle in families on the tree-tops; while the deer and other creatures on the floor of the jungle, whose sharp ears had detected the sounds of death and the alarm of the monkeys, raced uphill and away from that valley of doom.

Time passed, and the life of the forest resumed its normal course. The birds forgot the tragedy in a matter of seconds; the monkeys and the other animals took perhaps an hour to calm down; while the poojarees in the distant hamlet of Manchi would undoubtedly have forgotten the death of their clansman Keera in a month or two had not another of them been killed a fortnight later; and, ten days after that, a third.

These things the poojarees could not forget. A dreadful fear overshadowed them. A scourge lay upon their tiny village; a man-eater had come to stay!

4

These people belong to a tribe that lives on the produce of the forest. They gather wild honey from giant combs built on high rocks and trees; they catch the iguana-lizard which they eat or sell for the aphrodisiac properties said to exist in its tail; they pick medicinal herbs and roots and berries which are traded as medicine; and they cut and collect bamboos, grass and the pods of the tamarind fruit, according to the season of the year. All for a pittance, less than an ordinary person living in Europe or America would spend on feeding his pet dog. Their work, their very existence depends upon the forest, and into that jungle a fearful menace had now come. No man who left his miserable grass hut in the morning knew whether he would return that night. No woman or child was safe; for the second and third victims had been, respectively, a young girl of nine years and a pregnant bride of fourteen!

None of them did anything about it except one man, and that was my old friend and instructor in jungle-lore, Byra the *poojaree*. Once before had he summoned me, in the case of the 'Marauder of Kempekarai,' about which I have written elsewhere,* and once again he asked me to come to the help of the people of Manchi.

This time Byra arrived in person rather than convey the message through another. He walked ten miles or more from Manchi to Aiyur village, and thence nine miles to Denkanikota town, whence a bus brought him to Bangalore.

From the story he told me it was clear that the three killings had taken place in comparatively quick succession, within a total of twenty-four days and all within a radius of four miles from Manchi, in the vicinity of the track leading from Aiyur to Kempekarai along the deep valley that I have

---

* See *Man-eaters and Jungle Killers*, Chapter 1.

elsewhere referred to as 'Spider Valley,' because of the large spiders to be found there.

These killings indicated that the perpetrator was a comparative novice so far as man-eaters go. Either he was a young animal that had, for some reason or the other, just launched out on a career of man-eating; or he was a wounded tiger that had been almost incapacitated and was desperately hungry; or perhaps a tigress, killing merely to feed her cubs. This third alternative was extremely unlikely, as there was still a fair amount of game on the surrounding hills, while cattle were plentiful around the villages of Aiyur, Gulhati and Bettamugalam.

The facts pointed more to his being a beginner. No experienced man-eater would have killed in such quick succession or almost in the same place, as had this tiger. Veterans are far too cunning to do that. They follow a circuitous beat of many miles, covering a large tract of land, and slay at sudden and infrequent intervals, all of which habits combine to make them extremely difficult to shoot.

The course for me to follow would be to strike quickly and bag this beast before he began to learn from experience and became more cautious and adept. That caution would come as soon as the villagers tried to retaliate by shooting him or by some other means. He would be frightened then; or perhaps he would be wounded. That would make him a wiser and far more dangerous antagonist.

I knew the terrain well. For many years I had tramped that dense bamboo jungle in the deep, narrow valley flanked by the two parallel ranges of towering hills, running north and south, closely bordering the banks of the narrow stream that also flowed southwards to merge finally into the Chinar river at a place called Sopathy. The eastern range was the loftier of the two, culminating in a high peak named Gutherayan, near

6

which was a picturesque forest bungalow known as the Kodekarai Forest Lodge. Kempekarai hamlet lay on the slopes of the other and western range, a short distance above the little stream. The locale was almost the same as in my earlier adventure, except

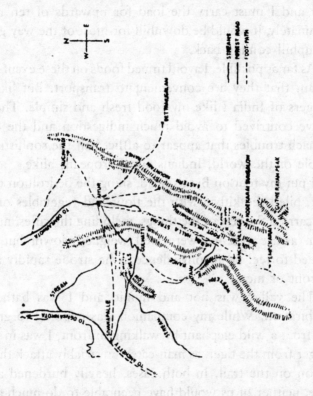

that the 'Marauder of Kempekarai' had been a more experienced man-eater, hunting in an area west and south of the little hamlet of that name. The present animal had so far confined his activities to the north of the settlement of Manchi and near to the Aiyur track, as I have just told you. For this reason he should be a comparatively easy proposition to bag.

Bundling Byra and my camp kit into the Studebaker, with food to last for about a week in the form of flour for *chappattis*, bread, butter, vegetables—especially potatoes—and of course tea, coffee and sugar, together with my little tent and bedroll, we set out for Denkanikota and Aiyur. From the latter place we would have to walk to Manchi and that would mean that Byra and I must carry the load for upwards of ten miles. Fortunately, it would be downhill for most of the way going, but uphill coming back.

As far as possible, I avoid tinned foods on these excursions. I grant that they are convenient to transport. But like the villagers of India I like my food fresh and simple. Thereby I have contrived to avoid much indigestion and the other stomach troubles that appear to afflict half the sophisticated people of the world, Indians and Europeans alike.

I put my tent on Byra's head, slung the bedroll on to my back, piled the kitbag with the flour and vegetables on his, and carried the rest of the things, including the rifles, myself. I can assure you we were well weighed down, but Byra seemed to feel no inconvenience as he strode rapidly along in front of me.

The valley was hot and humid and I was bathed in perspiration. While my companion was exposed to greater risk from a wild elephant by walking in front, I was in more danger from the tiger, as man-eaters invariably attack the last person on the trail. In both cases, heavily burdened as we were, neither of us would have been able to do much about it. But I don't think we thought about elephants or tigers, being more bent upon reaching the journey's end as quickly as possible and ridding ourselves of our abominable loads.

We arrived at last, and with a sigh of relief I threw down the things I was carrying (except the rifle) just beyond the little pool of drinking water that was to figure so prominently in this adventure. The first requirement was tea—gallons of it—and I asked Byra to fill the kettle from the pool and light a fire quickly. Very soon we were pouring scalding tea down our throats and life seemed to be rosy once more.

By this time some of Byra's friends from the hamlet had gathered around us. They were all poojarees—an underfed, skinny and scantily-clad group—but all as tough as nails. The men wore little *moochas* and nothing else; the women were bare-breasted, the rest covered by threadbare saris that hung in shreds and hid nothing; the children, both boys and girls, were completely naked.

There were the usual greetings, whereupon Byra launched into a prolonged account of how he had travelled to Bangalore to bring his *dorai*, who had immediately come to their help. There was a murmur of amazement and, being of a practical turn of mind, I took advantage of the situation to despatch some of the elder boys to gather firewood from the brambles growing around the pool, and one of the men to lay in a store of water in the aluminium carrier and the water-bottle I had brought with me. These mundane but essential matters attended to, I set about munching the roasted meat, jam and buttered bread brought from home, while I asked my companions to tell me all they knew about the tiger.

I acquired little information other than the bare facts that Byra had already recounted, but there was one new item. Byra had set forth for Bangalore the previous morning. In the early afternoon of the same day, as nobody would go near the pool later than three o'clock for fear of the man-eater, four of the women had gone for water together. They had kept close to one another, relying on their numbers for safety.

The women had finished the task and were turning away when the eldest noticed a slight movement under one of the bushes bordering the jungle some fifty yards away. She looked closer. Her companions, noticing her staring at something, had all looked the same way. On the ground under that bush

9

was the head of an enormous tiger. It was glaring at them hungrily and snarling! With screams they threw down their water-pots and bolted for the hamlet, less than 200 yards away. This time the tiger did not attack and they all got back in safety.

Two of those four women were among the group around me. One described the tiger's head as 'that big,' indicating a distance of a yard between outstretched hands. The other, who was a very matter-of-fact and comely young girl, and somewhat of a wit to boot, said it was big enough to eat all four of them and me as well. Her subtle smile after this statement was perhaps a hint that, after it was all over, I would at least be in good company inside the tiger's belly!

The news gladdened me and I noticed the gleam of satisfaction that sprang into Byra's eyes. Old hunter that he was, he knew that things would be easier for us now. If the tiger was there yesterday evening, as likely as not it would come again this evening. For all we knew, it might be watching us at that very moment.

This fresh development made me change my mind about pitching my tent near the pool. It would not fit into the plan that now came to my mind. To make camp within the hamlet itself was a far from attractive proposition, as the poojarees, who have many good attributes, do not count cleanliness among them. So I got some of the men to carry my things a little beyond the village, to where a wild jack-fruit tree was growing. Beneath its shade I pitched the small tent and put my belongings inside.

The plan that had come to me connected the tiger with the pool. Strange, indeed, that a situation of this nature should be twice destined to arise in waiting for a man-eater. In that earlier adventure at Kempekarai, just a few miles away but many years ago, I had waited all night long at a well for the 'marauder' to make an attempt to kill me. But I had waited in vain. Perhaps this tiger, which was certainly not such an experienced animal, would be more obliging and I was glad I had not made the mistake of pitching my tent, that was more or less white in colour, within sight of the pool. Whereas the 'marauder' of years ago might have been tempted to attack the occupant, this recruit among man-eaters would surely be frightened away. Or so I reasoned, and Byra agreed with me. Events that night were to prove both of us quite wrong.

At sunset I ate an early supper, finishing the last of the roast I had brought. This time I made no tea and drank hardly any water, for experience had taught me that imbibing liquids does not help when a nightlong vigil for a man-eater is contemplated. Nature cannot be diverted from her normal practices, and the slightest fidgeting or movement on the part of the hunter will betray his presence to the tiger when he comes.

The night would be dark, for which reason I did not follow quite the same plan as I had with the 'marauder.' That had been a moonlit night and I had deliberately advertised my presence at the well by working the squeaking pulley and pretending to draw water in order to attract the tiger. But this night would be totally dark and it would be foolish to show myself openly. He would hear and see me all right; the only trouble being that I certainly would not be able to see him, and might not be able to hear him either till it was too late!

So I decided to modify the scheme a little by sitting with my back against the *babul* tree some twenty feet from the water and facing the jungle. I would sit quite still and with no movement whatever. The man-eater could hardly attack from the rear. He would have to come from in front or from either side and sitting motionless would not only help me to hear him but it would puzzle him also. He might not notice me at all; or if he did, as a novice he would be perplexed at my immobility and decide to investigate. I hoped he would make some sound in the process.

When Byra heard my plan, he told me that it was a very stupid one. The tiger might attack without making any preliminary sound. He might come from behind. I would hear nothing and see nothing in that darkness; but the man-eater would certainly see me, while he (Byra) would never see me again. For that matter, the tiger might not come this way at all. Why should he be snooping around a pool of water at dead of night? The beast knew very well that people drew water from it—but during the hours of daylight and not at night.

While he was speaking, Byra looked at me significantly, and the meaning of his glance became quite apparent. He was trying to put me off.

'I know all that,' I interrupted testily, 'but it's the only way.'

The old fellow was bent upon complicating the situation.

'I never meant that you should not sit for the tiger.' he said aggressively. 'What I meant was that you should be beside me. We should await his return together.'

'Idiot,' I interrupted, being as rude as I could, 'you have not the brains of a flea! In what way will your presence lessen the darkness? Keep out of this and let me try the plan I have in mind, at least for tonight. Tomorrow you may tell me a better one if you can think of one.'

'If you are here to listen,' he concluded pointedly.

And so, an hour before sunset, I took up my position near the little pool, my back to the *babul* tree and facing the jungle, the small stream beyond and the pathway along which we had come that morning. Inwardly, I hoped that the tiger would arrive early and see me and that in turn he would show himself as he had to the four girls, so that the episode might be closed before darkness fell. Unfortunately, the man-eater did not oblige.

The poojarees in the hamlet drew great clumps of thorns, which they had cut earlier, around the low entrances to their wattle huts, stepped gingerly between them and slipped inside. I could hear the thatched doors of the huts being barricaded from within with large stones, gathered from the stream for the purpose. These people believed in self-help, and it was evident they did not have much confidence in my ability to save them from the killer that now threatened their lives.

The sun had sunk behind the range of hills to the west, outlining their heights against a background of blue, which turned to pink and then to orange. As I was facing northeast, I could just catch brief glimpses of the beauties of this sunset. The orange deepened to blood-red, and then to crimson, green and yellow and violet and purple. An instant later it was quite dark.

While I had been watching the sunset abstractly, I had been listening to the sounds of the jungle which at all times are pleasant music to my ears, particularly at the close of the day and again at dawn. Two families of langur-monkeys, one on each of the slopes of the opposing ranges of hills, called to each other across the narrow, deep valley. 'Whoomp! Whoomp! Whoomp!' cried the males of one batch as they leapt from branch to branch, and back came the joyous notes from the other group on the hill slopes across the stream: 'Whoomp! Whoomp! Whoomp!' and 'Cheek! Cheek!' from the females and young.

Then the sounds of pleasure suddenly turned to those of fear and danger as the monkey-watchman of the more distant clan issued his staccato barking alarm cry: 'Ha-aah! Harr! Harr!' which he continued to repeat at short intervals.

13

The group nearer to me and on the same side of the valley fell silent, while their watchman in turn took up the note of warning, answering the more distant calls of his colleague: 'Haaah! Harr! Harr!' The two monkey sentinels kept answering one another and my nerves tingled pleasantly in expectation.

To one accustomed to such sounds there was a wealth of difference in the timbre of the calls. The voice of the distant watchman was filled with great fear and apprehension, and it was evident that he could see the source of danger. The watchman on this side of the valley, although sounding the alarm also, was merely doing his duty to alert his tribe. His notes were flat and matter of fact. This could be detected by the fact that he called each time immediately after the other watchman, like an echo.

The calls of the two monkeys were becoming less frequent when a junglecock, somewhere on the stream, screamed suddenly in fright: 'Kuck! Kuck! Kuck!' The hen with him, hearing the cries of fright made by her mate, flew quickly away crying: 'Krr-r-r-r! Keek! Keek! Keek!' Silence and a great stillness enveloped the jungle. Then a peacock gave sign of nervousness; 'Quank! Quank! Quank!' His metallic notes broke the stillness and a moment later I could hear the distant heavy flapping of wings as he launched his weighty body into the air to reach a place of greater safety.

I knew the tiger was afoot! He had descended the opposite range of hills and been discovered by the distant langur-watchman. He had crossed the stream and disturbed the jungle fowls and the peacock. He was now coming straight towards the pool and the spot where I was seated.

It was growing darker with the passing of each minute. Would the keen eyes of the nearer langur-watchman detect him? Although the monkey had the advantage of elevation, he was comparatively far away, and no tiger—not even a beginner among man-eaters—will betray his presence unnecessarily. My doubt was settled the next instant when the watchman on the hillside to my left broke forth hysterically, fearfully: 'Ha-aah! Harr! Harr!' His cries were quick now, and independent of his distant colleague, who was still calling, but at long intervals. The note of fear was there this time— of danger and sudden death. He had seen the man-eater. And it was much closer to me than I had thought.

But of the tiger itself I could see or hear nothing. It was growing darker all the time. The bushes at the edge of the jungle before me had lost their individual outlines. They appeared as grey masses against a background of deep chocolate, turning rapidly black. A frightened hush fell over the forest, permeating it, enveloping it. The further langur-watchman had stopped calling altogether, and the nearer one barked only intermittently. He could see the tiger no longer and, having fulfilled his duty by alarming his tribe, was wondering what next to do about it.

The summits of the ranges of hills to my right and left showed themselves as ragged lines of intense blackness against a background of lesser darkness, studded by myriads of stars, flashing and blazing in a distant glory all their own. I concentrated upon one of them. It seemed to change its colours constantly, like a heavenly gem.

While staring into the blackness before me I glanced alternatively from right to left. I slowed my breathing, even tried to hold my breath altogether, in an effort to hear the very faintest of sounds. But I saw and heard nothing.

Then, with nerve-shattering abruptness, a sambar belled in the thickets just the other side of the pool: 'Dhank! Oonk! Oonk!'

The brambles crackled to his departure as he crashed his way through. The sounds of his running were lost in a few seconds, but he continued to call with alarm as he rattled over the pebbles in the stream and scrambled up the slopes of the opposing range of hills, 'Oonk! Oonk! Oonk!' came his cries as they grew fainter with the ever-increasing distance.

Grateful, indeed, was I for the warnings of my jungle friends, for they told me as unmistakably as if I had seen him with my own eyes that the tiger was within a few yards of where I was sitting. The questions were: Had he seen me? Would he see me?

I know the value of stillness in the jungle, and so I sat absolutely motionless, hardly daring to breathe. That was my only hope of escaping the tiger's immediate attention.

The seconds ticked interminably by. They appeared to pass into minutes and then into hours, though I knew that they were only seconds. Then I heard a gentle rustle to my right: the faintest of sounds, as of a leaf being turned over, and it came from a direction in line with the pool. Not a breath of air passed which could have caused that dry leaf to be moved and I knew that the author of the sound was moving through the undergrowth, hidden from my sight, and passing the pool at that moment, and that in a few moments more he would have passed behind me.

Holding my breath I listened intently, but I heard no further sound. Every instinct warned me that the tiger had now passed and was somewhere behind the bushes on the other side of the *babul* tree against which I was leaning. I was filled with an urge to turn around and face the danger, but I knew that if I did so I would certainly make some faint noise. However slight it might be, the tiger would hear it and in all probability would turn to investigate. So I overcame the urge, but turned my head around to see if the beast was creeping upon me from the rear. All I could see was the trunk of the *babul* tree only a few inches away, and beyond that darkness.

I do not know for how long I endured this suspense, but suddenly the silence was shattered by the high-pitched, fear-laden yelping bark of a village dog in the poojaree hamlet so close behind me. The tension was relieved for the moment and I breathed more easily. Two things were evident to me now. The tiger had passed the well without detecting my presence, and had gone towards the wattle huts, obviously in search of human prey. Secondly, and beyond any doubt, it was the man-eater, as no ordinary tiger would deliberately wander near human habitation.

At that moment a perfectly silly notion entered my head. I reasoned that I could achieve no useful purpose by remaining where I was. Assuming that the man-eater did not succeed in finding a human victim, there was little chance that he would retrace his steps and pass the pool again. He might wander away in any direction, while if he did return, he would come upon me from the rear and this time he might not fail to detect my presence.

I cannot tell you, however, why I did not think of doing the most obvious thing; just sit where I was, but facing the hamlet. Instead, I made up my mind to go towards the hamlet myself, shine my torch when I came close enough, and pick up the glare of the tiger's eyes in its beam. That should afford me an easy shot.

This was a silly thing to do. Had I remained where I was, the tiger might have returned to drink at the pool, while I would have been in a fair position, behind the stem of the *babul* tree, for an easy shot. Instead, I got stealthily to my feet, and in a half-crouching position, started advancing towards the hamlet which, as I have already told you, was hardly 200 yards away.

Within a few steps I realized my foolishness, for although there was a well-defined pathway leading from the huts to the pool, in the intense darkness I could not see it and began stumbling among the bushes, making enough noise to scare away the man-eater or urge him to attack. I then thought of going back to the friendly *babul*, but again decided to advance, this time with the full knowledge that the man-eater might be five yards away, behind any bush, and I would not be able to see it.

The hysterical barking of the cur was taken up by others of its kind, and by now some half-dozen village dogs were yowling their heads off in a perfect frenzy, making enough noise to unnerve the boldest of man-eaters. It was extremely doubtful that the tiger would pursue his original intentions in the face of this din; he would either slink off or turn back. And if he did turn back, he would run into me, face to face, at any moment.

With this thought in mind, I made the second mistake of the evening. I switched on my torch—far too soon, as it turned out! As the bright beam cut through the darkness the tiger, of which I did not catch a glimpse, true to the cowardly code of most man-eaters, roared shatteringly from somewhere in front, and I could hear him crashing into the dry scrub beyond.

There was no point in further caution. My quarry had fled and I followed the torch-beam dejectedly towards the *poojarees'* wattle huts while cursing myself repeatedly for the idiot I had been. Upon reaching the hamlet, I called softly to Byra, who emerged from one of the huts. He had been awake and had listened to the alarm-cries of the langurs at sunset, followed by those other sounds. The barking of the dogs had mystified him till the tiger had roared. Only then had he realized that the man-eater was in the village itself. He was even more surprised at finding me there also.

Quickly I related what had happened and was not comforted with Byra's brief comment, heavy with sarcasm.

'Did the *dorai* think he was following a rabbit? Perhaps the years have affected his wisdom!'

It was now just after eight o'clock, and with nothing better to do, I walked to my tent, which you will remember I had pitched under the jack-fruit tree beyond the village, lit the small hurricane lantern hanging from the ventral pole, and made myself a pot of tea. That done, I closed and fastened the flap of the tent, spread my bedding on the ground, not having burdened myself with the weight of a camp cot, extinguished the lantern because I do not like sleeping with a light burning, and was soon fast asleep.

Something awakened me with a start. In the jungle one does not wake as city folk usually do from the snug warmth of a comfortable bed, to yawn and stretch in luxury and maybe spend another five minutes contemplating with dismay the tasks that have to be performed. The forest teaches its inhabitants to sleep alert. When they awaken, they are keyed to instant action, for a second's delay may be their last.

When I opened my eyes, the vague feeling of danger that filled my mind synchronized with my groping hand and outstretched fingers as they fumbled for the rifle I had placed loaded on the ground beside me. Its comforting hardness brought assurance as I sat up to discover what had awakened me with that urgent, oppressive sense of peril.

For a second I could hear nothing, and then came the faintest of scratching sounds, which stopped and started again after a moment or two—scrape, scrape—stop—scratch, scratch—silence, and then once more. The side of the tent moved slightly and something entered from underneath; something that groped about here and there with a sinister purpose. Was it a snake?

That something encountered the edge of my bedding as it lay on the ground to my left barely a foot away, became entangled with it, and pulled away sharply, wrenching canvas and groundsheet with a sharp, tearing noise. Claws! The man-eater was outside!

He had sensed the presence of a human being within the tent, but fortunately, with no knowledge of its flimsy structure, had tried to feel with his paw under the canvas and along the ground in the hope of reaching his prey, whom he would drag out before the victim was aware of what was happening.

A neat little plan, indeed; the only fault being that the victim was myself! Fortunate, indeed, that a premonition of terrible danger had awakened me in time.

I quickly pulled the rifle across my body as I lay on the ground, pointing the muzzle towards where I knew the tiger must be, and slid my right hand towards the trigger.

Remember, it was pitch-dark in the tent when this happened and I did not know exactly where, and in what position the tiger was standing outside. I waited for the next movement and it came again as the groping paw wrenched once more at the bedroll.

Then I pressed the trigger!

There was a deafening explosion and I scrambled to my feet, working the underlever of the .405 Winchester feverishly to fire two more shots blindly through the canvas side of my tent.

There was no sound from the tiger. Was it dead? Even so, it should have uttered a last gasp or gurgle. Was it wounded? Then surely it would have roared with pain. Had it got away? I must have missed. That could be the only explanation for the unaccountable silence.

Like a fool I had once again made an inexcusable mistake. My torch was clamped to the rifle. Why had I not switched it on for a brief moment before firing? A second or two of torchlight would have sufficed to indicate the direction from which that groping paw was coming and where the tiger was standing outside the tent. Instead I had pressed the trigger blindly in total darkness; three times, moreover, hoping to hit an animal whose whereabouts I did not know.

With torch alight, I hastily opened the tapes closing the entrance to the tent and stepped forth cautiously, to direct the torchbeam in every direction. As I had already guessed, the man-eater had escaped, nor was there the slightest sound to indicate in which direction he had fled.

My three shots had awakened the poojarees in Manchi hamlet. I could hear the voices of Byra and some others calling anxiously, inquiring if all was well. Knowing that if I did not go to them soon, the poor felows would brave the darkness and come to find out what had happened, I walked the short distance to the huts by torchlight and told a huddled, frightened group of little jungle men just what had taken place.

They insisted on coming back with me right away to see the three bullet holes in the canvas of my tent for themselves, and the ragged edges in my bedding made by the tiger's claws. They called loudly upon God in thanks for protecting me. Then I had to leave them back at the hamlet, where Byra implored me to share the hut in which he slept for the rest of the night and not risk going back to my tent.

But this invitation I declined and marched back once again, and lay down to continue a much disturbed sleep this time with the hurricane lantern brightly burning. Sheer disgust with myself and things in general caused me to awaken long after sunrise. Voices outside greeted me, and opening the tent-flap I found all the poojarees from the hamlet squatting around in a semicircle.

The reason for their visit was a simple one. My foolish actions of the previous evening and night, and the misses I had made with the three shots I had fired, was to be explained in just two words, both of them very simple: black magic! Someone had cast a spell upon me and my rifle, so that I and the weapon did not act in coordination. Who had done it? Why? When? How? The spell would have to be removed if I hoped to kill the man-eater.

Superstition of this sort is rife amongst the simple people of the Indian forests, and large numbers of townsfolk as well. I knew that no amount of reasoning, persuasion or argument would make the poojarees think otherwise. If I ignored their belief, they would just cease cooperating with me, and then blame my failure on the spell that had been cast on me and my weapon. The shortest and easiest way was to agree.

I said, 'Yes; some misbegotten son of a ... has cast a spell without doubt. Will you please remove it, if you can?'

In turn, the eldest among them replied, 'Yes, but it will cost five rupees to do this,' going on to explain that this sum covered the cost of a fowl that had to be sacrificed, and various other articles, together with the fee for performing the *pooja*.

I agreed again, paid the five rupees, and went inside the tent to snatch another hour of sleep. But disgust with myself prevented me from sleeping and I fell to thinking about the man-eater. The raucous screeching of an unfortunate chicken having its throat cut, followed by the acrid smell of smoke and incense, announced that *pooja* was being performed.

In due course Byra's voice called to me from without: '*Dorai! Dorai!* Wake up and come out. The spell is broken. Let us search for the tiger now. We will surely find him, and this time he will fall to your rifle with a single shot, for the weapon will obey your command.'

The *pooja* was not quite complete, however. The grey-beard, who was also the sorcerer of the hamlet, asked for my rifle. Laying it on the ground he made various marks in red and white, using *konkam* powder and lime (*chunam*) respectively, on both sides of the stock. The entrails of the chicken were next looped into a circle and passed up and down the length of the barrel half-a-dozen times to the accompaniment of muttered mantras and some more incense smoke. Finally he scattered the fire in four directions, calling loudly to the tiger to come forth and be shot.

The sun was high in the sky by the time all this was over. Byra and a poojaree lad of about twenty years of age, who turned out to be the grandson of the old man who had conducted the *pooja*, then invited me to accompany them into the forest in search of the man-eater. As everybody knows, to look for a tiger in any jungle, especially a man-eater, by walking about in broad daylight is not only hopeless but foolish and a waste of time. My regard for Byra's junglecraft was boundless, but that a hunter of his experience could lend himself to this sort of foolishness surprised me.

My looks must have shown my disapproval, but Byra and the lad together urged me to waste no further time in idle talk. Evidently they had implicit faith in their sorcerer. We started, Byra leading, then me and next the boy, but as soon as we were out of sight of the hamlet I insisted on altering this marching order and exchanged places with Muthu, for that was the lad's name. If the man-eater did see us, regardless of all the hocus-pocus that had just been performed, the chances were that, like all man-eaters, this one would decide to attack the last individual in the line of march, and the unarmed youngster would not have a chance.

We walked downhill to the streambed where we cast around in the loose, dry sand for recent tracks. Difficult as it always is in such terrain to differentiate between fresh and old spoors, the two poojarees were not long in finding the tiger's tracks where he had approached the pool, with me sitting near it, the previous night a little later, and nearly a furlong away, they found his trail again, this time leading away from the village. Whether this was the spoor left by the tiger when my light near the hamlet had alarmed him, or later on after I had fired my three shots through the tent, was settled by the fact that the scooping out of the grains of sand at the toe portions of the tracks, and the marks of all four feet separately on the ground, showed that our quarry was moving very fast when he made them, with no attempt at concealment or caution. Evidently he was hurrying away after being badly frightened and this appeared to indicate we were following the trail left by the man-eater after I had fired those foolish shots. The absence of blood anywhere confirmed that he was uninjured.

We had not gone far when the trail veered abruptly to the right and led straight up the hillside on the eastern bank of the stream. I remembered that this was the direction from which the monkey-watchman of the first batch of langurs had voiced his alarm the evening before, when the tiger was descending the hill. Now the tiger had returned the same way. Very probably his lair was in a cave somewhere higher up that hill, or perhaps some distance further away, on the slopes of the Gutherayan mountain.

With this discovery came difficulties. The ground became hard and stony once we had traversed the low-lying belt of bamboos. Clumps of spear-grass grew in between rocks and small boulders and all signs of pug-marks vanished entirely.

The two poojarees, experts though they were in woodcraft, were soon at a complete loss. They moved around in small circles, trying to pick up the trail. At times Byra, and then his young companion, would come upon a broken stem of grass or an overturned stone that showed the way the tiger had gone. But this was not for long and very soon they were forced to a halt. Beyond knowing that the tiger had gone up the hill, we had no further indication of his whereabouts.

We discussed the matter in whispers and decided to climb the hill ourselves in the vague hope of coming upon a cave of some sort in which the man-eater might be hiding. To proceed in single file meant covering only a single line of advance, so we decided to fan out slightly in order to search a wider area. Byra went about a hundred yards to my right but remained within sight, while Muthu moved off about the same distance to my left. Then the three of us started to advance cautiously.

The ground became more stony and the boulders increased in size and number, but we came across no signs of a lair. The hillock we were climbing might have been about 500 feet high, but in due course we reached the top and were able to look down the other side. Here the ground dropped sharply to a lush valley, thickly covered with bamboo, before it started to climb the next foothill. Above that hill rose the peak of the Gutherayan mountain.

At a signal from me, and maintaining the same distance apart, the three of us began the steep descent. On this side the hillock was more fertile. There were fewer rocks and boulders, larger and taller clumps of grass, and even bushes and stunted trees that increased in number till we had reached the region of bamboos, where we found ourselves in a green twilit valley beneath the towering fronds. Now we could no longer see each other, and very soon I felt that my companions, unarmed as they were, had exposed themselves to terrible risk, for I could not help them should the tiger decide to attack. The bamboos and heavy jungle afforded ample cover and even the keen eyes of the two aborigines could not possibly penetrate the green wall that enveloped the three of us.

It was as if this thought gave rise to action, for just then I heard a shrill scream of terror from the poojaree boy, who was about a hundred yards to my left. This was followed by short, sharp 'woofs' as the tiger charged him. The roars ended abruptly when Byra, to my right, gave voice to a volley of shouts. Knowing he was doing this in an attempt to frighten off the attacker I added my yells to his as I turned and crashed towards the spot from which the scream and the roars had come.

Short as the distance was, Byra had caught up with me before we found the lad. He was lying on his face just beyond a pile of boulders and long grass, the back of his skull crushed in, while deep fang marks at the base of the neck and over the right shoulder showed where the tiger had first bitten him before smashing his skull with a stroke of the paw. Possibly the man-eater had been seized by a mixture of fear and rage at hearing our shouts, intended, as I have told you, to save the boy's life. But in this instance they had sealed his fate, for the tiger had killed him.

The flattened grass on the opposite side of the pile of boulders showed where the man-eater had been hiding, waiting till the lad had passed before pouncing upon him from behind. We turned the young poojaree over and were confronted by a ghastly spectacle. The force of the blow upon the back of his head had caused the eyeballs to protrude, while the boy had bitten through his own tongue so that the end hung loosely from his mouth, held by a shred of flesh. Blood seeped into the sand where it was forming a little pool.

Shaken and feeling sick, I turned to my companion. His jet-black face had turned to an ashen hue and his features worked violently with emotion. But not a word did he say. Nor did I. What was there to say? We—and most certainly I—could only blame ourselves for our carelessness and for exposing this unarmed youth to the fiendish cunningness of the tiger.

My watch showed it was just eleven o'clock and the sun beat mercilessly down upon the scene.

It took some minutes to recover from the shock.

Then I said, 'You were so sure that we would kill the tiger after that silly *pooja*. Instead, he has slain one of us!'

Byra did not answer at once. When he spoke there was resentment in his tone. 'The sorcerer should have sacrificed a cock. Instead, he slew a hen, for the hen cost him a rupee less. But it has cost his grandson his life!'

I was scarcely listening. An idea had flashed into my mind. I walked through the long grass to the boulders, stepped on one, and looked back at the body. Barely ten yards! The distance was almost too close. There were only four boulders lying haphazardly together, and the largest of them, the one on which I stood, was about three feet high. The others were much smaller.

The idea then became a definite plan. Since there were already some stones on the spot, would the tiger notice if a few more were added? Perhaps not, provided the extra stones were so placed as not to give rise to undue suspicion.

I turned to Byra and said, 'The night will be dark and this will tempt the devil we are after to return to his kill early, provided we leave the body where it is. For he is hungry, remember. He was hungry last night. That was why he went so boldly to the huts at Manchi. And he has not eaten since then. Tonight he will be very hungry indeed. So we will bring some more boulders to add to these four and make a hide in which I will sit. At this close range, when my torchlight falls upon him, I cannot miss.'

'*Dorai* you're completely mad,' commented the old hunter. 'As soon as he sees the hide he'll suspect something. Perhaps he may go away. Maybe not! If he should spring over the boulders, he will be on top of you before you know where you are.'

'Besides,' he continued, 'it's our duty to return to Manchi and tell that rascally grandfather what has happened to the poor boy. Then the men from the village will come and bear his body away and burn it tonight. Thus his soul will gain peace. If we leave his remains here to be eaten by the tiger, and not burn them, the soul will wander in these jungles and torment us for failing to do our duty.'

'The tiger will not eat them,' I cut in sharply, 'for I will be among the boulders to prevent him. That I promise you. Is this not a good chance to be avenged upon this devil? If I succeed in slaying him tonight, will I not save many lives, perhaps your own among them? As a hunter yourself, don't you agree it would be foolish for us to lose such a golden opportunity?'

Byra did not reply. I could feel him weakening. Finally he looked at me and there was complete innocence in his expression.

'We've searched everywhere and cannot find the body, *dorai*. Let's go back now and inform the others. Tomorrow ·morning we will search again. Tonight you will sit at the side of some jungle *path* to await the tiger, should he pass by, while I will perch like a monkey on a tree, out of sight but not out of hearing, in case you should need my help.'

Thus Byra settled the issue with his conscience and we got to work in right earnest.

In order not to arouse the tiger's suspicion, we moved quite 200 yards away to another area strewn with boulders, big and small. Together we carried half a dozen of the larger ones, one at a time, and placed them in a rough circle with the four boulders that were already there. On this foundation we placed smaller stones, so that in time we had built a circular wall maybe three feet high. I realized it would not do to make this wall any higher, for the additional safety thus gained would be of no avail should the tiger become suspicious on seeing a construction before him that had not been there on his last visit.

Next, into crevices between the stones we stuck handfuls of the tough grass which we tore from tufts and clumps growing some distance away. All this took a long time and was strenuous work, for you must realize the sun beat down on us mercilessly, and the stones and the grass had to be brought from a distance to avoid creating suspicion.

When we left Manchi that morning, boosted by the sorcerer's confidence that we would kill the tiger, I had brought only my rifle and no torch or water-bottle. It would be dangerous to send Byra back alone to fetch these things. Either we would both have to go back, or I could go myself and leave the poojaree up a tree, and if I did that there was always the chance that the tiger might return during my absence and carry away the cadaver of the unfortunate boy to some more remote spot where it would be difficult for us to find it again.

After considering all these factors in whispers, we decided that we had no choice but to take up our positions straight away. I within the small three-foot fort we had constructed and Byra on some tree within hearing distance, and remain in our places till next morning, in the hope that the man-eater would remember his human victim and come back for a meal. We could only hope that the tiger had not been in hiding within hearing distance all this while, for then our movements during the past three hours would undoubtedly have alarmed him and he would have moved off long ago, not to return. Our only chance of success lay in the hope that he might have gone higher up the hill in search of water and had not heard us. It was most unlikely that he had returned to the stream in the valley for, as I have told you, it was quite dry at this time of the year.

We cast around in a wide circle for a suitable tree for Byra, and came upon one about half-a-furlong away, slightly lower down the hill from the spot where the boy had been killed. This was a fairly large tamarind and offered ample scope for the old poojaree to shelter in comfortably till I called him next morning.

It was two-fifteen in the afternoon, perhaps the hottest time of day, when Byra climbed the tamarind after earnestly advising me to be careful and not fall asleep at any cost. Leaving him there, I returned to my little fort, scrambled over the scorching stones we had placed there to form the wall, and tried to settle down inside. I at once encountered the first difficulty. The ground was so hot that I could not sit on it, but had to remain crouched on my haunches. Apart from being a painful and uncomfortable posture, the wall was not high enough for it. My head showed above the top and would be easily seen from outside, so I had to sit with head bowed to try to conceal myself.

It did not take me long to realize that such a position was absurd and dangerous, for I would not be able to see the tiger should he creep upon me.

I got out of the hide then, walked some distance away, and plucked several handfuls of tough grass stems which I stuck very closely together into the *pugaree* of my 'Gurkha' hat. This took a little time, but I was satisfied with the task eventually. When seen from a distance, there was no hat to be seen, only another clump of grass.

Donning the hat, I returned within my fort of stones, crouched once more on my haunches and attempted to remain motionless. I was just able to look over the rim of the rocks in a half-circle, before and to both sides of me, and by turning my head ever so slowly to right and left, I could even see behind. This movement would not be very noticeable, I felt, as the whole 'clump' of grass on my hat would turn with it and might be mistaken by the tiger for the effect of the hot breeze that was blowing from the valley and the streambed towards the hill-tops and was rippling the bowed heads of the dried grass in waves from time to time.

I soon found that I could not remain still in that crouching posture for very long. My ankles became painful and the calves of my legs became numb. I had to move this way and that, slowly and a little at a time, till after four o'clock, when the earth cooled sufficiently to allow me to sit down.

Up to this time the surroundings had been abnormally silent. Not an animal or bird had indicated its presence by sight or sound. All creation—and no doubt the tiger, too— was sheltering from the devastating heat. Only twice had I seen movement, firstly when a giant iguana lizard attempted to cross, caught sight of Muthu's body on the ground, turned abruptly and scrambled away, and later, when a small python, hanging unnoticed head downwards from a low tree, had dropped upon a passing ground squirrel to crush it to death. I had seen the squirrel, but had not noticed the snake till I saw the python's coils squirming in the grass and heard the squeaks of the victim being crushed to death.

There was a marked cooling of the air by five o'clock and this reminded me that I had drunk no water since morning. There was not a drop to drink anyhow, and worst of all, I would have to remain thirsty till I returned to Manchi the following morning—a truly formidable thought!

A partridge on the hillside to my left broke the long silence at last 'Kee-kok-kik! Kee-kok-kok! Kee-kok-kok!' he

31

called in challenge and within minutes came the acceptance
to a fight from another male bird slightly higher up the hill:
'Kee-kok-kok! Kee-kok-kok! Kee-kok-kok!'

The two partridges challenged each other frequently as
they drew closer together, hastening to the fray, till finally
they met. Then with hysterical cries of 'Kok! Kok! Kok!',
the duel started in earnest. Unfortunately I could not see
the birds but could picture the battle in my imagination for
the ten minutes or so that it lasted, before one of the
contestants gave way to the superior prowess and stamina
of his adversary. He flew helter-skelter from the scene of
battle. I was just able to glimpse his brown form sailing
precipitately downhill to safety, while the other bird
remained to voice the victory cry 'Kee-kok-kok! Kee-kok-
kok! Kee-kok-kik!' once again.

The battle of the partridges had served to while away
the time. It was now 5-40 p.m. and the calls of junglecocks
from the streambed in the valley rose to announce the
advent of eventide. 'Wheew! Kuck-kya-kya-kuckm!' they
crowed from down below, to be answered by other cocks
on the hillsides in all directions. Occasionally a peafowl
voiced its meowing cry, while *bulbuls* in hundreds, on bushes
and thickets, joined in the general symphony of calls that
remain indelible in the memory of all that have known these
beautiful jungles.

But it would not do for me to pay too much heed to these
sounds much as I enjoyed hearing them. I would have to remain
keenly alert from now onwards, for with nightfall drawing
near, the man-eater would remember his victim and might
decide to return at any moment. At this time the two tribes
of langur-monkeys, one of them on the hilltop above me and
the other somewhere on the adjacent hill across the stream,
started their eventide gambols, frolicking among themselves

and calling boldly to each other across the intervening valley. 'Whoomp! Whoomp! Whoomp!' they screamed as they leaped from branch to branch. I could not see them from where I was sitting, but could hear the bang and thud of their bodies as they landed heavily among the branches of the trees.

I was grateful for the presence of the langur-monkeys. I knew that each tribe would have its own watchman, sitting alert on a tree-top, serious, silent and intently scanning the ground below for movement and danger.

The sun set behind the range of hills at my back and the shades of evening spread rapidly around me. The grasses and bushes and boulders that had been so clear all this while now became hazy and blurred. Distances lost their perspective. In a few moments there was no background to be seen at all; just the few indistinct bushes that grew in my immediate vicinity. All else was a dark-grey void, rapidly turning to chocolate and then to blackness. Muthu's body, only ten yards away, lost its shape and became merely a darker heap upon the rapidly darkening ground.

There was a whirring flutter of movement behind my head that startled me, accompanied by high-pitched, creaking squeaks. The long-eared bat, intent on its search for insects, had thought there might be a few in the clump of grass adorning my hat and had come to investigate. Softly a nightjar fluttered on to one of the stones forming my rampart. It was so close that by stretching out my hand I could have caught it, and I was pleased with myself at having sat so still, for I had even deceived this bird into not noticing my presence. The nightjar snuggled low on the hot rock, puffed out its throat with air, and voiced its usual cry:

'Chuck! Chuck! Chuck! Chuck! Chuckooooooo!'

Then it noticed poor Muthu. Suddenly it took fright, fluttered both its wings like a giant moth, and sailed into the heavy air and out of sight. A little later I could hear it again, this time from far away, where the bird thought it was quite safe, voicing its jerky call.

Now I could no longer see the bushes, the grasses, the stones, nor even poor Muthu. A curtain of blackness closed over me with the falling of night. The stars that to a certain extent illumine the darkness in a jungle were few this night as I raised my eyes heavenwards in search of them. The steely blue-black of the usual night sky was covered by a ruffled blanket of small, broken, cirrocumuli clouds, resembling the ringlets of wool on a sheepskin. They stretched between the two ranges of hills and all but hid the stars from sight.

It was a perfect night for the man-eater to discover my presence and add me to his menu without my ever being aware of his nearness. To see him in such darkness was impossible, and I was entirely at his mercy. Suddenly I became very frightened and began to shiver. Why had I been so foolhardy as to place myself in this predicament by not listening to the old *poojaree*'s experienced advice? I felt like shouting to Byra. I felt like getting up and dashing away from this horrid place to the faraway tamarind tree in which I knew my friend, the jungle man, was sheltering. A feeling of being closed in, of suffocation, of claustrophobia, gripped me. Panic all but overwhelmed me and the sweat of nervous terror streamed down my face. In the distance, a horned-owl hooted dismally: 'Whoo! Whoooo! Whoo! Whoooo! Whoo! Whoooo!'

At that moment the calm of the night was shattered by the dying scream of a sambar stag from the stream bed down in the valley.

'Aar-aar-aarrhh-aaarrhh!' it shrieked in its agony, and once again 'Aaahhh-gggrrrhhh!' Then there was silence.

I knew the animal that was being done to death at that moment was a stag, for a doe would have uttered a cry of far higher pitch, while the shriek of a spotted deer would have been quite different. Three possible foes could be killing that stag; a pack of wild dogs, a panther or a tiger. I decided against the dogs; a pack would have raised its hunting calls and I would have heard them long ago. Besides, these dogs do not hunt on dark nights. So the slayer was either a large panther of the tendu variety, or a tiger. Nothing else could be killing an animal as big as a sambar stag. Even a tendu would have all its work cut out to bring down a victim of that size.

Very likely the killer was a tiger after all. But was it the man-eater, who was reputed to eat only human flesh? Or was it some ordinary wandering tiger who happened to be in the vicinity too? I knew that the man-eater could not subsist on human flesh alone. His kills were too few and far between. He must be devouring animals as well, and I remembered he was very hungry that night, not having eaten for some time. Very likely it was he who had attacked the stag after all. Perhaps he had been returning for Muthu and had come upon the deer by chance.

The sambar was dead now and all sounds had ceased. The tiger would spend the rest of the night feeding on this new victim and would not come near the body of the poojaree lad. My vigil would have been in vain. The thought was very mortifying indeed.

Mixed feelings of relief from immediate danger, and sheer disgust with myself at my cowardice, set in when I realized that only a few moments earlier I had been trembling, scared out of my wits at nothing but the darkness and the thought of the man-eater's proximity.

I knew that the old poojaree, too, must have heard the sambar's death-scream. Like me, he would wonder if the killer was the man-eater or some other animal. I wondered what conclusion he had reached. The slaying of the sambar had brought to an end the nervous tension under which I had been labouring. I was quite calm now as I wondered over and over again whether the man-eater would return or not.

For the next half-hour or so the forest was hushed and strangely silent. It was as if its denizens were aware that danger lurked by the streambed, and that sudden and violent death awaited any of them who betrayed his presence. I glanced at my watch. It was not yet ten o'clock. I had many hours of tiring vigil before me.

After that the jungle gradually came to life again. I could hear the stealthy nibbling of grass by a barking-deer a few yards to my right. Down below, on the banks of the stream, an elephant was breaking bamboos.

As the heated air from the valley started to rise, the colder air from the hilltops rushed down to take its place. This caused fitful gusts of breeze to blow and carried to the munching barking-deer the smell of Muthu's body that was now beginning to make itself felt. There was a sudden noise as the little animal dashed away for a few yards. Then it came to a halt to voice its barking alarm-cry: 'Kharr! Kharr! Kharr! Kharr!'

The barks came at intervals of a few minutes. It seemed incredible that such a small animal could make such a loud noise. I knew that the call of a barking-deer can be heard for over a mile on a still night.

Shortly afterwards the elephant in the valley, in his hunt for fresh bamboo-shoots, moved upstream. This brought him to the remains of the stag that had been killed a short while earlier. Probably the killer, panther or tiger, was still there, feeding on his prey. Whatever it was, the elephant became excited and began to trumpet repeatedly, the brassy scream of each note disturbing the silence of the forest.

And then I heard it clearly. 'Wr-aagh! Wrr-aagh!'—the roars of an angry tiger coming from the same direction. The elephant screamed again and again, and the tiger roared its defiance in between, answer for answer. I could imagine the scene. The tiger had been feeding, or perhaps just sleeping by the sambar's remains, when the elephant had blundered upon him. Would the encounter develop into a fight, or would one or other of the animals lose its nerve and retreat?

The screams of the elephant began to change in timbre. The high-pitched note of fear gave place to the longer, slightly lower note of anger. I could make out that the animal was a bull. He resented the tiger's presence amongst the bamboos, which he no doubt regarded as his own property, and was rapidly losing his temper.

What would the tiger do? The matter was not left in doubt for long. He suddenly lost his nerve and decided to give way to the irate elephant, even if it meant abandoning his kill. There was sudden silence when the tiger beat a retreat, while the bull elephant, finding his bluster had succeeded in driving away the foe, slowly regained his composure and ceased to trumpet.

Silence once again descended upon the forest. The fleecy clouds that had been hiding the stars since sunset had disappeared about an hour before, and I could now see the dark form that was Muthu, and the nearer bushes and grasses, reasonably clearly in the light of the stars. Now at least I might be able to see the man-eater should he decide to return to Muthu's body. This caused me to wonder again whether the tiger that had just had that altercation with the elephant was the man-eater or not. His display of cowardice tended to offer an affirmative answer.

My thoughts were disturbed at that instant by a growl! I heard it only once and so I could not quite locate the sound or where it had come from, but it was an unmistakable growl. I fancied it had come from somewhere behind me and lower down the hillside, but I was not quite sure.

As quietly as possible, I turned my body a few inches to the left, so as to be able to observe whether anything was approaching from that direction, but I could still see the smudge that was Muthu, by looking to my right.

And then I heard it again: another growl, louder and closer this time. There was now no doubt whatever: the tiger was coming up the hill, he was coming in my direction.

I could not help smiling to myself as I thought of the great service that the elephant had done me in driving the tiger from his kill. The angry tiger had now been forced to remember that he had made another kill, one of those tasty human beings, earlier that afternoon and higher up the hill. So he was returning to it, voicing his anger all the while against the elephant that had disturbed him.

My luck had been stupendous. Not only was the tiger advertising his presence, which was much in my favour on a dark night, but the bad temper he was displaying, and his smouldering resentment against the elephant, would prevent him from being too cautious when he eventually reached poor Muthu. After all, perhaps he would not discover my presence. I was elated at the thought.

Twice more the tiger growled. Then I dimly saw a long, dark ill-defined shape to my left and a little below me. It seemed to move. It disappeared completely. Then it appeared again, this time much closer. It was certainly moving towards me.

The tiger growled again Apparently he was still thinking of the elephant and could not get him out of mind. The throaty, rasping note came from the long, moving object that was rapidly approaching me.

The dark shadow disappeared behind an intervening bush. A few seconds later the slinking shape moved dimly from left to right, and came to a halt over Muthu, just ten yards away. It had not even glanced at the little stone fort that Byra and I had so painstakingly constructed.

The tiger was in such a vile temper that he voiced a series of loud growls when he bit savagely into the poojaree lad's dead body and began to worry the carcase. His recent undignified retreat before the bull elephant, and the fact that he had to abandon his sambar kill, was annoying him intensely. He felt he had to vent his spleen on something.

Only now did I realize how difficult was the task that lay before me. I had to kill the tiger with my first shot, or at least cripple it effectively so that it would not turn upon me. My quarry was a mere ten yards away, but I could just see it as a blur. I had no torch, no nightsight, no white card as an index, that we read about so often, to fit to the sights of a rifle to make night shooting easy. My old .405 did not even have a phosphorescent foresight.

I realized I would have to act quickly while the tiger was still venting its wrath upon poor Muthu's remains. Once it became calmer and settled down to feed, it would notice any slight movement of my rifle and attack me. In fact, if it had eaten enough of the sambar it might just pass on, to return later in the night when it became hungry again, or perhaps not return at all.

Very cautiously I raised the stock of the .405 to my shoulder, taking the greatest care not to knock the barrel against any of the stones we had erected. Holding it firmly, I pointed the barrel as best I could at the front portion of the dark shape that was the tiger.

I knew there was no possibility of picking my shot of firing at some vital place. I would have to take a chance.

Perhaps I would miss altogether. Very likely I would just wound the tiger superficially and it would then turn and attack me. There was a hundred-to-one-chance that I would kill it with my first shot.

Steadying my hand and holding my breath, I pressed the trigger.

Pandemonium broke loose as the sharp report of the rifle thundered out and echoed against the opposing range of hills. The tiger roared lustily. Fortunately it had been facing away from me when I fired. Not knowing whence the shot had come, it imagined the foe was somewhere in front and sprang upon the nearest bush and began to tear it to shreds. As I feared would happen, I realized I had only wounded the tiger. It had been in a bad temper then. Now it was furious.

And then I made a mistake. Had I done nothing, the tiger would have reduced the bush to nothing and probably have gone away after that, without discovering my presence. But I fired again at its dark shape.

After that the tiger's behaviour was fearsome. Hit a second time, it catapulted itself into the air, fell to earth with a thud, and then began grubbing around in a circle. Evidently the spine was broken, for the animal appeared to be unable to stand upright. But this time it knew where its attacker was concealed, and the grubbing circle it was taking brought it directly down upon me.

Scrambling to my feet, I fired my third shot into its head at a range of scarcely two yards. Then I vaulted over the stone parapet by using my hands and promptly fell down the other side. My feet pricked as if there were a thousand needles in each, for I had been sitting crosslegged for some eleven hours and they were numbed.

Fortunately the tiger remained on the other side of the stones. A dreadful bubbling, gurgling sound was coming from it, showing that the animal was still alive but grievously hurt and probably dying.

I scrambled to my knees as the blood flowed back to my legs and peeped cautiously over the intervening boulder. The tiger lay on the other side, twitching and gasping and gurgling. My fourth shot ended its suffering.

When the noise died away, I could hear Byra calling to me frantically, asking if all was well. I answered him in the affirmative and told him to come along. A few minutes later my friend appeared out of the darkness and I told him the whole story. On the streambed the elephant trumpeted again.

Unerringly Byra led me through the dark jungle back to Manchi hamlet. There, for the second time, I repeated all that had happened. The inhabitants turned out to the last child, brought lights and returned with us to bring in the bodies of Muthu and the tiger.

My first shot had entered the stomach. My second had smashed the spine high up at the shoulder. It was this second shot that had anchored the tiger and prevented it from escaping. As we had anticipated the man-eater turned out to be a young animal, and this accounted for his inexperienced, erratic ways. The poojarees asked why we had used the body of Muthu as a bait. We asked them why they entertained a sorcerer of such poor calibre in their midst. We also reminded them we had rid them of the man-eater. The end justified the means.

To this they said nothing.

# Two

## The Lame Horror of Peddacheruvu

IF YOU WERE TO TRAVEL FROM GUNTAKAL BY THE METRE-GAUGE railway eastwards towards the city of Bezwada, now known as Vijayawada, you would traverse some of the best-known and densest forests of the state of Andhra Pradesh soon after leaving Dronachellam Junction, when you pass Nandyal and go through the stations of Basavapuram, Chelima, Bogoda and Diguvametta.

The forests on either side of the track are the only areas in southern India where the once-numerous giant antelope, known as the nilgai or blue bull, are still to be found. They are especially numerous in the jungles around the Forest department Rest House at a place named Chinnamantralamanna. These great animals, which once abounded everywhere, are now extinct in all the other forests of the South.

In addition to the blue bull, the others found in the Indian subcontinent are numerous here, together with huge sounders

42

of wild pig, and all these animals in turn attract tigers and panthers who are always to be found where sufficient food is available. But when this natural food becomes scarce for any reason, the carnivora are forced to prey on the herds of cattle, sheep and goats tended by the herdsmen who live on the outskirts of the villages. Then, and only then, do they fall foul of the men who attend the herds, and who naturally endeavour to drive away the marauders with spears, traps, bullets and other devices. Tigers and panthers are wounded or hurt in other ways too. This incapacitates them for normal hunting, and in time they take to man-eating as the easiest way of appeasing hunger.

In the course of years many man-eaters have appeared in these areas. I have already told of one of them that haunted the railway tracks between some of the stations I have named* and what follows is the story of another that appeared in the same general locality, but some miles to the north.

To reach the spot, you do not alight from the train at Diguvametta, but travel another forty miles to Markapur Road. You detrain there and go by road in a northerly direction for another forty miles. The road winds down a picturesque ghat to an insignificant place known as Srisailam, overlooking the winding course of the Kistna river that formerly separated the Madras Presidency in the south from the dominions of the Nizam of Hyderabad in the north. The British have now gone, and so also have the Nizam's dominions, all these areas having been brought within the extensive state of Andhra Pradesh, the second largest in India, while Srisailam, hitherto merely the site of a large temple and of only religious significance, is becoming famous as the centre of a great twin project involving an irrigation and electricity scheme.

* See *The Black Panther of Sivanipalli,* Chapter 4.

In former years, when conditions were undisturbed, this road from a point about twenty miles from Markapur Road railway station as far as the Kistna river was covered with the type of forest that tigers delight in—not too dense and not too thorny—with sufficient high grass and low trees to afford cover for themselves and grazing and shelter for the wild deer and pig that form their natural diet. Low, rolling hills with interesting streams provided plenty of water for them in even the hottest weather, while the tiny jungle-ticks that are the scourge of the forests further south, and the voracious leeches of the Western Ghats, both of them hateful to all carnivora who cannot rid themselves of these pests, seem to be entirely absent. At least the leeches are, while the ticks appear only after the rains and then in insignificant numbers.

So tigers and panthers, particularly the former, were plentiful. They fed on the Nilgai and the deer, and sportsmen did not visit the area very often. Elephants and bison strangely enough, are entirely absent from these jungles. The rare blue bull makes up for them in a way, but as it is protected and there is a total prohibition against shooting them, these areas have never been popular with tourists or sportsmen. The climate, too, is difficult: hot in winter and savagely hot in summer.

Another factor that has saved the carnivora to a large extent is the paucity of motorable tracks into the interior. If you want to travel away from the main road, you either walk or travel by bullock-cart. But all this made the jungles of Srisailam very pleasant to me. In their fastnesses I could lose myself, away from the crowd.

There is a village named Peddacheruvu situated to the west of the road from Markapur to Srisailam. To reach it you go by bullock cart through eighteen miles of forest where you generally do not meet another human being. Peddacheruvu is a small village, and to the south of it lies a pretty lake. The bullock-cart track passes this lake and wends southwards for a few miles more till it reaches a hill. At an impossible gradient the track descends this hill to the hamlet of Rollapenta, where it meets another main road leading from the village of Doranala to the town of Atmakur. Further south yet is the Rest House of Chinnamantralamanna, where the Nilgai abound.

The lake I have just told you about is ringed by the jungle, and in this jungle many tigers are to be found. So many, in fact, that they have killed and eaten all the panthers that at one time lived there too. From November to January each year, during the mating season, after sunset and often during the daylight hours too, you can hear the moaning call of a tigress seeking her mate, and sometimes the awful din of tigers fighting for the female whose roars have summoned them from afar.

I have told you in earlier stories that the natural food of tigers and panthers is the wild game of the forest, and when these become scarce, the herds of domestic cattle and goats that are taken out to graze. Man-eating is invariably the result of a tiger or panther becoming unable to hunt its normal food by some injury caused, in every case in my experience except the one I am going to tell you about, by a wound inflicted by man. Generally it is a gunshot or rifle wound, or injury brought about when escaping from a spring trap, when the animal has had to tear itself free from the teeth of the steel jaws that have fastened on its face or foot.

But in the case of the man-eater of Peddacheruvu it was none of these things. For after I shot him I found that this tiger, well past his prime, had been involved in a fight with another tiger. He had lost an eye and an ear as the result— both on the right side, where his adversary had gripped him— and the tendons of his right foreleg had been chewed through and through, causing him to drag that limb as he walked and to leave a distinct trail behind him. These disabilities, together with his advancing years, had prevented this animal from being able to kill his normal prey. A tiger's forepaws, and particularly the right one, are essential to him in normal attack, for with them he grips his victim while he bites the neck or throat, causing the animal to topple over and break its neck by its own weight. With his right foot maimed, this tiger could not hold any animal larger than a mouse-deer. So he went through months of starvation while his wounds healed, and then he took to killing and eating every human being that came his way, for he found them slow in movement and quite helpless to resist him, even with his handicaps.

The people of Peddacheruvu told me later that they had heard a tigress moaning for some days. That was when this story really began.

It was just before Christmas and the mating season. Two tigers had begun to fight for her. The quarrel had started at sunset and had lasted half the night. Both contestants had evidently been badly hurt, for one of them had come down to drink water at the edge of the lake, where he had left a pool of blood on the muddy edge. The other had crossed the sandy track leading from Peddacheruvu to Rollapenta, on the Doronala–Atmakur road. The soft earth showed a distinct blood trail and three sets of pug-marks, while a faint furrow in the sand showed that the animal had been dragging one of his limbs and could not put his weight on it.

Time passed, and then a sheep or goat here or a village dog there disappeared, while as often as not the pug-marks of the 'limping tiger,' as he came to be known, showed that this contestant at least had survived the epic fight.

The older men in the village shook their heads and conferred in whispers. Some of them had heard of such cases before. A few had actually seen them. But they all knew that the taking of the sheep, the goats and particularly the village curs, meant that a man-eating tiger was in the making. For tigers disdain such food and will only stoop to kill and eat such insignificant prey when they are on the verge of starvation, or when they are unable, for some good reason, to kill anything bigger.

The first human victim was taken very soon after that, and the old men wagged their heads and their tongues yet more. He was a cartman and had been returning to the village in the evening with his cart laden with bamboos that had been cut in a valley five miles away. The cart track skirted the lake I have told you about, and here the man had stopped to water his bulls without unyoking them, for his cart was too heavily laden and it would have been impossible for him to re-yoke them again single-handed.

Perhaps just before or after watering his animals, the man had got down from his cart to drink himself. That was when the 'limping tiger' took him.

The bulls, terrified at the sight of the tiger, had dashed madly away, dragging the laden cart behind them. They had not kept to the road, as a result of which the cart had fallen down an incline, the weight of the bamboos dragging the two unfortunate bulls with it. One had broken its thigh and the bone, protruding through the outer skin, had stuck into its belly, while the cart lay on top of the animal, effectively anchoring it. The second bull had been more lucky. The yoke had slipped off its neck, leaving the animal free to dash to the village. Its arrival there had caused consternation, but as night had fallen already nobody would listen to the pleadings of the cartman's wife and three children that the men should form a search-party with lanterns to look for the breadwinner.

The sun was already up next day when the able-bodied men of the hamlet, two of them armed with matchlocks and the rest with spears and sticks, eventually left the village. Very soon they came upon the capsized cart, and the unfortunate bull with the broken thigh. Of the owner there was no trace.

They followed the tracks of the cart to the edge of the pool and there they saw in the mud the prints left by the limping tiger. Some of the searchers had wanted to look for the remains of the cartman, but the two individuals armed with matchlocks had become faint-hearted. One said his weapon was useless and would not fire. The other, more truthful, admitted he was too afraid. As a result the whole party returned to the village and the remains of the cartman were never found.

The second victim was a woman. This incident also took place in the evening, but at a spot within a hundred yards of the village where she had taken her water-pot to the community well. No jungle grew there, but nearby was a grove of peepul trees which, in turn, adjoined a coconut plantation. A thick hedge enclosed this plantation, and on the further side was wasteland, covered with scrub and grass. The jungle proper began more than half a mile away. The well was at a spot where no tiger had ever been known to come within the memory of the oldest inhabitant, and he was well over a hundred years old.

But the limping tiger came that evening. Two other women saw him in the act of carrying away his victim when she screamed. They turned around at the sound and were dumbfounded to see a great tiger, with a distinct limp, dragging the woman by her shoulder and moving at a fast pace towards the peepul trees. They had waited no longer and fled screaming to the village.

Human kills had followed in rapid succession after that, and one day I received a letter from an old friend of mine, a Telugu Indian gentleman named Byanna, who lived near the Markapur Road railway station, telling me of the goings-on at Peddacheruvu village and asking me to come and shoot the tiger. Moreover, Byanna offered to accompany me in order to render what assistance he could, and suggested I should travel by train to Markapur Road, from where he would take me in his Land Rover to our destination.

Such a summon is impossible to resist, so I sent Byanna a telegram informing him I was leaving by express the following night. The next forenoon found us together on the platform of Markapur Road railway station.

Mr Byanna is meticulous, and looking after a guest is to him a matter of great importance, so important that at times it is all rather embarrassing. I was taken to his house where a hot bath had been ready for the last two hours. Then a huge dish of chicken pilau was placed before me and I was almost commanded to eat it all. I knew I would have to put up a good show, for Byanna is rather sensitive and would be greatly offended if I did not do justice to the meal.

When this feast was over, I was taken to the garage at the rear of the house. There stood Byanna's Land Rover, laden to the brim with all manner of unnecessary things intended for my comfort. There was a spring-cot and mattress, camp chairs, camp tables, a canvas camp tub, a camp basin and stand, a small refrigerator and a fan, both worked by kerosene oil, and heaven knew what else. As for foodstuffs! There were gunny bags in large numbers crammed with stores; enough, I should think, for a whole month. Four Primus stoves, one of them with a double-range cooker, had been provided; and pots, pans and storage drums for water were tied on at inconceivable points and at incredible angles. Where he and I were going to sit seemed an insoluble problem.

Byanna asked me if I would like to sleep the night in his house and start next morning, to which I said I was as fresh as a daisy after that hot bath and marvellous chicken pilau. Could we start right away? Wonderfully obliging, he consented at once, and an hour later the Land Rover, looking more like one of those covered wagons from the prairies of America, took the road northwards that led to Srisailam.

We left the main road a little beyond Doranala village and negotiated the rough track of eighteen miles that eventually brought us directly through the jungle to the village of Peddacheruvu, passing another hamlet named Tummalabayalu on the way, the scene of an encounter with a man-eater in my young and inexperienced days. There I tumbled out of the Land Rover and sat on someone's doorstep, while Byanna rattled away in the Telugu dialect to the throng of villagers that gathered around us.

It transpired he was trying to find a suitable room for us to occupy. This did not take long, for the headmaster of the local school who had joined the crowd to learn the purpose of our visit, at once volunteered to let us live in the main hall of his little school.

We drove the Land Rover there and unloaded. By the time we had taken everything out of the vehicle we had crammed that room to capacity, though more than half the objects were quite unnecessary.

Water was fetched for us in pots by several willing villagers. We were conducted to the bathroom, in a separate building, where we bathed; and we were shown the lavatory, in yet another building. It was a long time before we could sit down to our first meal of curry and rice that Byanna had brought from his home at Markapur.

Dusk had fallen by now, but people from the village still kept coming and going, to stare at us and ask innumerable

questions which Byanna answered in Telugu at great length.
Finally I took matters into my own hands. Selecting three or
four of the villagers who seemed to know something about
the man-eater, and carrying my rifle, I asked them to follow
me outside.

It was moonlight. The main street of the village led directly
to the track that skirted the lake on its way to the Doranala-
Atmakur road. Half a furlong away the lake began, and I
could see the water glinting in the moonlight.

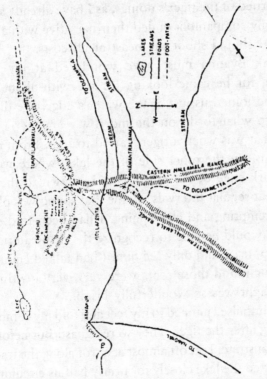

I walked along the street with my companions, who very
soon told me that it would be dangerous for us to leave the
precincts of the village because of the man-eater. I said I
wanted to talk to them where we could have peace and

51

quiet, which was impossible in that infernal schoolroom, and I reassured them about the tiger. Finally we reached the edge of the lake and sat down by the water. It was delightfully cool there and the moonlight was so bright that we could see right across the wide expanse of the lake to the jungle on the other side.

I noticed that my companions kept glancing nervously around, but as we were in the open with no cover for the tiger, there really was no justification for their fear. Little by little I learned of the tiger's doings, as I have already set them out, and my companions ended their narrative with a fervent plea that I should shoot the beast at all costs.

I think Byanna must have wondered at my sudden departure, for he came looking for me with about twenty people and joined us just at the water's edge. We discussed plans as to what to do on the morrow.

And that was when a tiger started to roar. From directly opposite us, on the other side of the lake, where we could see the dark edge of the jungle coming down to the water, he roared at regular intervals. To me that sound was pleasing, exciting, tempting and challenging. I had been told enough to know I would be able to recognize the man-eater at once by his limp, if I could only see him. I had talked enough and eaten enough; and those roars were very, very inviting. And the moonlight was so wonderfully bright.

On an impulse I jumped to my feet and told my companions I was going after the tiger. They were aghast. But before they could remonstrate, I set off almost at a trot along the track that I knew skirted the lake closely for nearly half its circumference till it reached the other side, before breaking away into the jungle. I judged the tiger was roaring at least a mile away, maybe further, and I wanted to reach him before he stopped. Obviously he was coming down to the lake for a drink.

In less than fifteen minutes I was almost there, and the tiger was still calling, although at longer intervals. I knew that very soon he would stop. He was so close now that the earth seemed to tremble with each roar as I left the track I had been following to cut through the jungle towards the sound. That was when my difficulties began.

I knew very well that if I attempted to walk through the undergrowth the tiger would hear me. He would either go away then or, if he was the man-eater, he might creep forward to ambush me by a flank or rear attack. My hope lay in finding a footpath if possible, and in following it in silence so as to try to see him first—an almost impossible thing to do.

Luckily I discovered that footpath. Rather it was a game-trail that went down to the water and not a footpath; but it offered salvation, for it was leading more or less in the general direction from which the tiger's roars were still coming, although at longer and longer intervals.

I started to follow the *path*, glancing down frequently to make sure I did not stumble or tread upon something that would betray my presence. I judged the tiger was well within 200 yards when he ceased to roar. I stopped advancing as soon as I realized this, for it would be impossible for me to locate him. Whereas he would assuredly hear my footsteps in spite of all my precautions in the complete silence that now enveloped us both. I thought quickly and had an idea. An acacia tree grew to the right of the game trail. Its trunk was hardly thick enough to hide my body when I sheltered behind it, but provided I remained absolutely motionless there was a hope that the tiger would not detect—at least, not too soon.

Quickly I stepped behind the acacia, drew in my breath, and imitated the roar of a tiger with all the force of my lungs. Twice I did this, in rapid succession. Then I remained silent to await events. And happen they did, in real earnest. The tiger in front of me, apparently amazed and greatly annoyed at the impudence of the intruder who dared to come so close to him and roar twice, although those roars must have sounded miserably puny and weak, lost his temper. I could hear him coming, grunting and snarling as he bounded forward. Fortunately, the acacia had been growing at a spot where the pathway followed a straight course for a few yards, rather than at a bend.

Before long, down the pathway came the tiger in short bounds, so intent upon looking for another of his kind that he failed to notice me behind the trunk of that acacia tree. He had passed when I was forced to put him to the test. I coughed almost imperceptibly.

The tiger whisked around in his tracks to face this new sound. He knew it did not come from another tiger but from a man, and his reaction would show whether he was the man-eater or not.

I did not move a fraction of an inch as the beast stared at the acacia. Having no sense of smell, he could not locate me exactly, although he must have seen some part of me and knew that something was sheltering behind that tree. He hesitated, and then stepped three or four paces to his left from where he would be able to get a better view of me.

Recognition came to both of us at once. He found out what I was and where I was standing, while I found out that he was not the man-eater. For there was not the faintest trace of a limp in his walk. We stared at each other.

The next three or four seconds would decide our fate. I certainly had no wish to shoot a harmless tiger provided he left me alone. But would he? I had excited and irritated him by roaring, and had made matters worse by coughing. An angry tiger cannot often control itself.

The tiger sank to his haunches and I knew the charge was coming. I aimed and was about to press the trigger when one of those unaccountable events, that often make a tiger's behaviour unpredictable, occurred. He turned and bounded into the bushes!

Allowing time for him to get away and for my nerves to calm down. I retraced my steps along the game-trail to the roadway and back to the village where I told Byanna and the others, who admitted they had never expected to see me again, what had happened.

To say I was disappointed would be putting matters lightly, but I was glad I had not made things worse by shooting the wrong tiger.

During the next three days we bought four baits and tied them out at the most likely spots where *nullahs* and pathways crossed each other, and within a mile or so of the big lake, and above each bait we constructed an almost perfect *machan*.

That was how I came to meet an individual who, as events were to prove shortly, was as brave a man as any I have met. He was a Chenchu—the name by which the aboriginal jungle men of these areas are known—and he carried a bow and a quiver of arrows like most Chenchus do. These, and a filthy rag as a loin-cloth, were apparently his sole pssessions. One more thing he had, and I think it was his greatest asset. Appu—for that was his name—had a most infectious smile, a marvellous sense of humour. He was as happy as the day was long.

Appu offered his services in selecting suitable places in which to tie my baits and in building the *machans,* and I was quick to accept, for his smile won me completely. What wonderful *machans* he built! He concealed them so cleverly that, even when staring at one from the ground and knowing its location, it was difficult for me to realize a *machan* was there. Indeed, little Appu added greatly to my knowledge of the art of *machan*-tying, for with him it was an art indeed!

Nothing happened the first night, nor the second. The buffalo heifer that we had tied a quarter of a mile from the spot where I had met the roaring tiger was killed and half-eaten on the third night, so that on the fourth night I sat over this heifer's remains, awaiting the return of the killer.

Would it be the lame tiger, the man-eater, or would it be the 'roaring tiger'—as I had come to call him—that I had encountered a few days earlier? Unfortunately the ground was so hard that no tracks were visible to answer this question in advance. The tiger returned before darkness had set in, which is something rare for a tiger to do, although sunset is the usual time at which panthers come to their kills. He did not even glance upwards at Appu's perfect *machan* but walked boldly up to the heifer's carcase and gazed down upon it.

There was nothing wrong with his walk. He was not the lame tiger I had been told to look for. He was not the man-eater.

The thought came to me to try a little experiment from that wonderful *machan*. I made the grating call of a panther. The effect on that tiger was astounding; he was galvanized into fury. He whirled around to locate the puny but audacious panther who had dared to challenge his right to his own kill. Where was this intruder?

'Hah-ah! Hah-ah!' I called again. Then stopped.

'Wrauff! Wrauff! Wrauff!' roared the tiger, and charged directly at the tree in which I was hidden. I had carried the joke too far. The tiger was furious and hellbent upon exterminating what he thought to be his spotted foe, hiding in the tree. Moreover the tree was an easy one to climb and I was only about fifteen feet above the ground.

The tiger disappeared from view as he got below the platform of my *machan*. The tree shook as he sprang into the first fork and I could hear the scraping of his claws upon the bark as he scrambled upwards, growling furiously. It was not a big tree and his efforts, together with his weight, set up a strange trembling that made my whole *machan* vibrate.

Matters had gone far enough. In another moment those enormous paws would reach up and tear the platform on which I was seated to shreds. I would be thrown off the tree and the tiger would probably jump down upon me before he could realize I was no panther.

'Shoo! Shoo! Shoo!' I screeched in desperation, leaping to my feet as I pointed the rifle downwards, waiting for his head or paw to show over the edge of the platform. The unfortunate tiger really got the shock of his life. He recognized the human voice and must have wondered what sort of panther could be above him, since it had, all of a sudden, turned itself into a man. And courage was not his strong point, as he had shown a few days earlier when he had met me behind the acacia.

The growling stopped and the tree shook furiously as the tiger hurled his bulk to earth. He did not stop for a moment, but bounded into the undergrowth; then I heard the noise of his precipitate departure through the dry bushes.

When I got back to camp I told Byanna and Appu and my other friends of the joke I had at the tiger's expense. They were all amused, but little Appu was tickled to death. He slapped his thighs with the palms of his hands and laughed and laughed and laughed. Almost gasping for breath, he choked over his words: 'But yesterday, the tiger heard a tiger that turned out to be a man. Today it heard a panther that became a man. It must be thinking it's going mad!'

Next day, I replaced the heifer that had been killed, and that very night this new heifer was killed. We had not changed the spot nor the *machan* where I had teased the tiger the day before. We were after the lame tiger, the man-eater, so it was an advantage to use the *machan* from which the other tiger, the stupid 'roaring tiger' as we had named him, had been driven away. By using this *machan* again, we could at least be sure the 'roaring tiger' would not interfere. So it followed that, when the slaying of the new heifer was reported at about 9 a.m. by Appu and the half-dozen men armed with axes and staves, who had gone to inspect the various baits, my spirits rose in anticipation. At last I was to come to grips with the man-eater himself, for surely here he was at last!

Filled with this hope, I climbed into the *machan* early that afternoon and had not been there long when a mongoose appeared. He must have been extremely hungry, for he nibbled at the dead heifer and then started bolting mouthfuls of flesh until he was bloated and could hardly walk, before he toddled away.

As if they had been awaiting his departure, a bevy of what are known in this part of India as 'gerjers'—a species of small quail—appeared in the clearing within a short time. They did not touch the putrefying flesh but started pecking at the myriads of tiny beetles and other insects attracted by the stench from the carcase that was increasing with the heat of the day. Bluebottle flies settled in hordes upon the exposed flesh. There they would lay eggs that in a short while would hatch into myriads of white grubs. These would eat up the flesh and would, in turn be eaten by birds and insects that would come to prey upon them. In less than twenty-four hours that carcase would be reduced to mere bones by the action of maggots alone, apart from the scavengers of the sky, the vultures, that were already gathering for the final feast, and the scavengers of the night—hyaenas and jackals—that would arrive for the scant remains after darkness had fallen.

Then, of course, there was the rightful owner—the lame tiger as I hoped he would be—who should turn up by eight o'clock at the latest.

My reverie was rudely interrupted by the raucous but happy crow of a junglecock nearby: 'Wheew! Kuck-kaya-kaya-kuck'm' he called, and I knew without looking at my watch that it was nearing half-past five. Evening had come and I began to hope that the man-eater would be as obliging as his inoffensive cousin, the roaring tiger, by putting in his appearance before nightfall.

Down by the lake which, incidentally, was behind me, two families of peafowl began to call to each other: 'Mi-aow!' while what is known as the 'Golamothy Bird,' from far away, gave her mating call: 'Gol-a-mothy! Gol-a-mo-thy!' Every male within earshot, hearing that irresistible, enticing cry, would fly to her and before sunset she would have a number of suitors from whom to make her choice.

Twilight soon enveloped the jungle, that period of uncertainty between daylight and dark, when the eyesight is most easily deceived and innocent shrubs and bushes assume the menacing appearance of crouching, watching beasts.

Phutt! Phutt! Phutt! A number of birds flapped heavily in headlong flight from a tree somewhere behind me. They gave voice to a shrieking alarm 'Kee-ya! Kee-ya! Kee-ya!'

Something had aroused a flock of crimson-headed parrots from their roosting place and they fled to seek another. Now why did the parrots do that? Maybe they saw a wild cat on the prowl. Or could it be the tiger?

Time slipped by.

'Keech! Keech! Keech! Keech!' A number of miniature bats of the insect-eating variety swooped and dived at their invisible prey, taking them on the wing and screeching in sheer joy in such high notes, I am told, that it is beyond the human ear to register them. And I am right glad of that as the screeching, creaking noises they were making at the moment that I could hear were loud enough.

A nightjar fluttered overhead and settled somewhere behind me. He started the chorus of calls that would soon be repeated by a number of his fellows: 'Chuck chuck Chuck Chuck Chuckooooo; Chuck Chuck ...'

Then he stopped abruptly and took flight. I could see him sailing over the treetop to my right. And a second later I heard a deep sigh beneath my *machan*, followed by complete silence. Although I could not see him, I knew the tiger had arrived.

He was standing directly below me, and I sensed that he was inspecting the kill and his surroundings with the utmost care to make quite certain no hidden danger threatened. Would he look up and discover the *machan*? A nerve-straining period of inactivity followed. Then I heard a continuous small sound which I shall not try to describe, although I could easily identify it. The tiger was answering the calls of nature.

I was elated. This was a good sign indeed. It showed he was not at all frightened or suspicious.

The next instant the tiger walked boldly into view from under my tree. In spite of the fact that it had become very dark I could make out those cautious but purposeful strides that took him to the kill. There was not the vestige of a limp in his walk. He was certainly not a lame animal and therefore not the man-eater.

I voiced my disgust beneath my breath. The tiger stopped as if he had heard me. Then he continued till he reached the dead heifer, where he halted to look down upon it.

Without doubt he was my old friend, the roaring tiger. For a moment I was tempted to shoot him, for this animal was becoming a nuisance. He had taken two of my baits and probably would take a lot more. And baits cost money.

Then I stopped to think. Could he be the man-eater, after all? What evidence did I really have that the man-eater was lame, beyond hearsay? Perhaps the story was all wrong. Maybe this was the man-eater, standing there, just waiting to be shot.

But I recalled his behaviour on the two occasions when he had seen me and found I was a man. That was not the conduct of a man-eater: he had acted more like a scared rabbit. Nevertheless, there was no getting away from it. This animal was becoming a nuisance. So I raised my rifle, aimed quickly at the ground under his belly and fired.

The bullet struck the earth between his legs and in spite of the near darkness I could see the puff of dust it raised as it buried itself in the ground. As for the tiger, he arched his back like a frightened cat, then became elongated as he stretched himself for a mighty spring that took him clean out of sight.

I came down from the *machan* in disgust, shouldered my rifle, and using a pocket torch to light the way in case I trod on a snake, made my way back to the village.

The next day I bought yet another heifer and tied it out at the same spot. Surely the roaring tiger would not take it this time? And I made up my mind that, if he did, I would shoot him without compunction.

This time he did not kill. Oh, he came there all right. The whole village and I heard him. He roared from about ten till near midnight. He had seen the heifer and was very hungry. But, mindful of a tiger that had turned into a man, followed by a panther-man or shall we say a 'leopard-man', and then of some strange thing that made an awful bang and hit the ground between his feet with tremendous force, he could not summon enough courage to kill the tempting bait. He roared his frustration and displeasure instead.

Next morning no kills were reported. But little Appu had some news to give. He had found the trail of the lame tiger near one of the further baits. It had passed within a few yards of the heifer, even halting to look at it. Yet it had not killed the buffalo. Appu said he felt that the man-eater was averse to buffalo meat and would therefore not take any of our baits, however long we might try. He suggested I exchange the buffaloes for bulls and try again.

He said he had another plan in mind. I inquired what it was. Appu grinned hugely as he suggested that he and I might go looking for the man-eater every night until we found him.

A good idea, I replied. As good a notion as looking for a needle in a haystack.

It took a little time for Appu to understand me. With haystacks he was familiar. But not with needles. After all, why should he want one? He wore no clothes! I suggested a pin, instead of a needle. That did not register, either. What had Appu to do with pin? Then I had a brainwave. I picked up a dried twig and twisted off the largest thorn growing on it. I went through the motion of hiding the thorn in a haystack and asked Appu how long he might take to find it. He shrugged.

I said that this was like looking for the lame tiger in an area of jungle that extended for miles and miles. Appu's face brightened as he caught my meaning at last. He laughed and he laughed and he laughed.

All this talk had made breakfast late, but we set out as soon as I had finished. Appu led me in a southwesterly direction from the lake, over the brow of a low hill and into a valley on the other side. A dry streambed wound along this valley and one of my baits had been tied at a spot where a fire-line crossed this stream.

The *path* we had just followed from the lake also crossed the stream at its intersection with the fire-break and led onwards to a Chenchu settlement about three or four miles away.

Chenchus do not live in villages. One stumbles upon a tiny circular hut of sticks and grass, scarcely noticeable in the surrounding jungle. A whole family of ten persons may live in one such hut. There may possibly be another hut nearby, or you may have to cover many miles before reaching the next.

We had deliberately selected the junction-point as the best spot for tying the bait, for a tiger coming upstream or downstream, or from either side of the fireline or footpath—that is, from any one of six directions—would see it immediately. And now, clearly in the dust of the footpath and coming from the opposite sides, were the footprints of a tiger.

I studied them closely. There were the pug-marks of three feet, instead of the four distinct impressions a tiger makes when he is ambling along, or the two marks he leaves when he is stalking by placing each hind foot upon the place vacated by the corresponding forefoot as it is moved forward to avoid treading upon a dried leaf or a twig. There was no doubt about it: this animal was using only three of his feet, and there was something wrong with the fourth. Hence he was unable to leave the quadruple trail normally made by a roaming tiger.

At last I was looking at the man-eater's pug-marks. The uneven distance between them indicated that he was limping badly, almost hopping along, while an occasional drag-mark in the dust showed where he had tried to put his weight on that right foreleg but could not do so. It was clear that the injury was severe and that the wound had not yet healed. I came to the conclusion that it could not be a very old one.

By tracking backwards for about 200 yards we reached the place where the tiger had come out of the jungle intending to cross or follow the footpath. Here he had spotted our bait and had deliberately walked up to it. We could see where he had halted to inspect the heifer from a distance of ten feet and then continued on his way.

This conduct puzzled me. Judging from the severe handicap from which the beast was suffering, he must be very hungry indeed, if not in a state of starvation most of the time. In that emaciated condition, why had he refused a meal that was his only for the taking? One could only conclude that he was not so very hungry after all, for hunger is an urge that neither a starving human nor a starving tiger can resist.

We followed the tiger's trail after leaving our heifer. He had continued along the pathway for only another five or six yards and had then broken into the jungle where he had turned back to recross the streambed and enter the forest on the other side. Here we lost the trail among the dry leaves and hard ground. It appeared as if the tiger had decided to resume his walk to wherever he had been going before he had spotted our buffalo and moved closer to examine it.

Appu and I decided we would ramble in his wake, or rather in the general direction he had been going, for as I have just said, the dry ground afforded no further trail. In a little while we came upon a game-*path*. The ground was still too hard for us to see any pug-marks, but we could make out the abrasions and scrapes left upon the baked earth by the pointed hooves of sambar and spotted deer, while a little further on a bear had recently been engaged upon heaving over boulders that bordered the *path* in his search for grubs and roots.

Appu suggested that, after all, the lame tiger might have been making for this game-trail and had probably followed it, although we could see no traces, and I agreed with him. The track seemed to be much used by wild animals, for not long afterwards we found the marks of a sounder of wild pig, coming from the opposite direction. Of the tiger there was still no trace.

But a little further on we found we were right. A *nullah* cut across the *path* almost at right angles. The trail we were following led sharpy down an incline into this *nullah* and up the other side, and clearly imprinted upon the loose earth of this *nullah* were the tracks of the lame tiger, leading away from us. They had been made the previous night and we had been correct in thinking that the game-trail we were following was the tiger's route. We were interested and decided to find out where the tiger had wanted to go.

We had covered more than a mile along that game-trail when we reached the crest of a small hill and looked down the other side. Below us, leading across a small clearing, we could see a distinct pathway and knew that it was the rough road that led to the Chenchu settlement I have told you about. The game-trail we were following had been but a short cut that had led across the hill instead of going around it, and the lame tiger had been moving towards the settlement.

We continued, and within the next half-mile we discovered that our game-trail led across the Chenchu roadway. Here the tiger had left the game-trail and had walked along the roadway, for his tracks lay clearly in the dust before us. We followed him for nearly another mile, when we heard voices approaching from the opposite direction. Around a bend appeared some ten Chenchus, walking rapidly and talking loudly among themselves. All carried bows and arrows and half of them were armed with crude spears and axes in addition.

They caught sight of us and came forward, talking excitedly, but before they could reach us we had overheard and knew the reason for their agitation. The man-eater had carried off a Chenchu from the hamlet the previous evening.

When they reached us they told us the story. They had all known of the presence of the man-eater for some time and went about, when they had to, in groups armed as they were now. But Kalla, one of the their number, had always been a hunter and held all tigers, including man-eaters, in contempt.

He had proclaimed that he was afraid of no tiger, while on the other hand every tiger walked in fear of him. Kalla had taken his axe and his bow and arrows and his long spear that morning and gone out hunting. He had returned for a late lunch and had informed his wife that he had failed to kill anything, but consoled her with the news that he had discovered a beehive in a hole in a tree almost within a stone's throw of the village.

Kalla had left his bow and arrows and spear behind as unnecessary impediments and had taken his axe, a box of matches and some straw with which to hack out the hive and smoke the bees away, and also an empty tin in which to collect the honey. In a short while, some of the Chenchus heard the sound of his axe and had wondered how they had been so foolish as not to detect the presence of the hive before Kalla had done.

At that moment they were startled by a scream: 'Tiger! Tiger!' Kalla had shrieked, and 'Help! Help! Help!' Then there was silence.

Kalla had not been popular and nobody, including his own wife, was in too great a hurry to rush to his rescue. They waited to see when he would return, but Kalla did not show up. In due course the menfolk gathered together, armed themselves as best they could, and went to the hollow tree where Kalla had found the beehive. The tree and the bees were there, and the axe, but no trace of Kalla. Instead they found fresh gum oozing from the deep abrasions that had been made in the trunk of the tree as the tiger had stood on his hind-paw and grabbed at Kalla with the only forepaw he could use—his left. Necessarily, the operation had been a clumsy one, as the handicapped tiger must have had to support his weight against the tree trunk while reaching for his quarry with one foreleg. This had given Kalla time to scream for help. Had the tiger not been maimed, the Chenchu would not have heard or seen his attacker, while had the tree been a few feet higher, Kalla would have been beyond the reach of the man-eater, which could not have followed him.

The man-eater had dragged Kalla through the bushes into the jungle, where they came across blood and the remnants of his *loincloth*. They had followed for a short distance after that and then stopped, for nobody seemed to have liked Kalla very much. They knew he was dead. What was the use of following? Then they remembered that somebody had told them a couple of *dorais* had come to the village of Peddacheruvu to shoot this man-eater, and they had decided to go there to tell them. But it was too late and darkness had already set in.

So next morning some of the Chenchus had leisurely finished breakfast before setting out to bring Byanna and me the news. That explained how Appu and I came to meet them on the way. My guide and I now knew where the lame tiger had been heading when he had observed our buffalo, and we also knew why he had not killed and eaten the heifer.

Evidently he had made a good meal of the Chenchu the previous night and had then wandered away for water. As likely as not he had visited the lake for a drink. There he had remembered his human kill and had decided to return and finish off what was left. He had been on the way back when he saw our bait but was not hungry enough to kill and eat it, and as likely as not he preferred the taste of the Chenchu's flesh to tough buffalo meat, even though by now there could be little of the Chenchu left.

We told our part in these happenings to the Chenchus, who now became enthusiastic and offered to help in trying to trace where the tiger had gone. We knew that if we succeeded we would find Kalla's remains. But to them this appeared of little importance. Primarily, they wanted me to shoot the tiger, for as long as he remained their lives were in danger. With the eleven Chenchus to follow the trail, we went in the wake of the lame tiger for another few yards before we found he had again turned into the jungle. This time his passage could not escape those eleven pairs of searching eyes and in due course we came to a small, dry *nullah*, up which our quarry had turned. We could see his footmarks, while one of the Chenchus whispered that their settlement was hardly a quarter of a mile away. Within a short time we got the smell of the cadaver, and a little later we heard the hum of a thousand bluebottle flies. At last we had come to what remained of the unfortunate Kalla, the man who had been a little too cocksure. He had met the fate of many a hunter before him, and the fate that is in store for many more the world over. The fate that comes to those who are over-confident and careless.

There was very little left of the Chenchu. His head had been spared. Also his hands and feet, the usual portions of the human anatomy left by a man-eater. Even his shin-bones had been chewed and splintered, and some of his ribs, while sections of his spinal column lay about with hardly any flesh on them.

The man-eater must have been very hungry. Indeed, he must have been almost starving to have made such a meal. Again I wondered why he had spared my buffalo bait, which would have provided him with a far bigger repast.

A short distance away one of the Chenchus discovered a thigh bone. Of the other there was no trace. A hyaena or jackal had probably carried it way.

We discussed the situation in whispers. My companions were divided in their opinions. About half said that I should sit up for the tiger that night in a *machan* they offered to construct, while the other half were convinced it was a waste of time, as the man-eater would never return. There was nothing left for him to eat. Yes indeed: a hyaena would come, certainly jackals. A tiger? Never. Tigers were not carrion-eaters!

Then I remembered that the lame tiger appeared to be a very hungry animal, and I had no doubt of the course I should follow. I would sit over the remains of Kalla that night, come what may. There was a chance, albeit a slim one, that the tiger would return. I told my companions this and even the doubtful ones now saw my point. With enthusiasm, one and all set to work, and under the direction of that expert on *machans*, Appu, once again a wonderful structure took shape before my eyes.

Appu had selected a bushy tree that grew some thirty-five yards away, and from the *machan* the Chenchus built on it, rather higher than usual, being some twenty feet off the ground in order to gain an uninterrupted view of the remains, I would await the doubtful return of the man-eater. We brought the solitary thigh-bone to where the other bones lay, so as to keep them as closely as possible together and offer a more tempting sight that might at least bring the man-eater forward to sniff at them.

Leaving Appu to the task with the other Chenchus, I hurried back to Peddacheruvu for something to eat and also for my night equipment. Byanna was excited when he heard the news and wished me luck.

It was past four o'clock when I returned to find Appu and two others perched on the *machan*. They had covered the few remains with leafy branches to conceal them from the keen sight of vultures, and these branches they removed when they left for the Chenchu settlement, where Appu had elected to spend the night with the others.

With the departure of my henchman, I began to think about the lame tiger. I wondered if he had really been maimed

69

in a fight with another tiger as reported, or by a gunshot wound fired by some poacher, as frequently is the case. Undoubtedly the animal was very severely handicapped, so much so, in fact, that he must have lacked the confidence to tackle the heifer I had tied out for him. I concluded that this was the real reason why he had left it alone. This tiger would indeed prove to be in a very emaciated condition, necessarily dependent on the few small animals and other creatures that he could stalk and tackle upon his three sound legs till such time as some lucky chance presented itself and he found and killed some unfortunate human being.

With this thought came fresh hope. A tiger as hungry as this would surely be tempted to return to the scraps that were left, even after the full meal he had made the night before.

The evening drew to its close in comparative silence. There were few birds and small animals, such as monkeys, in this part of the jungle, or they were strangely quiet for some unaccountable reason. This was unfortunate, for not only are the sounds of the forest for me endless source of delight, but it is upon the cries of alarm made by these smaller creatures, as well as the members of the deer family, that I largely rely to tell me of a tiger's movements. Once or twice, in the distance, a partridge called, but of jungle fowl and peafowl there was no evidence. I wondered about this till the answer came suddenly. The Chenchu settlement! Those little marksmen, with their bows and arrows, had wiped out all the edible birds within a considerable radius.

Darkness began to fall and the birds of the night, being less edible in Chenchu opinion than their unfortunate cousins of the day, and certainly far more difficult to hunt, began their calls. I welcomed the sounds that broke the monotonous silence of the evening I had just passed. A night-heron wailed in despair from the bed of some dry stream, and his cry was answered by a companion further down the valley. Far away, a pair of jackals raised their haunting call.

A squat kind of wood-cricket inhabits the forests of Andhra Pradesh in large numbers, which I have never come across nor heard in the jungles of Madras and Mysore. This little insect chirrups loudly, and when hundreds of them chirrup together the noise is loud enough to drown all other sounds. At times these vibrations synchronize and the resultant throb has the intensity of a tractor working nearby.

I had been listening to this noise that had started soon after sunset. It appeared to be growing steadily in volume and intensity as more and more of the insects joined in the chorus. Nothing else could I hear. Suddenly there was a sharp diminution of the sound. The crickets in the distance appeared to have stopped chirruping, and in a matter of seconds those nearer to me, becoming aware of the silence of their distant companions, stopped chirruping too. It was as if the tractor had come to a sudden halt.

The ensuing hush was relieving to the nerves in one sense but in another way it was strangely foreboding and terrifying. Just what had made the crickets stop their chorus?

The night-herons were still wailing to each other in the distance when I first heard the cause: the call of the man-eater! He roared in the valley. Once, twice and again.

Now I knew why the crickets had ceased their chorus so abruptly. They had heard the first roars of the tiger that had been inaudible to me because of the din they were making. Only after they had stopped was I able to hear him. But what had the man-eater got to do with crickets? Why should they fear him? I fell to wondering at the answer to this question. It intrigued me so much that I decided to put it to a friend of mine in Madras, who is a naturalist. The answer, as I found out later, is a simple one, and I shall tell you about it before I end this story.

The tiger was still roaring. He roared and roared as he came closer and closer. Obviously he intended returning to the remains of Kalla, the Chenchu, but why was he roaring in this fashion? It was as strange as it was unusual. When a tiger returns to his kill he does so in absolute silence, using the utmost caution to conceal his every movement with each step he takes. He certainly does not advertise his presence by roaring.

I was intrigued and awaited the answer in what he would do in the next thirty minutes.

He came as close as about fifty yards from my *machan*, but there he stayed put, hidden in the undergrowth, while he continued to roar. Never for a moment did he come out or show himself, although after some time he started to move around my *machan* and Kalla's remains in a wide circle, while his roaring grew louder and more fierce.

It did not take long to realize that the man-eater knew all about my presence in the tree overlooking his kill. But how could he have found out? He certainly could not have discovered my *machan*, for he had started roaring a long while back and quite a considerable distance away. Thus it was clear that he had known about me and the *machan* from the very start, and that he was trying to frighten me away.

There was only one way in which he could have found out. The man-eater had been lying in concealment all the time and had watched us build the *machan*. He knew some hated human enemy was awaiting his return, and that a return spelt great danger to him. Like all man-eaters, this tiger had an inherent fear of the human race, but in this instance the urge to eat again, in spite of his last big feed, was making him bold enough to think he could drive his foe away by roaring loudly and often. He had evidently followed Appu and the other Chenchus as far as their encampment and had now come back in the hope of being able to gnaw a few bones.

The man-eater continued to roar as he circled again and again, and I waited in patience to see what he would do. There could be only one answer to this intriguing situation within the next half-hour or so. Either the man-eater must become impatient and take a chance, or I would become impatient and go down in search of him. The third alternative was that the tiger would go away and I would lose him. At all costs, I must not allow that to happen.

Time passed. Half an hour. Then another ten minutes. But the man-eater did not show himself. Instead of continuing to move around in a wide circle as he had been doing, the tiger was now evidently lying on the ground, or perhaps sitting on his haunches, in a thicket that I could just make out as a big, black void in the darkness that was softened by the stars that shone brilliantly from a clear sky. And from this thicket he was roaring and roaring with unabated vigour and fury to drive away the person or persons he well knew were hidden in the tree where he had noticed such activity in the afternoon.

When there is something to be done, I am not a very patient person, and the urge to act was growing stronger with each moment. So at last I started to descend the tree as silently as possible. As stealthily as I moved, I knew the man-eater would hear me. If only he would give me time to reach the foot of the tree and walk the few steps to where Kalla's bones lay! Danger lay in the risk that he might attack while I was halfway down. Then I would be helpless, as I would not be able to use my rifle. I could feel the sweat of fear pour down my face and my hands were slippery with it. But I controlled my feet to move as silently and surely as possible. To fall now and hurt myself would mean lying on the ground entirely at the man-eater's mercy.

I was about halfway down when the roaring ceased. He had heard me and guessed that his quarry was on the move. Would he come closer to investigate? Naturally, he would. He might even then be only a few feet away.

The thought made me shaky and I quickened my descent, almost slipping once or twice. I had to feel for each foothold, although the stars gave enough light to make the ground visible. A great feeling of relief and thankfulness surged through me as my foot touched the earth at last. Quickly I brought my loaded rifle, which I had to sling over my right shoulder while making the descent, to the ready, while I stood with my back to the tree to meet the charge I expected at any moment.

The quietness was intense. Not a leaf stirred. The crickets were silent. The man-eater must be creeping towards me now. Surely he would make some sound, the faintest of rustles that would tell me where he was and give me a chance. But he made no sound. There was no rustle. Only an unearthly stillness.

Then it happened! The strain on the tiger had been as great as it had been on me, and he could contain himself no longer. With a shattering roar, he charged.

But he came from quite a different direction from what I had expected. He launched his attack from behind and not from the bush in which he had been hiding.

I heard the roar and whirled around. The tree-trunk was in my way and I could not see him coming, although I had switched on the torch. The stream of light was thrown back into my eyes by the trunk before me and a dark void lay beyond.

The tiger could not now check himself despite the bright light that faced him. A mass of snarling fury, he was suddenly before me, appearing out of the darkness from behind the tree-trunk and to my left. I leaped to the right, desperately keeping the tree between us, and fired hastily from the shelter of the trunk at the massive head, not more than two yards away.

The tiger tried to turn while continuing his blind rush forward and had reached the tree before my scattered wits responded to the urge to work the underlever of the .405. The spent cartridge case flew out of the breach and I had time for a hasty second shot at the confused, blurred hindquarters of the tiger.

He disappeared, and silence fell once more. I listened intently for the sounds I hoped to hear: the gurgling death-rattle of a dying animal, or the deep, sad moaning of a badly-wounded beast. At least the angry roar of an infuriated creature that has been hit in some place. I listened for the crackling, crashing noise made by a wounded animal in headlong flight, heedless of where it is going so long as it succeeds in getting away.

But none of these sounds was to be heard: absolutely nothing at all. I waited perhaps for ten minutes—or fifteen—with the beam of my torch still on the spot where the tiger disappeared from view.

Still the silence continued. No distant alarm-cries from sambar or spotted deer marked the movements of the man-eater. Could my first shot have been fatal? Perhaps the tiger had dropped dead a few yards away.

Then at last I heard a sound. It was the chirruping of a cricket. Others joined in, singly and in twos and threes, till once more the jungle was filled with that vibrating, rasping, uneven sound. It was as if the hidden tractor had been put to work once again.

Of one thing I could then be certain: the man-eater was no longer in the vicinity.

Relieved of the tension, I lowered the beam of the torch on my rifle to examine the ground at the spot where the tiger was when I fired at his head. Then I moved slowly forward, looking closely at the earth in the direction he went. I passed Kalla's bones and reached the place where he disappeared. But nothing was to be seen.

I moved forward till I reached the thick undergrowth and the ground was hidden from view. I examined the leaves, the twigs and the blades of high grass as I moved on in the direction taken by the fleeing man-eater. But there was not a drop of blood to be seen, nor any sign of disturbed, bitten or clawed undergrowth, no evidence of any wounded creature having passed that way.

Then I remembered the deep silence that followed my two shots and was convinced at last of the shocking fact that I had missed, not once, but twice, and the first at point-blank range.

Not knowing the way to the Chenchu settlement in the darkness, I climbed back into the *machan* and spent the rest of the night in bitter self-recrimination. The man-eater would now become more cunning than ever and would never return to a kill again. As a result he would be hungry more often, and this would lead to him killing more frequently. The Chenchus, and other unfortunate people who lived in that area, would have to pay the penalty. The man-eater would now exact an indirect payment for my poor shooting.

It was 4 a.m. before I fell asleep, to be awakened shortly after dawn by Appu and nearly a dozen Chenchus who had accompanied him to ascertain the result of the shots they must have heard the previous night. Shamefacedly, I related what had happened. Appu said nothing. He merely looked at me with one raised eyebrow. There was a wealth of disdain in that look, and he knew I knew it.

There was nothing to do but ask our Chenchu friends to report at once if they heard or saw anything more of the man-eater, and then Appu and I took the weary trail back to Peddacheruvu. Neither of us spoke the whole way. We both felt that, under the circumstances, the less said the better.

Byanna tried to cheer me up when he heard the story by giving a short discourse on the law of averages. In effect he said I had to miss some time if I did not want to miss every time. I was not impressed and went to sleep.

Nothing happened during the next two days and Byanna said that we would have to return to Markapur very shortly for fresh supplies, for, incredible as it might seem, that great stock of foodstuffs we had brought with us was running low. Personally, I think he had given up hope and had come to feel that the man-eater was too cunning for us.

Here was where little Appu showed his mettle. He told Byanna to go to town for the fresh supplies while he and I would scour the jungle from dawn to dusk in an attempt to meet the tiger. My friend agreed, but added that he thought we were wasting our time.

Byanna left for Markapur at six next morning, while Appu and I set off at the same hour to try to meet the lame tiger. This time the Chenchu brought not only his axe but his dog, a lanky, cadaverous cur, whose ears had been cut off as a puppy to avoid attracting the hordes of 'horse-flies,' as they are called in India, that pester horses and dogs in later life by collecting on their ears. I do not know the real name of these pests, but I am told that they belong to the same family as the African tsetse fly. Their bite, unlike that of their African cousins, is quite harmless, although very sharp and painful.

This apparition of a dog, which Appu addressed as 'Adiappa,' looked as if he had not eaten for at least six months. Now Adiappa is a man's name in the Telugu dialect and definitely not that of a dog. I asked Appu the reason and he replied that Adiappa was his neighbour's name, a person

whom Appu disliked intensely. He had, therefore, named the
cur after him to insult the neighbour. In this strategy, however,
Appu had come off second best, as he went on to add with
great resentment that the neighbour, who washed clothes for
a living, had retaliated by giving the name Appu to one of
his donkeys, which he used for carrying the bundles of dirty
linen to the tank for washing.

So Appu and I, with the cur Adiappa dodging between
our legs, circled the lake once again, this time along the
eastern shore and not by the western approach where the
track from Peddacheruvu made its way to the Atmakur-
Doranala road. The scrub was thinner at this end of the lake,
and as a consequence feathered game like peafowl and partridge
were quite plentiful. We also put up a small herd of blackbuck,
an animal normally not found in the vicinity of big jungles
and usually confined to wastelands bordering the cultivated
areas. One old stag, with a jet-black coat and white underbelly
and an enormous pair of corkscrew horns, regarded us with
studied indifference till Adiappa took it into his head to give
chase with a series of hungry yelps. The stag and his harem
disappeared and the cur came back to regard us with mournful,
accusing eyes. Very plainly he was upbraiding us in his
doggie mind for having missed the chance of giving him
something to eat.

The blackbuck, which is the most beautiful of the few
species of the antelope family in India, was also at one time
the most plentiful and roamed the wastelands all over the
peninsula in thousands. Since those days they have been
relentlessly pursued with bows and arrows, firearms, dogs and
all manner of ingenious traps, till today they are but few and
far between, scarcely to be seen in their old haunts and in
real danger of extermination. Rules for their protection exist
on paper, written in Government offices and printed in

notifications and gazettes, but nobody pays heed to them, and the eventual disappearance of this beautiful creature from the face of this earth seems a certainty.

To make matters worse, the blackbuck belongs to the order of animals that chew the cud. That is, their food is swallowed after being partly masticated and passes into the stomach where digestion begins. From here it is returned to the mouth again for further mastication before being finally swallowed. During this process the animal is incapable of quick or prolonged movement and tires easily. If chased for a distance, it falls to earth exhausted and helpless. The indigenous hunters and village poachers know this, and they also know exactly how long after grazing the second digestive process begins and for how long it lasts. So when they observe a herd feeding, they watch patiently till the animals squat down to 'chew the cud.' They wait for a few minutes more and then give chase with packs of dogs, guns, bows and arrows and what not. The frightened antelope tries to escape, but the younger members and the females cannot go far. They collapse exhausted and are either torn to bits by the pursuing dogs or killed at close range when the men come up.

To continue with my story! Appu and I had not gone far after seeing the blackbuck when we crossed the tracks of a family of four nilgai or bluebull, as they are better known. As a rule these animals graze alone. This quartet had gone down the previous night to water at lake. These big antelope leave tracks that look very like those of their cousins of the jungles, the giant sambar deer, the difference being that the former are much more pointed and rather more elongated. At this point we halted. For, superimposed over the tracks of the four nilgai were the pug-marks of a big male tiger.

Appu and I studied the ground carefully and started to follow the tiger's trail for a short distance. Soon we confirmed that he was not our quarry; the lame man-eater. This animal had all four of his feet intact and was suffering no handicap whatever. Undoubtedly we were looking at the pug-marks of our old friend, the roaring but very timid tiger that seemed to insist on haunting us as well as the precincts of the lake. He was no good to us anyhow, while the lame man-eater, being also a male, was hardly likely to keep him company.

We went on and on, working southwards, till by midday we judged we were at least ten miles from the lake which, according to my pocket compass, lay directly north of us. We did not want to go too far as the man-eater had hitherto confined his activities to within about this radius. So after a whispered consultation Appu and I changed direction and set off on a northwesterly course that should, before evening, bring us to a point due west of the lake and within a couple of miles of the little Chenchu settlement where I had met my last adventure.

Here we ran into difficulties. Such game-trails as we did cross ran at right angles to our course, from southwest to northeast, as the animals that had made them through the years had gone towards the lake for water. So we could not avail ourselves of the natural assistance they afforded by following them, but had to follow a direct course towards our destination by struggling through the jungle. This made for very hard going and slow progress. Every few yards we would come up against thorny bushes or clumps of heavy vegetation. These we had to circumvent. Thus the distance we had to cover was more than doubled and took much more time than planned and required frequent reference to my compass.

The sun was scorchingly hot at 3 p.m., and we were both bathed in perspiration when we reached a small hillock. There was an overhanging rock facing us on one side of this hillock, and from the base oozed a tiny trickle of fresh water, only a few drops at a time, which had formed into a puddle no more than a couple of feet in diameter. The supply of water was so small that a stream could not form and the liquid soaked into the ground at about the same rate as it dripped from the rock. As a result the water was fresh and crystal-clear, and to our overheated and tired bodies as welcome as an oasis in the Sahara.

But there was this difference. Clearly imprinted in the moist earth were the tracks of the tiger we were looking for; in fact there were many pug-marks to be seen, for by accident we had discovered his regular drinking-place. Among the tracks was the blurred drag of his limping foot in places where he had rested it on the ground while he drank.

There was no doubt about it. We were looking at the tracks of the lame man-eater at last! Jubilation filled us, both at discovering the tracks and at finding water to drink. I placed the .405 on the ground and lay on my stomach with just one thought for the moment and that was to drink, and drink and drink. I never bothered to see what Appu was doing or even to think about him. I suppose with the usual *sahib's* accustomed attitude of taking things for granted, my subconscious mind, if it thought at all, expected Appu to wait till I had finished.

It was good that Appu actually did so, for my subconscious mind was apparently not up to form that day. For, as I was enjoying the ice-cold water, the man-eater decided to charge.

There came a tremendous roar from the right of us; 'Wrr-off!' And again: 'Wrr-off! Wrr-off!' And then the man-eater was upon us!

Groping for the rifle with my right hand, I crouched on my knees, turning around as best I could to face the rush.

A terrifying apparition greeted me. The snarling form of the tiger was racing towards us in lop-sided, bobbing bounds. He was but fifteen feet away! Appu stood his ground, maniacally flourishing his axe in sweeping circles to meet that onslaught. Yelping frenziedly in front of his master, the dog Adiappa, which up to this moment had showed no sign of being any more than a ludicrous, half-starved cur, stood with bared teeth to meet that awful onslaught.

I suppose the tiger, too, thought the sight before him frightening. The people he had so far killed had been taken by surprise. They had screamed but offered no resistance. In this case a man stood before him, whirling something round and round, while a despicable cur, that he would not have condescended to look at, seemed to want to fight. The only craven thing in the scene and up to the tiger's expectations was the second individual who was rolling on the ground, evidently in abject fear and unable to get up.

The tiger halted for a moment, and in that moment the man-eater had made his greatest and last mistake. The man on the ground—myself—had found his rifle at last and did not get up because he was kneeling to take aim. I fired then, and twice again.

An examination of the dead animal confirmed what I had been told. He had been turned into a man-eater by the severe damage to his right leg suffered during a fight with another tiger. At least, in this case, man was not to blame!

To Appu and his dog, Adiappa, I am grateful that I was able to tell Byanna, when he returned from Markapur very late that evening with a fresh stock of foodstuffs, that his labour had been in vain. Had the stocky little Chenchu and his large-hearted dog not stood their ground but run away, the man-eater would never have paused in his rush and I would not have lived to tell the tale.

To conclude, I will explain why the crickets ceased their chirruping when the man-eater started roaring. My naturalist friend at Madras says it is because the tiger's roars made the ground vibrate. Apparently crickets cannot hear, but they have an acute sense to touch. The vibrations had given them cause for fear—perhaps even an earthquake in the offing? The crickets had stopped shouting at least.

# Three

## *The Queer Side of Things*

VISITS TO THE JUNGLE ARE NOT ALWAYS FOR THE PURPOSE OF HUNTING and killing. Far from it. As I grow older, I find that I have no urge to slay, except when occasion calls for it. So for a change I will tell you of a few incidents of another kind that I have experienced in my forest wanderings.

Among the foothills to the north of the Nilgiri range of mountains lies undulating country, covered by heavy forest to the west where the rainfall is plentiful, and slightly lighter jungle to the east where the monsoon, having expended itself against the lofty Nilgiris, is unable to bring so much rain. Centuries ago, all this land was cultivated and densely populated too, and the remains of quite a number of ruined villages, temples, forts and viaducts are to be found in the forest, covered now by the jungle, where evidently civilization thrived in days gone by.

I have in mind the cattle *patty* of Chemanath, where half-a-dozen wattle huts now stand, enclosed within a rough circle of perhaps two acres of land. The circumference of the circle is outlined by a low barrier of cut, piled thorns, three feet high. The surface within is inches deep in cow dung, accumulated over decades by the hundreds of cattle that have sheltered in this 'patty.' In summer time, when there is no grazing in the forest and the cattle are taken away, this cow dung dries as hard as cement. Then the rains come, and the cattle return. The rain, and the urine passed by hundreds of animals quartered within the thorn enclosure at night, make a quagmire of the accumulated dung. The herdsmen live in the centre of the enclosure, so if you wish to speak to them you must be prepared to wade through the malodorous morass, which may reach to your ankles or higher.

It is not about this *patty* itself that I intend to tell you, but about the ruins of a great temple that stand perhaps half-a-mile away. The roots of massive fig trees grow within the temple walls, but the sanctuary, the holy of holies which only the Brahmin priests were allowed to enter, remains fairly well preserved. A courtyard encloses this sanctuary, and you pass great pillars of hewn rock, leaning at a crazy angle, till you reach a massive wooden door at least six inches thick. It is studded with great brass knobs and has a mighty lever for opening the door from the outside. The huge draw-bar that closes it on the inside is still there. The rusty hinges, made of crude wrought-iron, still exist, and the two doors creak eerily when you open them to pass inside. Of their own weight, perhaps, or maybe due to the angle at which they hang, they come together and once shut you are immured within the sanctuary and can never escape.

The temple itself is built of solid granite, and a few yards in front are the remains of what must, in its day, have been

85

a magnificent stone well. It is lined with granite and is over 150 feet deep by about the same in diameter. Many of the granite blocks have fallen in now and no sign of water is to be seen at the bottom of the well.

Just over a mile from this temple and well, as the crow flies, stand the remains of a stone fort, surrounded by a moat. The forest now covers everything. Nobody goes there and the Irilas of the jungle give the area a wide berth. For they say the spirits of the thousands who perished there in a matter of a few days still haunt the place. No one knows exactly when the catastrophe happened. The story has been handed down from father to son for many generations and has always been the same. It may have occurred two or three hundred years ago or it may have been much earlier.

The Great Fever came at that time, so they say, and it mowed the people down in thousands. The victims never saw the light of a second day. There were no remedies and no doctors. The people just died where they collapsed and there was nobody to bury them. It is said that the stench of death and decay was so great that people at Kalhatti, seven miles away and halfway up the mountains, could smell it. The few that survived fled from the valley of death, not waiting to take their belongings with them, and civilization came to an end. The jungle took over and blotted out human habitation, while its creatures fed on the rotted flesh and the countless bones of the dead for a whole year.

What this great fever could have been nobody knows, but from the havoc it wrought, its contagious nature and quick end, people say it could only have been that most dreaded of all infectious diseases, the plague, in one of its most virulent forms. Certain it is that human habitation in the area ended completely, and it has never returned.

Into the holy of holies of the temple no outsider was ever allowed in times past, particularly a meat-eater or one of foreign race. The ancient priests, all Brahmins, would attend bare-bodied and with bare feet. This makes you wonder whether you are right when you stand within the sanctuary with your boots on.

There is a raised earthen platform at one end, and resting upon it are a number of images, carved in stone, of the sacred animal of the Hindus, the bull. There are about five of them if I remember correctly, varying in size. The bull is always depicted in sitting posture. The largest stands a little over a foot high by about two and a half feet long; the smallest about four inches by ten. To one side is an ancient lamp, perhaps six inches high. It is made of brass, completely dulled with age and oxidization, and consists merely of a hollow cavity to hold the oil, and a lip to support the wick that rests in the oil, the whole standing on a pedestal which is a carving of some deity.

And thereby hangs a tale, for some years ago I went to this temple accompanied by some tourists. They were strangers whom I had met casually in the jungle. They had heard of the temple and asked me where it was, and because it was difficult to locate I had brought them there in person. They were four. We stood inside the holy of holies, looking at the stone bulls which, incidentally, are called 'nandies,' when one of the tourists, let us call him Captain Neide, who came from Australia, noticed the brass lamp and took a fancy to it.

'I think I'll keep this as a souvenir,' he remarked, picking it up and thrusting it into his pocket.

'You shouldn't do that.' I remonstrated, and his wife supported me. 'Put it back, John; we don't need it,' was her comment.

'But why not?' argued John. 'I need it.'

The top of the lamp protruded from his pocket as we went away and I could not help thinking to myself that it was a shame that the lamp was leaving its abode after no one knew how many hundreds of years. I returned to my camp, while the party of tourists went up the hill to the town of Ootacamund, seventeen miles away. They had mentioned they were spending four or five day there, before moving on.

Four days later I was walking along the main road when a black and yellow taxi, coming down from Ootacamund, overtook me and then halted. Taxis do not generally come to jungles, so I approached it curiously to see who was inside. To my great surprise I saw Captain Neide at the back, propped up with pillows, covered with a blanket, and looking very sick. Next to him sat Mrs Neide, pale and anxious.

'Thank heaven we met you, Mr Anderson,' she burst out. 'Something terrible has happened to John.'

Then she went on to explain that the very evening her husband and their friends reached Ootacamund, he developed a high temperature and became extremely ill. A doctor was summoned, who diagnosed sunstroke and treated the patient accordingly.

But during the night Neide's temperature rose to 106 degrees. He became delirious. His distraught wife and her friends called the doctor again. Neide was taken to hospital, where it was thought he was developing blackwater fever, or an extremely bad bout of malaria. Quinine was administered, but there was no improvement. On the third day Neide was desperately ill, and the hospital staff confessed they could not discover the cause. Neide himself provided the solution on the morning of the fourth day. Delirious most of the time, due to his high temperature, there were short periods when he regained his senses, and during one of these he gasped to his wife, 'Margaret! That lamp! I must take it back to the temple. Get a car, a taxi, anything. I must take it back to the temple today, or I shall die tomorrow. I must take it myself.'

Haltingly he explained that he had had a dream in which he had seen the lamp back in its place on the altar of the old temple. His wife told the house doctor, who merely smiled and said briefly, 'Delirium, madam; he imagined it all.'

But Mrs Neide knew this was not so. On the table in their room at the hotel stood that dreadful lamp. It seemed to draw attention to itself and she could not take her eyes from it.

'I think I shall take him and the lamp by taxi, doctor,' she argued. 'I feel something dreadful is going to happen if we don't return it.'

'Mrs Neide, if you move your husband in his present condition, I'll not be responsible for what happens. He is far too ill and I will not give my permission.'

She went back and told Neide what the doctor had said.

'If you don't help me to return the lamp, I shall be dead by tomorrow. I know it, Margaret,' he gasped.

'I'll take it back in the taxi for you John,' she offered.

'No, no,' he was adamant. 'I brought it away and I must return it,' he insisted. And that was how I came to meet them on the road.

Without comment, I got in beside the driver and directed him to the track that led off the main road to the Chemanath *patty*. A little beyond was the temple, but the car could go no further. Captain Neide, who was conscious now, wanted to carry the lamp to the temple, but it was obvious he was quit unfit to walk.

So I said to him, 'John, I think you have done enough to show you're sorry for taking the lamp away. You've brought it back as far as you possibly can. The temple deity will understand that. Let Mrs Neide and me take it back for you while you rest here.'

He was too exhausted to reply but nodded his consent and, with his wife carrying the lamp and me leading the way, we went back to the temple. The ancient door creaked open and closed of its own volition behind us. We stood at the altar before the five nandies and Mrs Neide reverently replaced the old brass lamp on its pedestal. She was weeping, and I could see she was praying. Then we returned in silence to the car.

Neide was sound asleep. Involuntarily, I stretched out my hand to touch his forehead. He was perspiring profusely, the sweat running down his forehand and cheeks. The fever had left him, and he was quite cool to my touch. Helped by his wife, I tucked the blanket more closely around him, wound up the glass windows to prevent a draught, and instructed the driver to take him back to the hotel at Ootacamund.

For there was no need to go to the hospital. Neide was cured. There were tears of joy on his wife's face as the taxi drove away.

That, my readers, is exactly what happened. You may offer any explanations you like. Autosuggestion? I will not argue with you. All I know is that it happened!

\* \* \*

Another curious incident that I witnessed recently at a hamlet within half a mile of Mavanhalla settlement, which is exactly fifteen miles from Ootacamund, was a case of avowed black magic.

A comely girl living in the hamlet was engaged to be married to man living in the village of Garupalli, twelve miles away. In India couples do not get engaged of their own volition. These things are arranged for them by the parents of both parties, who barter and bargain till they arrive at a settlement. Normally, the principal parties do not even see each other till they are actually married. But in this case there was a difference. The man and his parents visited Mavanhalla. He saw the girl and approved of her, and the date of the wedding was tentatively set.

These people are known as Irilas, and it is their custom for the man's parents to pay the girl's parents a certain sum of money for her hand in marriage. In plain words, they purchase her. This is different from the normal Indian custom of dowry, whereby the girl's parents are required to put down an agreed sum.

In this case, however, the boy's parents at the last moment said they could not, or would not, pay. The girl's parents, in a rage, broke off the engagement and found another candidate willing to pay the price they had fixed for their daughter.

Then things happened. The Garupalli lad, furious at being turned down, and mad with jealousy, walked through the jungle for a distance of over a hundred miles to the town of Kollegal, near the banks of the Cauvery river, where lived a black magician of very great and evil repute. He had to spend money through the nose, for the magician made him buy a whole sheep for sacrifice, its blood being offered to the spirit which was now to take a hand in matters, while its flesh went to the magician. The unholy ceremony was performed at three in the morning of the night of the full moon.

A hundred miles away the girl was sleeping in the hamlet near Mavanhalla when, at precisely three that morning, she awoke with a pain in her stomach and hastened outside the hut to answer the call of nature. A few yards to the rear of each hut is the spot where the inhabitants usually go for this purpose.

She reported that she had finished and was just coming away when two unknown men materialized as if from nowhere, laid hold of her sari, and urged her to come at once with them to Gorupalli. Sensing that this was a ploy by her late betrothed to entice her away, the girl said she would try to come as soon as it was daylight. To this the men replied that she should come immediately, when the girl said that the distance was too great. At this they offered to carry her.

The exchange of words had reached this stage when the girl happened to look down. Horror gripped her when she noticed that neither of the men had feet; at least their feet did not touch the ground, which she could plainly see in the brilliant moonlight. Rather, she could see the ground in the brilliant moonlight, but no feet where there should have been feet!

She screamed after that. The men vanished and people came tumbling out of their huts in response to her yells. She told them what had happened, but the neighbours thought she had had a nightmare, for no men were to be seen.

The girl was upset for the rest of that day and would not eat, but at the usual time of about 7.30 p.m., sat down for her supper, a simple meal of curry and rice. In the usual way she fashioned with her right hand a ball of rice and curry and put it into her mouth. Then her mouth burned as if on fire and the food appeared to become hard. In a panic she spat it out. But what came out of her mouth and into the plate was a stone.

This sort of thing continued for eight days. Then I happened to visit Mavanhalla and was told about it. Apparently the girl could eat her morning meal undisturbed, and also at any other time of the day. The phenomenon occurred only after sundown, when she attempted to eat her supper.

Being always interested in things unusual, I hastened to the hamlet, where I saw the girl and her parents and spoke to them. I spoke also to the neighbours; in fact nearly every adult in that settlement. They had all witnessed the phenomenon and told me the story that I have just related. The father had collected these stones and some other miscellaneous articles that the girl had spat out. I asked him to give them to me, which he did, and they are before me as I write. The items are as follows: stones of various sizes and shapes—six items, the largest weighing three ounces; broken bits of pottery—six items; charcoal—two pieces; lastly, a piece of broken bottle-glass.

As I have said, the time for these phenomena to occur was at the evening meal. So I returned just after seven o'clock that evening to witness things for myself.

The girl was lying on the ground in a sort of daze, with more than a dozen people around her. Her face was damp with sweat, and every little while her mouth would work, twist and pout, as if something was inside.

By nature I am sceptic. The thought came to me that the girl was putting on an act and the reason seemed simple enough. She wanted to marry the man at Garupalli and had invented the whole story. In the course of the day she herself, or perhaps an accomplice acting for her, would procure a stone or a piece of tile in advance and conceal it somewhere on her person. This object the girl would put into her mouth some time before the evening meal and keep it there till the time she spit the object out, together with the food. So I determined that I would expose her trickery before all the people who had gathered around her.

I told her to open her mouth widely. She did so. I had brought my torch with me, as it was dark outside. I shone the torch into her mouth. Nothing appeared to be there. Suddenly, and without asking her permission, and risking a bite from her, I thrust my forefinger beneath her tongue to see if anything was hidden there, then into both the cavities formed between her cheeks and jaws, holding her firmly with my left hand by the back of her neck in order that my probing finger would find the stone I was convinced was hidden in her mouth.

The girl choked, but surprisingly enough did not struggle or protest. Rather, she appeared to be going to sleep. There was nothing in her mouth and finally I released her. The working and pouting and twisting of her mouth stopped after that, and time passed.

In about half-an-hour her evening meal was brought to her. She sat up to eat it, stretching forth her hand to take the first mouthful, but I stopped her. Calling to her mother, I asked the old woman to break up the rice in the girl's hand as the thought came to me that a stone might be concealed in the rice or curry.

The girl stretched out her hand again, took up the grains we had examined between her fingers, mixed them with the curry, made a small ball of them and put it into her mouth. Then she started to chew. Everything was normal. I smiled to myself in satisfaction. The vixen has not been able to dodge me.

The next instant I heard it. A jarring, crunching sound as the girl's moving teeth came down on some hard object in her mouth. The look of abject terror that came into her face was genuine enough. I could see fear in her eyes, genuine fear, not assumed. With a muffled scream she spat the object out. A stone fell with a dull plop into the earthen plate containing the curry and rice.

At that moment I shouted to her to open her mouth, seized the back of her neck again with my left hand, and thrust my right forefinger into her mouth. Believe it or not. There was not a grain of rice or food of any sort in her mouth! The mouthful she had just taken had vanished entirely. The stone had taken its place!

Now the girl had not the time to chew the food, nor could she have swallowed it, for I had been watching intently all the time. To swallow a fistful of rice and curry requires a visible swallowing movement of the muscles of the mouth, throat and gullet. There had been nothing of that sort. The stone she spat out that evening is the one weighing three ounces which is now before me.

But the story does not end there. I witnessed the same thing the next evening. Once more I looked into the girl's mouth and searched carefully for any hidden object as she began to eat her food. As if to reward my diligence, the piece of broken bottle-glass, with jagged edges, emerged this time. It also lies before me as I write. How the broken edges did not cut her tongue and mouth I do not know. And once again there was not a grain of food left in her mouth after the glass had dropped out. This time a larger crowd of people than ever before witnessed the incident.

News of these happenings, as may well be imagined, had spread far and wide, and the next afternoon a healer arrived. He was an Indian of about my own age, a Christian, and an unpretentious individual. I had gone a little early to the girl's hut that evening, for I was still curious and wanted to see this thing once more for my own satisfaction. The strange Indian was squatting at the door when I arrived. He rose and smiled affably. Speaking softly and in faultless English, he introduced himself and said he was on a visit to Ootacamund. He had heard about the girl there and had come down by the evening bus, walking the three miles alone through the jungle from the village of Masinigudi, where the bus had dropped him.

Very modestly, but with strange self-confidence, he claimed that God had given him the power of healing and that he had come to heal the girl. Rather taken aback, I am afraid I spoke somewhat caustically.

'What you mean is, you have come to try to heal her!'

'No, sir, I have come to heal her. I was impelled to come from Ootacamund for this purpose. God will not fail, sir. He cannot.'

I felt rather sheepish, faced with such simple confidence, and said nothing. Then this stranger, who had introduced himself by the simple Indian name of Puttaswamy, began to question the girl and her parents. In a short while these, together with several of the bystanders who had witnessed the phenomenon on many occasions, told the whole story. Finally I told him of my own experiences on the two preceding days.

By this time the girl had begun to perspire and her mouth had begun to work. The symptoms I had seen twice before were starting. Puttaswamy sat beside her and said nothing. Hie eyes were closed and his lips were moving faintly. He appeared to be muttering to himself—perhaps he was praying.

Once again, regardless of the healer's presence, I made the girl open her mouth and examined it more carefully than ever before, looking down her throat questing with my finger beneath her tongue, between her jaws and cheeks, everywhere I possibly could. Very definitely there was nothing concealed in her mouth.

Then came the final act in this strange drama. The evening meal was brought to the girl in the form of the usual rice and curry, for the Irilas knew no other. The girl made and put the ball of food in her mouth and started to chew. Peremptorily the silence was broken by Puttaswamy. In a strangely confident, loud voice, he cried:

'In the name of Jesus Christ of Nazareth, whoever you are, I command you, come out of her!'

There came the unmistakable crack and crunch of stone in the girl's mouth. She screamed and rolled on the ground in a frenzy as if in an epileptic fit, tearing her hair and grinding her teeth. Puttaswamy knelt beside her. His eyes were like coals and were moist with emotion. Once again he cried:

'In the name of Jesus Christ of Nazareth, leave her this instant!'

The girl was violently convulsed, bending backwards as if in the throes of tetanus. She spat out the rice and curry she had taken. A horrid screech came from her throat. She shuddered, then was still. A few minutes later she moved again. Gently Puttaswamy sat her up. There was no stone in her mouth—only a few grains of rice and curry.

Softly, but quivering with deep emotion and joy, Puttaswamy said, 'Thank you, Jesus.'

The girl was cured. Instinctively we all knew it for we could feel the power that radiated from this strange and simple man.

I saw these for myself and know they are true!

* * *

The man I am now going to tell you about was a dacoit—a thief and murderer of nine people!

The story began many years ago. The man's name was Selvaraj. The police records described him as: 'aged 36 years; height 5 feet 7 inches; of average dark complexion; usually sporting a heavy, twirled moustache reaching almost to his temple; has a distinctly protruding upper lip and a scar reaching from the corner of his right eye to the lobe of his right ear.'

The trouble started with a family feud. Selvaraj's father had quarrelled with a neighbour. The latter assembled a gang of relatives, waylaid the elderly man one night, murdered him and tied the corpse to a tree bordering the highway for everyone to see as an example the following morning.

Selvaraj was a young man then. He knew about the feud, but had contrived to keep himself aloof. But the cruel murder of his father was too much for him. With his brother to assist, and five others, the seven avengers raided the home of the murderers and hacked all nine of them to death with wood-choppers.

There was a hue and cry after that, the cause of mass murders and the identity of the perpetrators being well known. Three of Selvaraj's relatives, who had assisted him, were caught, convicted and hanged. He, his brother and two others went into hiding.

The feud spread and police help was not asked by either side. The relations of the nine men who had been killed came to find out where Selvaraj, his brother and the two others were hiding. As usual, it was because of a woman that the information leaked out. Selvaraj's brother had taken up with another man's wife and was living with her, along with Selvaraj and the other two men. The aggrieved husband gave the information to the relations of the nine men. They came at night with petrol and set fire to the hut in which their enemies were sleeping. The brother and the woman were burned to death, while Selvaraj and his two companions escaped.

The police came again, arrested the avengers, and got two of them convicted and hanged. Both sides had now gone into hiding in the forest, afraid of the police and thirsting for each other's blood.

Bereft of all his possessions, lands and livelihood, Selvaraj had to live somehow. He could not earn an honest living in any town because the police would arrest him on sight, so force of circumstances compelled him to turn to robbery, but even this he tried to do in an honourable way, if one can associate such a term with crime.

Selvaraj became a dacoit, a sort of Robin Hood of South India. He robbed the rich to feed the poor. Landlords, wealthy business men, shopkeepers and thriving merchants were his prey, but he kept only a portion of his extortions for his own maintenance. The rest he gave away to the maimed, the poor, the sick and the needy. So much so, indeed, that there was a sharp division of feeling about him. The large majority of people, including the farmers and poor ryots, loved and respected him. The small majority of the rich, and of course the police, feared and hated him intensely.

Selvaraj, at about this time, began to acquire a nickname. He had a protruding upper lip and became known as 'Mumptyvayan' meaning 'the man with a mouth like a 'Mumpty.' 'Mumpty' is the local name for a shovel. He lived entirely in the jungle and his domain was here, there and everywhere, over an extent of many miles, ranging from the banks of the Cauvery river into the eastern portion of the district of Kollegal, into Salem district, up Doddahalla or the Secret river and across the mountains to the Chinar river and the outskirts of the town of Pennagram.

He appeared and disappeared like the Scarlet Pimpernel, and the authorities could never catch him. Like Man Singh, the notorious dacoit who ranged the fastnesses of the Chambal valley of Rajasthan in the north of India, Mumptyavayan in the south was equally loved by the poor who inhabited the forest regions and their borders. The authorities could never gain information regarding his whereabouts and could not lay hands on him. On the other hand, people would inform him about the movements of the police when the latter sent armed squads periodically into the jungles to try to catch up with him.

Mumptyavayan's *modus operandi* was simple. From a host of willing informers he would gain information about the sources of income of landlords and merchants. Mysteriously he would then appear at dead of night in the homes of these gentry, threaten them with knife and gun, and make away with the large sums of money they would hurriedly hand over to him in order to save their lives.

Another thing he did was collecting money from timber thieves. At dead of night these poachers would bring lorries and a gang of workers to some quiet corner of the jungle, hack down a tree, cut it up into sections, load the wood on to their vehicles, and disappear before dawn. But just at the crucial moment, as the engine was being started, Mumptyvayan would appear at the driver's cab, his gun pointed at the people inside, and demand fifty rupees as the price of his silence. Invariably the sum was paid.

But on one occasion the enterprising driver engaged his gears and tried to make a run for it. Mumptyvayan did not shoot the man; he shot at both the rear tyres in quick succession. The driver paid up after that. He was put out of business too, for the lorry carried only one spare wheel. Daylight came before the party could go to town and return with a second spare. The poachers tried to off-load the lorry and hide all the timber they had stolen, but they were discovered, arrested and sent to jail, while the lorry was confiscated. In any event, each tyre cost Rs. 600 and the dacoit had only asked for Rs. 50. Mumptyvayan gained much prestige after this incident, while the poacher greatly regretted having refused his reasonable demand.

From reports that were made to the police, it was estimated that Mumptyvayan collected Rs 25,000 a year by robbery, on an average, but the figure could be doubled to include amounts that were taken by him but not reported to the police, as Mumptyvayan was astute enough to rob many whose activities were such as to make it inconvenient, if not impossible, for them to seek police aid.

He invariably worked alone for, very wisely, he distrusted accomplices. His usual costume was a Khaki shirt, rather ragged khaki shorts, a belt around his waist to which a huge knife was strapped on the left side and a dagger on the right, a cartridge-belt across his shoulder, filled with home-loaded 12 bore cartridges, both ball and shot, while he carried an old but well-kept harmless .12 bore Geco gun that he had stolen. Sometimes he wore a green turban to simulate the uniform of a Forest Guard, but generally was bareheaded.

Mumptyvayan was extraordinarily courteous to women, of whom he was, unfortunately for himself, rather overfond. His legal wife lived at the village of Mecheri, ten miles from the Mettur Dam, and he never forgot her in spite of his many concubines who ranged, like his activities, all over the jungle. For six months the police watched the wife's house at Mecheri and still the husband visited her. He came once, disguised as a woman and all covered up; the police only knew about it after he had left.

A month later another muffled figure approached. The police pounced on this one, knocked it down and fastened handcuffs on hands and feet. But to their chagrin, and the open derision of all the villagers who had turned out to enjoy the fun, this figure turned out to be a real woman. She abused the police, but also grinned widely and admitted that Mumptyvayan had sent her to make of them a laughing-stock.

This incident appears to have increased the vagabond's confidence in himself and he regarded the custodians of law and order with contempt, for overnight a notice appeared on the gate of the police station, duly signed by the dacoit, intimating a week in advance that he would visit that very village on a particular day. Two wagons, loaded with constables were rushed to Mecheri and every one of the men was ordered to learn, by heart, a description of the rogue so as to be able to recognize him on sight.

Nobody answering to the description put in an appearance, but at the time of the midday meal a rather troublesome mendicant, without a vestige of hair on head or face and who had met with an accident and lost his right eye, turned up at the police station and begged for food from the constables who were squatting on the verandah and eating their food. One or two of the more kindly-natured gave him a fistful of rice, but the others kicked him out unceremoniously.

Later, they found that a small aluminium tiffin carrier belonging to one of them was missing. The beggar must have taken it—for all beggars are thieves! At dawn, two mornings later, a bleary-eyed policeman found the tiffin-carrier at the gate of the police station. Inside it was a note from Mumptyvayan thanking the owner for the loan of the carrier.

Greatly incensed at this, the authorities are rumoured to have sent about 300 armed policemen, in gangs of fifty, to scour the jungles and bring the dacoit in, dead or alive. They were particularly enjoined to be very alert in dealing with him because, shortly after the tiffin-carrier incident, the rascal had purloined a rifle from a landlord whose house he had raided, although the weapon had had no ammunition with it and it was felt the dacoit would not be in a position to secure any.

While the police were out in the forest searching for him, Mumptyvayan came to town and visited a travelling cinema that had come to the large village of Pennagram. He sat through the show till it was half over, then visited the box-office and relieved the cashier of all the evening's takings. The cashier pleaded that he would be sacked and jailed, as the management would say he had invented the story in order to take the money himself. So the chivalrous dacoit, seeing his point, hastily scribbled a note certifying that it was he,

Mumptyvayan, who had taken the money and not the cashier. He also gave the latter a five rupee note from the takings to buy himself a good meal at the local hotel before news of the robbery was given to the owner and trouble began.

The very next morning he visited the largest shop in the hamlet of Uttaimalai, eleven miles away, and relieved the owner of sixty-three rupees. On that occasion he appears to have been wearing a black muffler, closely wrapped around his neck and up to his ears, and an overcoat, from beneath which he produced two straight double-edged daggers, holding one in each hand to frighten the shopkeeper into silence.

About this time a jail guard, whose home town was the same village of Pennagram, but who had been working at the prison situated in the city of Salem, was dismissed. He returned to his home at Pennagram very disgruntled and heard there about the recent exploits of Mumptyvayan and how anxious the police were to lay hands on him. The thought came to this ex-guard that, with a little subterfuge, he might be able to find the dacoit and gain his confidence; then he could go to the police and make a bargain in advance. A promise would have to be made to reinstate him in his old job at Salem prison, in return for which he would deliver the dacoit, duly fettered, to the police.

With commendable cunningness the ex-jailer pursued his plan. He gave out that he was an aggrieved man who wanted to work for the dacoit and give him information as to where easy money was to be had from the rich landlords and merchants of Salem city. This news was carried to Mumptyvayan in due course and the dacoit fell for the story. Through an agent he contacted the man and had a preliminary talk with him. It was arranged that they should meet again under a certain tree at a secret place near the cattleshed of Panapatti, about eight miles from Pennagram, at ten the following night and come

103

to an understanding. The man hurriedly informed the police at Pennagram, who planned to swoop on the rendezvous at 10.30 p.m., next day, by which time the dacoit was to have been securely fettered. The police also promised to see that the informer was reinstated as jailer at Salem.

Promptly at 10 p.m. the next night the two men met and sat down to talk. Unfortunately, the ex-jailer was rather careless and allowed the handcuffs, which the police had lent him, to clank against a stone as he sat on the ground. Mumptyvayan's sharp ears caught the sound and he became suspicious.

'What have you got there that sounds like iron brother?' he asked.

'This,' replied the ex-jailer and, realizing that the game was up, leaped upon the dacoit at once. Both men were well-built, powerful individuals and a terrific battle was fought in silence, neither side asking nor giving any quarter as they struggled upon the ground like beasts.

Then, for the second time that evening, the stone on the ground aided Mumptyavayan. The ex-jailer was sitting astride him, trying to choke him to death, when the dacoit felt the stone sticking into his side. Gripping it in his right fist, Mumptyvayan smashed it against the side of his antagonist's head. Momentarily stunned, the ex-jailer tumbled off and the dacoit in turn got on top. Once more the struggle began, but Mumptyvayan had his dagger out by now. As his adversary reached up to grapple with him again, a quick slash of the razor-sharp weapon severed three of the man's fingers. He screamed with pain, realizing that the dacoit, in his fury, would kill him for his duplicity. He begged for mercy and said he was sorry for what he had attempted to do.

Just then, Mumptyvayan heard the sound of the approaching police van. He disappeared in the darkness of the forest, leaving the would-be police agent rolling on the ground while trying to staunch the jets of blood that spurted from his injured hand.

The dacoit became a little more cautious after this incident. He disappeared from the jungles for three or four months and was heard of in the towns of Dharmapuri and Krishnagiri, where he robbed shops and people on a petty scale. He also filched a pair of binoculars from the owner of a car three miles out of Dharmapuri. Then Mumptyvayan came back to his old haunts, and the manner of his return was dramatic.

The Superintendent of Police and his family went down to the Hogenaikal Waterfalls on the Cauvery river on a Sunday, to enjoy a picnic and a bath beneath the waterfall. They had left their jeep scarcely a hundred yards away. After completing their ablutions, they ate a picnic lunch and returned to the vehicle to find that the camera that had been left there had been stolen. Scribbled upon the grey paint of the jeep, in chalk, and in five separate places, were these words in the Tamil dialect: 'Mymptyvayan, the rajah of dacoits!'

During my visits to these areas from time to time, I had of course heard many tales of Mumptyvayan and his exploits. The early incidents in his history had aroused my sympathy, but this to a large extent disappeared when I learned of his more mundane actions and the thefts he had committed. I then regarded him as a complete rogue. But when I heard from the police of his daring, his sense of humour and his undeniable bravery, I confess I became attracted by this personality and entertained a great desire to meet him.

One day I brought a party of friends on a fishing expedition to Hogenaikal and found much excitement prevailing at that otherwise peaceful and sleepy hamlet. Mumptyvayan had struck again, and dramatically.

For at about this time an engineer from the government of Madras state had been commissioned to explore the possibility of constructing a dam across the river above the waterfalls, and survey work of every kind was in progress. Just a mile upstream, at a point where the actual construction was contemplated, a camp site had been made and over a hundred labourers were engaged in building a road, drilling holes and helping generally with the survey work. A shed had been erected for the engineer and his associates. A payroll centre had been established, and a clerk had arrived to pay the labourers at the end of each week.

So had Mumptyvayan just two days earlier and he had relieved the pay-clerk of Rs 350 from the pay for the following week without touching an anna of the pay for the week just completed and about to be paid out to the labourers.

Not content with his exploit, he had tapped upon the door of the quarters where the Inspector of Fisheries lived at the neighbouring hamlet of Uttaimalai, a mile away, announcing he was the forest guard and had urgent news of the presence of fish poachers. The Inspector opened the door to find Mumptyvayan, but no forest guard. In a flash the dacoit had stepped within and closed the front door. Then, drawing his usual two double-edged daggers, he had intimidated the official. Luckily there were only Rs. 51 in the house at the time and all of this was handed over to the dacoit.

I met the Fisheries Inspector, and then the engineer, who allowed me to talk to the pay-clerk, and they confirmed the tales I had heard.

But at the moment I was more concerned about the dam than the exploits of the bandit. A dam here would mean the destruction by inundation of thousands of acres of jungle. There would be the erection of quarters for the staff and the township that would follow in the wake of the dam. The whole hamlet of Uttaimalai, including the little hut I had built and owned there for over twenty years, would disappear beneath the water.

I questioned the engineer regarding these things and he very kindly offered to take me around in his jeep and show me exactly where the construction might begin. I accepted his invitation gladly. A third man then joined us, carrying what at first seemed to be a service rifle. He was bareheaded, with a white *dhoti* around his waist and a khaki shirt hanging over it. Great ammunition boots without socks adorned his feet.

As we drove off, I asked the engineer who the armed man might be. He grinned and replied that the man was a police guard deputed to accompany him whenever he went into the jungle, for fear of what was generally thought that he would certainly be robbed by the dacoit, if not captured and held to ransom. Actually my friend seemed to be enjoying the situation.

Very soon we reached the site of the projected dam, alighted and wandered down the river bank together, followed by the armed policeman, who thumped over the river stones in his great boots or dragged them through the soft river sand. Winking to the engineer, I opened a conversation with the policeman, asking him about the dacoit. The man soon gave voice to his pent-up feeling. He was a government servant, he admitted, but the government consisted of fools. Fancy deputing him, single-handed, with a ridiculous weapon such as he held in his hands, to guard so august a personage as the engineer against such a notorious person as Mumptyvayan!

I asked what was wrong with the rifle. The policeman spat with disdain, unslung the weapon from his shoulder, and handed it to me contemptuously.

'It's not a rifle at all, although made to look like one,' he asserted. 'It's only a gun.'

I took the weapon from him and was surprised to find it was only a .410 shotgun with a wooden casing to make it look like a .303 service rifle. The policeman then opened the leather pouch on his belt and showed me ten rounds of ammunition for the weapon. They were merely .410 cartridges.

'With this pea-shooter,' he continued bitterly, 'the government expects me to guard this great man and outshoot this rascal Mumptyvayan, who is a marksman, as everyone knows.'

'Besides,' he went on, 'these rounds won't carry for more than fifty yards. Mumpty has only to sit on a rock sixty yards away and laugh at me, and I can't do anything about it. From there he can kill me, and the engineer *sahib*, as full of holes as a sieve. Bah! Thoo!' and he spat again venomously.

Keeping a serious face, I asked, 'What will you do, then, my friend, if Mumpty should suddenly appear from behind yonder rock or tree?'

With a start, the policeman looked up fearfully at the big rock and the phalanx of trees beyond it, some seventy-five yards away. In a burst of confidence, he addressed both of us.

'Sirs, I'm a family man. I have a wife and six children, the youngest yet a baby. Who will feed them if this bastard kills me? Forgive me, sirs; but if he should appear this instant I shall down this toy gun and run away.'

We laughed to ease his embarrassment when he realized he had said the wrong thing, and I added, 'Please pass the word to everyone to tell this character Mumptyvayan that Anderson *dorai* is looking forward to meeting him some day.'

Three or four months had passed after this incident when I went to my twelve-acre plot of land on the banks of the Chinar river, a dozen miles upstream from the point where this river joins the Cauvery river at Hogenaikal, to camp for a few days. I had allowed my old friend and *shikari*, Ranga, of whom I have spoken in other stories, to live on this land and cultivate it for himself, and in his usual manner he urged me to spend the time with him in the hut he had erected at one corner of the land, rather than pitch the tent I had brought along with me, and usually occupied, at quite another spot.

'For there's a bad elephant about, *dorai,*' he urged. 'It sometimes prowls around at night. Seeing your tent, it may trample upon it you before you can wake.'

'Bad elephant?' I queried. 'How extraordinary! The Forestry department has not told me of any such creature.'

It was midsummer. Everything was bone-dry, and the jungle like timber. There was a not a drop of water in the Chinar river. This was scarcely the time of year for an elephant to be around. Elephants would keep strictly to the banks of the Cauvery river, the only place for many miles where water was to be found.

'Are you quite certain?' I asked again, and suspicion lurked in my tone.

Ranga tried to avoid my gaze. The he spoke in a whisper. 'Mumptyvayan is here,' he confided. 'He came to my hut by moonlight last night and spoke to me. He's known to me, and will not harm you if you stay with me, *dorai*. But if you stay alone—who knows? He may rob you! He may kill you! Who can tell?'

'That's just wonderful.' I exclaimed in ecstasy. 'I have for long wanted to meet this character. Just you go and tell him to come along to my tent tonight. I'd like to speak to him.'

Ranga feigned surprise and indignation. 'Why should I?' he asked. 'Am I the friend of a dacoit?'

'You are,' I affirmed 'just that. But have no fear, I won't tell anyone.'

So we pitched my tent at the corner of the land where I usually camped. That night, till about 10 p.m., I had a long talk with Ranga beside the camp fire and then retired, while he walked back to his hut at the other end of the plot. I remember that I did not leave the lantern burning, for it usually attracts mosquitoes, which are plentiful in that area. The moonlight made everything almost as bright as day, and I could clearly discern the heavy belt of trees, nearly a quarter of a mile away, that marked the course of the Chinar river. I fell asleep still thinking of the dacoit.

Suddenly I awoke. No sound had disturbed me, but I knew that I was no longer alone. The figure of a man stood at the entrance of my tent, brilliantly lit from head to foot by the moonlight. With both hands he held a shotgun at waist level, the weapon pointed directly at me. A khaki shirt overhung a ragged pair of short, and strapped to the man's belt were two long, wicked-looking daggers, one on either hip. Crosswise from one shoulder was strapped a cartridge-belt, the brass heads of the .12 gauge rounds winking in the moonlight. Across the other shoulder hung a pair of binoculars in leather case! A scarf was wound around his head like a turban, but I could see the enormous black moustache that curled upwards to his temples. Brown, rubber-soled shoes were on his feet.

I blinked and rubbed my eyes, but he was still there. My watch showed that it was exactly 2 a.m.

I sat up and spoke joyously: 'Welcome Mumptyvayan! I've wanted to speak to you for a long time.'

'This is no time to talk, white man. I mean business.' He spoke truculently, in a harsh tone. 'Don't attempt to run, or cry out, or I'll kill you. Just come out of your tent and stand here in the moonlight, where I can keep an eye on you, while I collect your rifle, gun and money. I want all three.'

I was disappointed. I had been looking forward to meeting this fellow, but our meeting was not going to be the pleasant one I had hoped it might be. Well, if he wanted it that way, he could certainly have it.

'Mumptyvayan,' I replied sternly, not attempting to move from where I sat, 'I had been looking forward to meeting you and to talking to you as a friend. I've heard of your exploits and I confess I admired some of them, but not all. At least, I thought you were a brave man. Now I'm disappointed—greatly disappointed. For you're a coward, a braggart, and a bluffer!'

The man choked with rage. 'Do not provoke me too far, white man,' he hissed, 'or—.'

'Look, Mumpty,' I interrupted firmly, but with my heart in my mouth. 'You can't get away with it. You know that. You know very well you are bluffing. For you dare not shoot me! As it is, the price upon your head is too high. If you murder a white man just to rob him, the government will really come down upon you with a heavy hand. They'll send the *paltanwallahs* (soldiers) here. They will scour every corner of the jungle till they ferret you out like a jackal. Then they'll kill you, like a rat! Besides, I had hoped to be your friend. I had looked forward to meeting you. What a pity things have ended in this way.'

It was a game of bluff. On my part and on his. Nevertheless, fear gripped my heart. This man had murdered many people already. Would he shoot me like a dog? Perhaps kill me with one of his great knives? I could see that he was a man of tremendous physique.

He knew I was bluffing, but I was not quite certain how far he was bluffing. I only wished I knew. He overrated me, for he was certain that I was certain he was bluffing, and the next second his actions confirmed this.

For Mumptyvayan grounded the butt of his gun and leaned upon the weapon. Then he spoke in a changed voice:

111

'*Dorai,* you're a strange man, indeed, and the first one who has not begged for mercy. A man after my own heart. Do you give me your word of honour that you won't try to arrest me or harm me? Will you promise that you'll tell nobody, not even our friend Ranga, that we met tonight?'

'I promise, most willingly, Mumpty,' I said in genuine relief, getting up and walking out into the moonlight. 'Let's shake hands on it.'

The dacoit laid his gun on the ground and very solemnly we shook hands. It would have been a strange sight to a watcher, to see this fierce and ragged multi-murderer vigorously shaking the hand of a white man in blue-and-white pyjamas, whose heart was still beating abnormally fast.

We squatted on the ground there, and we talked and talked. I was clear from the beginning that this poor fellow wanted the company of someone to whom he might talk freely, someone to whom he could pour out his heart. And he did just that. He told me his whole life story, every detail. When he began talking there was pride and boastfulness in his words, but as he proceeded a certain wistfulness crept in. I could see that he was genuinely sorry for all that had happened, that he was genuinely repentant. Mumpytyvayan was earnestly looking for a way out. I was deeply moved by his words and I wanted to help him all I could.

He came to the end of his story at last, and silence fell upon us for quite some time. Looking straight into his face in the moonlight, I began to speak:

'Two wrongs don't make a right, Mumpty,' I said. 'They never have; they never will. Just because those wicked men murdered your father you did not acquire the right to murder them. However, the harm has been done now. I think you can see that for yourself and you'll admit it, eh?'

The dacoit nodded in silence.

So I continued. 'The proper thing for me to do is to advise you to give yourself up, but I am not so sure it would be practical advice so far as your interests are concerned. You would probably be hanged; come to think of it, I'm sure you would be. If I were to advise you to continue as your are doing, it would be bad advice, Mumpty. For every man's hand is against you.....'

But here the dacoit interrupted vehemently. 'What about my friends, *dorai?*' he protested impetuously. 'What about my many informers, who tell me so many things, including every movement of the police? They even told me about you!'

Then in a burst of confidence he admitted: 'The policeman who escorted the engineer told a constable that you wanted to meet me. That constable passed the message to me, for once I befriended his father, who is very poor. And so he gives information to me about the' movements of his brother policemen. Even Ranga is my friend.'

I tried another line of persuasion. 'Don't you feel lonely at times, Mumpty? Don't you long for human companionship? A person to whom you might talk, to whom you may pour out your heart just as you're doing at this moment, to me? How many could you trust to talk to in this way?'

'Indeed I do, *dorai,*' he responded wistfully. 'I realize that inside myself I am most unhappy, most miserable, most lonely. But tell me what I can do!'

I was deeply touched by the man's quite evident sincerity, by the magnitude of the problem confronting him. Silence fell between us as I thought awhile. Then all of a sudden it came to me. I felt I had the solution.

'You can do this, Mumptyvayan. Go to the Cauvery river at night. Throw your rifle, your gun, all the ammunition, your knives, the glasses you stole, everything, into the "Big Bannu," the pool below the Hogenaikal Falls where the water is perhaps 200 feet deep. They will never be seen again. Keep nothing you now have, even your clothes, for they will incriminate you. Throw everything into the "Big Bannu".

'Remove your moustache and hair. On second thoughts, burn your khakhi clothes and shoes and don't throw them in the river, for they might float. Then walk to Biligundu and onwards to Dodda Halla. Traverse this stream three miles above the place where it reaches the Cauvery and go through the Tagatti forest to the town of Oregaum. Keep straight on, and you will soon cross the Madras state frontier and enter Mysore state. The police there will not know you. You will arrive at a main road eventually. Turn to your right then, and inquire the way to the town of Kankanhalli. Thirty-three miles north of Kankanhalli is the city of Bangalore, where I live. If you reach Bangalore and come to me there, I will help you further.

'It will take you some days to do this journey on foot. Don't ever let your hair or moustache grow again for if you do, you'll certainly be recognized. Try to get work along the way. The money you earn will help you. Don't carry too much money from here or it will make people suspicious. I will give you my address at Bangalore.'

'Money I have enough of, *dorai*,' he assured me, 'but write your address on a piece of paper, so that I may find you easily at Bangalore.'

I shook my head sadly. 'That I will not do, Mumpty. For, if you are caught and my address found on your person in my handwriting, I shall be in serious trouble. However, I'll give you clear instruction. Memorize them. Okay?'

Mumpty nodded, and I proceeded.

'My name is Anderson. Ask for "Anderson *dorai*." Repeat the name each day to yourself so that you don't forget it.'

He repeated my name several times. Then I proceeded. 'I live next to the "Tamasha Bangla" (the Museum), close to the statue of the "Great White Queen!" Queen Victoria). Remember that. When you reach Bangalore, ask the way to the statue of the "Great White Queen" and the "Tamasha Bangla" which is close to it. In between is a big red house. That's where I live. Anderson *dorai*. Got it? Now keep repeating these directions to yourself, several times a day, so as to be sure you won't forget.'

We were both sitting on the ground, as I told you, and the dacoit threw himself forward touching my feet. This big man was crying like a child.

'*Dorai*, You are my father and my mother' he cried, 'the only real friend I have in this whole world. And to think that only a little while ago I wanted to kill you. I will do as you say.'

There was a strange lump in my throat as I tried to remain calm while patting his matted hair. The muffler he had been wearing as a turban had unwound itself and lay on the ground.

When he began to regain control I raised him to a sitting position, placed a hand on each shoulder and, looking into his eyes, said earnestly:

'You must go now, my friend. You've not realized it, but it's past five o'clock. The junglecocks are crowing and the moonlight wanes before the coming sun. Soon dawn will break, and nobody should see you here. Be brave now, my friend; be determined; be true to yourself and to me and do as I have said. And may Krishna be with you till we meet again.'

Impetuously he dropped to his knees, bent to kiss my feet. Then he scrambled to his feet, *salaamed*, picked up his gun.

The next instant Mumptyvayan the dacoit had vanished into the fading moonlight. I was alone. Or so I thought. For within a couple of minutes my old friend and companion, Ranga, stood before me.

'The *dorai* does not appear to have slept soundly,' he inquired. 'There are dark circles under his eyes. I trust no elephant disturbed him, or was it just the mosquitoes?'

The man could be very annoying at times and I was in no mood for banter.

'I slept soundly enough,' I countered, cutting him short, 'and you know very well that I'm an early riser.'

Ranga coughed, then continued in a casual tone. 'Perhaps I ate too much last night, for I appear to have been dreaming since the early hours of this morning. In my dream I saw two figures sitting in the moonlight, before this very tent. One of them was you, *dorai;* the other was a man in khaki and he carried a gun. You just talked and talked. Wasn't it a strange dream, *dorai?*'

So he had been watching us all the time! Abruptly I swung around and thrust my face forward, almost touching his.

'It was a strange dream, indeed,' I said fiercely. 'But it was only a dream. Only a dream. Remember that always, Ranga. And now, forget about this dream. Don't ever talk about it again. For if you do—to me, or to any other man— our friendship that has lasted for over thirty-five years is over!'

In a changed voice, he spoke cheerfully. 'I slept soundly last night, *dorai.* Nor did I even dream after all that heavy dinner.'

I smiled and laid my hand on his arm, and he smiled in return. Our long friendship was to continue.

Often did I think of Mumptyvayan after that night and nearly three months passed. Then one day I had finished lunch at home when the dogs barked. My Alsatian, followed by a little woolly nondescript about one-tenth its size, dashed out of the back door. They were barking at a mendicant, one of the many that present themselves almost every day at everybody's house in India.

This beggar was leaning on a staff. He was bald headed and clean-shaven, wore only a dirty loin-cloth and an ancient, broken pair of sandals and large, rounded glasses. Around his neck hung a necklace of wooden beads, each the size of a walnut and covered with grime. Smeared horizontally across his forehead from temple to temple were white and red caste marks alternately.

His coal-black eyes looked at me haughtily, even disdainfully. Almost with contempt he asked, 'Can any charity be expected in the abode of a white man?'

Impertinent blackguard! I felt like throwing him out. I advanced threateningly, my intention to abuse him roundly. The proud black eyes stared back into mine. Then I noticed that, beneath the white and red caste marks, a scar extended from his right eye to his temple, only visible when one came near enough to see it.

Mumptyvayan! By all that was wonderful! He knew then that I had recognized him. His eyes were no longer haughty. They shone and were moist with pleasure.

Donald, my son, had gone to work. My wife was out. Only the *Chokra* (boy-servant) was on the premises.

Motioning with my hand to Mumpty to wait, I shouted to the *Chokra,* and when he came gave him instructions to go to the railway station nearly two miles away to inquire the time of the arrival of the mail train from Madras. That should keep him away for the next ninety minutes at least.

When the *Chokra* had gone, I called Mumpty inside, offered him tea and what odds and ends were to be found in the cupboard, and asked him how he fared.

'I did exactly as you instructed me, *dorai*. It broke my heart to throw my firearms and cartridges into the "Big

Bannu" in the river. But I did so. The rest was comparatively easy. I reached the Mysore state border and the town of Kankanhalli in due course. There I got work as a labourer under a rich landlord. *Dorai*, how that man oppressed his poor workers! How I longed to be Mumptyvayan again, if only for a few minutes, to deal with him suitably! His behaviour made me decide never to work for any other man again.

'But by this time I had noticed that there were many mendicants on the roads, most of them in some religious guise. None ever appeared to be hungry. Somehow, somebody fed them. So I decided to become a *sadhu*. My name is Omkrishna, and I am making quite a good living out of it. I'm touring the south and hope to make my way to the city of Madras, where I'll settle down eventually.'

'Not Madras, Mumpty—I mean, Omkrishna,' I corrected myself, 'Somebody in uniform might want you there. It's too close and you might be recognized. I suggest you go northwards instead, into Hyderabad state. The further you are from the scene of your operations the better, remember.'

He thought for a moment and then nodded. 'I think you're right, *dorai*.'

Then he rose to go. I offered him money, but the *sadhu* refused it. 'I'm indebted to you, sir,' he said, 'not you to me. Which reminds me, I've brought something for you. It's the only link I have with the old days.'

He rummaged in his *loincloth* and produced a ring—a gold ring!

'Where did you steal it?' I inquired sternly.

'I didn't steal it,' he replied. 'I got it from the engineer who went to Uttaimalai to build a dam.' Mumptyvayan was laughing now, as he thought of the incident. 'He was walking by the riverside with an armed policeman to keep guard over him. The stupid policeman had one of those toy guns disguised as rifles. They didn't know that I knew it.'

Omkrishna grinned more widely at the recollection. Then he continued: 'I called to the policeman from the shelter of a rock that I would shoot him dead if he tried to resist.'

'The poor devil was terrified. He threw down his ridiculous gun and bolted. I went to the engineer then, but made sure to throw the policeman's weapon into the river first. Strangely, the engineer *sahib* was not frightened. He was grinning at the policeman's hasty departure. In my usual rough voice, I demanded money from him. The engineer spoke strange words to me: "Don't threaten me, Mumptyvayan. Learn to ask nicely."

'He gave me ten rupees. He also took this ring off his finger and handed it to me. I tried to return the money and the ring, for the engineer *sahib* was indeed a good man and a brave one; a gentleman, too. But he refused to take them back. So I wore the ring myself for some time. I knew that if I tried to sell it, I might get caught. However, and this happened before I met you that night, *dorai,*' Omkrishna hastened to add, as if in apology. 'After that meeting I have kept straight and have never robbed again, I can swear to that. And I kept the ring as a gift for you.'

So the unexpected had happened! My friend, the engineer, had longed to meet the dacoit Mumptyvayan. They had met, and as a result I now had his ring!

Omkrishna went away shortly after that and I never saw him again! A whole year passed, during which I often thought of Mumptyvayan but never heard of him. Several times I visited Hogenaikal and other areas that were his old haunts, but nobody spoke of him, nobody had seen him for a long time. Apparently he had disappeared for ever. Two months later the land was agog with the news! Mumptyvayan was dead! He had been shot by a friend who then claimed the reward that the government of Madras had placed on his head two years earlier. The reward was Rs 500, I think, and five acres of land, dead or alive!

Various stories were abroad about how his death had come about. Some said that Mumptyvayan had gone back to visit his wife, others that he had returned to visit a concubine who had been a great favourite. Wife or concubine—the woman had betrayed him! She had a brother, who was in debt and needed the reward badly. The story went that she had prepared Mumptyvayan's favourite dish for him, but into the food she had put *follidol,* a very powerful chemical supplied to the ryots by the government for killing insect pests that attack their crops. Mumptyvayan ate the food. In a few minutes he was in the throes of death. At that moment the woman's brother, who had been awaiting the propitious moment, came in and shot Mumptyvayan dead! For the reward stipulated that the dacoit should be brought in alive, or shot dead in self-defence, but it did not say anything about poisoning him.

The story has it that the reward was granted. Mumptyvayan's dead body was brought by the police to the town of Dharmapuri, where crowds gathered to witness his hasty burial.

\* \* \*

My next story is about an animal and has nothing to do with magic or evil men. It is the story of a bull elephant, and an unusual one at that.

We met this elephant for the first time at about four-thirty one evening while motoring through the jungle, about two miles short of the forest lodge at Anaikutti and about ten miles beyond the old temple I told you about at the beginning of this chapter. He was grazing peacefully in the jungle some fifty yards to our right.

The car was filled with sightseers and amateur photographers, and they took innumerable pictures of the old elephant. He ignored us completely, both cars and people, behaving as if he were all alone, with no other creature within miles of him.

I was seated at the back of the car, on the right side, while a friend was driving. The other members were foreigners who had come to India to see the jungles. One of them, who had seen elephants before but only in zoos and circuses, stepped out from the car and, against our whispered advice, walked around the vehicle and half the distance towards the elephant. This was an extremely dangerous thing to have done and the rest of us called to him to return. So he stopped and took a picture. He took several more and then started asking for trouble by shouting at the elephant, waving his arms about, and finally by hurling stones at the animal. The first missed its mark by a narrow margin. The second struck a branch of the tree under which the bull was standing and bounced off, falling directly on his back. The third stone stuck the elephant in the face at the base of the trunk and rolled down, thudding against the left tusk before falling to the ground.

The bull did not retaliate. He merely turned his back on us, walked behind the tree, faced about and peered at us quietly as if to say, 'Can't you go away and leave me in peace?'

His behaviour was astounding. No other elephant would have acted thus, particularly no bull, after such provocation. The normal reaction would have been to make itself scarce at the first sight, or even the sound of the car. Allowing it had not done this, any wild elephant would certainly have been provoked by somebody repeatedly hurling stones at him. I confess I was certain it would charge, and the gentleman who had been so brave and foolish would soon cease to exist, together with the car and all of us in it. We could not have done anything to save ourselves, for it is against the rules to annoy wild elephants, to bait them, hurl stones at them, if they show resentment.

With difficulty we got our friend away from the place and continued on our drive in search of other animals to photograph.

It was 6 p.m. when we returned the same way, speculating on whether we would meet the elephant again. We had yet a furlong to go when we saw him once more, this time standing on the opposite side of the road, even closer to the track we were negotiating and facing us. We stopped again to watch, but he went on chewing placidly, every now and then stuffing his mouth with leaves from boughs he had broken down. We noticed that in the process he even ate the wood of the smaller branches on which the leaves were growing.

We studied the animal carefully. He appeared to be in good condition, not emaciated. There were no signs of a wound or of sickness to account for his oddly placid behaviour. The only thing noticeable was that he was an old animal, as could be judged by the fact that the tops of his ears folded over, and by the hollows in his forehead.

Once more my new acquaintance got out of the car and started his stone-throwing. The elephant was closer to us now than at the first encounter, being barely twenty feet away and facing head-on. Something was bound to happen.

But the bull turned his back in obvious disgust and went on feeding. His behaviour was quite unaccountable. Even a domesticated elephant would not have tolerated such treatment from total strangers. To say the least, he would have moved away! Finally our acquaintance—brave, or mad, or both—called out to us that he was going to walk up to the bull. The rest of us then got out and seized him, practically dragging him back to the vehicle, while the elephant continued to graze placidly.

'Rats to your Indian elephants!' he exclaimed in disdain. 'They're as harmless as rabbits.'

At dinner that night the subject was the same. Questions were fired at me that I could not possibly answer. Was this how fiercely wild elephants actually behaved? I was worried. Why had the bull acted in such a strangely docile manner? I fell asleep determined to solve the puzzle the following day.

After breakfast the next morning, I enlisted the aid of two Karumba trackers and taking my rifle we motored to the place where we had met the elephant the evening before. We left the car there and followed his progress through the jungle. This was an easy task for the Karumbas and we came upon him again, a little over half-a-mile away, headed in the general direction of the Anaikutti river, which was still about a mile and a half distant. He was not grazing now, but standing placidly under a tree.

The Karumbas, of course, acted with great caution; but emboldened by our experience of the evening before, I walked towards the bull, the jungle men following at a considerable distance and ready to take off at the first sign of trouble. Nothing happened, although I came as close to the elephant as had my friend the evening before. The bull took no notice of me whatever.

I walked around him. I was convinced he was sorely injured. Or perhaps he was a very sick animal. Then the idea came to me: maybe he was blind in one or both eyes. Or he was deaf. Or he could not smell. There was something seriously wrong with him; of that I was convinced.

For a second time I circled him. At that moment I noticed him following my movements with his small eyes. But they were not inflamed, and there was certainly no sign of the discharge that would show on a bull in '*musth*.' And the animal was not blind. He then lifted his trunk a little towards me and then I knew he could even smell.

What could be wrong with him? Lazily he lifted his trunk, broke a twig above him and stuffed it into his mouth. He could not be wounded or sick, for then he would not be eating so well. All that I was able to discover was that he was a very old animal indeed. Apart from the hollows in his forehead and temples, and the turned-down skin at the tops of his ears, the ivory of both tusks was blackened at the roots with age.

The two Karumbas had been standing at a safe distance while I had been circling the bull. One of them now called out to me, 'there's no mystery here, *dorai*. The Wise one (the manner in which the Karumbas usually refer to elephants) is very old. His days on earth are over, and he has come to the river to die in it peacefully.'

We left it at that and returned to camp. The following day I had some business at the town of Gudalur, nineteen miles away, which is the headquarters of the district. A string of carts, laden with lengths of sugar cane, passed me on the main street. I thought of the old elephant then and of an experiment I would like to try with him. So I bought a dozen pieces, each over six feet in length.

Next morning I went to Anaikutti again, this time with three Karumbas. Two of them carrying the sugarcane. We trailed the old tusker from the spot at which we had seen last and found him on the bank of Anaikutti river. He was standing in the shade of a *muthee* tree.

I approached cautiously with one of the Karumbas who was carrying six of the sugar-cane stems. I can assure you he came with the greatest reluctance. The bull saw us and half-turned slowly. Now he was facing us. The Karumba stopped. I took two lengths of the sugar cane in my left hand, holding my loaded rifle cocked in the crook of my right arm, and advanced slowly and deliberately towards the animal, staring into its eyes but with only conciliatory thoughts in my mind. The next few seconds would show whether this strange animal's behaviour would culminate in a sort of friendship or in enmity.

When I got to within a few feet, the bull became very nervous. He blew air through his trunk and began curling it inwards to protect it from possible harm. His ears flapped. They came forwards and then went backwards against the side of his head. Bad signs indeed! He was about to charge!

I halted, extending my arm to hold out the sugar cane towards him. I did not speak, for I know the human voice annoys and frightens animals.

The elephant became less restive and my arms began to ache with the weight of the sugar cane. After some minutes, I inched forward again, continuing till the broad leaves at the end of the six-foot piece of cane were within reach of his trunk. Then I stopped, holding it out invitingly. With a nervous swish of his trunk the elephant tore the cane from my grasp, pulled it towards himself, and then beat it repeatedly against the ground. He hesitated. I knew he was pondering the question as to what to do next. Put it into his mouth? Stamp upon it and crush it with his weight? Throw it away? Or perhaps attack the puny intruder?

Cautiously, the bull placed the cane sideways in his mouth and bit it. That did it! He tasted the sweet juice, perhaps for the first time in his life, for there were no sugar cane fields in this area. Or maybe he hailed from far-off parts and had eaten sugar cane before and remembered the taste. Anyway, he obviously liked it. For he munched at the cane, while his small eyes stared at me unwinkingly. There was no enmity in them, but there was nervousness still.

I handed him the second length of cane after he had finished the first. He took it readily enough and munched it.

The Karumbas, with the rest of the sugar cane had stopped some distance away and refused to approach any nearer. I knew they regarded my actions as sheer madness. As I was reluctant to dispense with my rifle, I had to make two more trips from the elephant to the Karumbas and back again before I had fed him the remaining ten pieces of cane. But at last they were done and the strangest friendship that ever was heard of had been established between the old wild bull and myself.

The next day I motored to Gundlupet, twenty-one miles away, where sugar-cane could be had, and bought a whole load of the stuff. On the return journey I passed my old friend, Mr Chandran, one of the Forest Range Officers attached to the Mudumalai Game Sanctuary that came very close to the area where the old bull was living out the last days of his existence. I told him the story and he was amazed, adding that he had never heard of anything like it in all his service with the forest department. Mr Chandran reminded me of an incident about two years earlier, when he and I had been in a government jeep, conducting a German friend through the sanctuary.

On that occasion, the jeep had been travelling downhill along a narrow track when we had turned a corner and almost run into a wild tusker feasting on a clump of bamboos he had knocked down, which lay across the road. The tusker saw us and came straight at the jeep. I forgot to tell you that none of us carried firearms, as the area was a game sanctuary and no rifles or guns were allowed. Fortunately the driver kept his head and did not capsize the vehicle by running down the steep slope to our right. The hill banked upwards on the left, so we could not escape that way.

126

The bull reached the radiator, halted, smacked the bonnet with his trunk and—did nothing more! The driver came to life then and backed the jeep as far as he possibly could. Meanwhile, the tusker had gone. After ten minutes we advanced once more towards the bamboo-clump that lay across the track and got out to cut a clearing for the jeep when back upon us in great rage came the bull!

We scurried into the vehicle while the elephant mounted guard over his precious bamboo. This time we had to reverse the jeep for about a furlong before the track was wide enough to turn it around. Needless to say, we left the tusker with the bamboo as his prize!

Mr Chandran related another incident that had occurred more recently. He was again accompanying a party of tourists in the same jeep and with the same driver. A baby elephant suddenly ran across the track, frightened by the sound of the jeep, and its mother came after it. Fury seized her when she saw this strange thing, which she took to be an enemy, so close to her calf. Without further ado she overturned the jeep and then herded her calf to safety. Fortunately, the presence of the calf and her anxiety to get it out of harm's way had distracted her and prevented her from killing the jeep's occupants. As it was, the vehicle was damaged and several of the inmates injured, although not by the elephant directly.

The docile behaviour of the old bull at Anaikutti was all the more amazing in the light of these occurrences.

I returned the next day to feed him again. He accepted the cane readily enough, but did not seem very hungry, as he took only two pieces. The third and fourth pieces I offered him he refused, merely touching them with the tip of his trunk.

The following day we were back once more, but this time the old bull would accept nothing. He just stood in front of me, acknowledging my offering with the tip of his trunk, but taking nothing. His eyes were watery and seemed to hold a sad expression. When I left him, he even turned his head as if to bid an old friend farewell.

For some reason I could not visit him as usual the next day, but at about nine o'clock on the morning of the fourth day, I went to see him again, along with the Karumbas and the sugar cane. But he was not there. However, we knew well enough where we would find him. He would be at the 'Big Pool', half a mile upstream, the 'place where the elephants come to die,' as the Karumbas call it in their own language.

And we found him there, right enough. He was dead. The weather had been dry and the pool was only four feet deep. But the tusker had deliberately lain down in it on his side and placed his head and trunk beneath the surface of the water to drown. His flank protruded above and that was how we found him.

There lies the answer to the great secret: where do the elephants go, and how do they die, when they become too old to live? They drown themselves in a river. I had solved the mystery and at the same time had enjoyed a unique friendship with a full-grown wild tusker, although it was but a brief one.

# Four

## The Dumb Man-Eater of Talavadi

I HAVE MET MANY UNFORGETTABLE CHARACTERS IN MY TIME AND most of them have been jungle men; Indian, Anglo-Indian and European. For the forest appears to develop a man's personality. The more time he spends there the clearer his personality becomes. One such character was my friend Hughie Hailstone, who lived in a wonderful home he had built for himself called 'Moyar Valley Ranch,' down at a place named Mudiyanoor, near Talaimalai, in a corner of the North Coimbatore district and not very far away from the Moyar river, which separates North Coimbatore from the Nilgiri forest division.

Now Hughie was a character if ever there was one. He attended the same school as I did, but passed out much earlier. From that time he followed a varied career. But the man had brains. Everything he touched turned to gold. With some of this money he bought a large tract of forest land and on it he built his Moyar Valley Ranch.

Hughie had a fine collection of firearms, the best that money could buy, but among these he had a great fancy for a .023 Mauser rifle with a hexagonal barrel with which, if I remember rightly, he told me he had shot nine elephants and over twenty tigers. Later, Hughie took a great liking to my son Donald and presented him with this very weapon. Donald was, of course, delighted. But what enhanced the value of the gift was the fact that it was Hughie's favourite weapon. Frankly, I do not believe I could ever part with my ancient, but lovable, old .405. It has been my companion and solace for over forty years.

My story begins at a point where in some part of India Hughie either found or heard of a special kind of grass, the stems of which when dry were stronger than the ordinary matchstick, and not so brittle. They would not break easily, and they burned readily. So Hughie conceived the idea of cultivating this grass on a large scale on the lands of his Moyar Valley Ranch with a view to starting a match factory that would turn out a product to be sold at about half the price of those already on the market, and of much higher quality.

He obtained seeds in quantity, ploughed his lands with the first shower of the monsoon rains, and sowed them. Up came the grass in fine style. Acres of it. The land was virgin and the grass grew to five feet and more. I remember watching it as it bent and rippled to the breeze. But before Hughie's grass could be turned into match sticks there came herds of deer, particularly chital, and large sounders of wild pigs. The deer, of course, ate the grass, while the wild pigs made it their home and did considerable damage by digging it up at places, though for the most part they burrowed a maze of low tunnels through it, leading here, there and everywhere. In these tunnels they sheltered and multiplied to the extent that Hughie wondered eventually whether he should persevere with the match factory or run a ham and bacon concern!

Best of all, with deer and the pigs came tigers and panthers to eat them. Rather I should say more tigers than panthers, for the former arrived in such numbers as not only to decimate the deer and pig population, but to kill and eat the panthers too, so that in the course of time the smaller cats learned to give the match-grass a very wide berth.

Now Hughie employed an assistant, a man named Sweza (a corruption of D'Souza), who came from Mangalore on the west coast of India. Sweza was a most versatile individual: he did everything for Hughie, whose problems he not only knew but anticipated.

He once said to me with reference to his employer, 'I don't know why master spend much money to make more money. Master got plenty money to enjoy and enjoy. But no; he want to make matchsticks, tooth powder from *babul* bark, fertilizer from jungle seeds mixed with elephants' dung, invention for finding underground water, digging ground for getting some stones master says got iron, all sort of things. Only spending money. Why for? This very good place. Master should enjoy. Plenty girls got it here. Young girls; not 'nuff husbands here. I tell-it master. He get very angry. He say-it, "Sweza, you bloody rogue you got it one wife and three more women already. I saved you from one more wife. Now you want to put me in the same trouble!"'

But he was a good fellow, this Sweza, game for anything and as keen as mustard. And he ate well! His paunch and his jolly smile showed this.

One Easter, Sweza felt that his master and himself were entitled to roast pork or venison. So he borrowed his master's small-bore rifle after confiding his good intentions to Hughie, and waded into the match-grass, now somewhat withered and thinned down by the summer heat, in search of quarry. Sweza had not gone very far when he saw the snout of a medium-sized wild pig regarding him with grave suspicion from between the stems of the grass. He fired. The pig fell, picked itself up again, and disappeared. Sweza started to follow hard on its trail.

Just then there was a great swishing in the grass where the pig had disappeared, a snarl, and the scream of a dying animal. Sweza beat a hasty retreat and told his master.

Hughie came out with one of his heavy rifles and Sweza led him to the place where he had fired at the pig, pointing out the direction in which it had gone. Hughie went on and Sweza made to follow him from behind, but Hughie very wisely objected to this. He did not want a bullet from Sweza's rifle in his back. So he asked his servant to go back and wait for him in the open.

Hughie came to the spot where the pig had been killed, but there was no trace of its body. The killer had carried it away. Bent and broken stems of dried grass showed the direction he had taken with his burden. Moving cautiously forward, he had gone for quite a hundred yards when suddenly a loud growl from in front told him the killer was feeding somewhere ahead and resented his intrusion. But Hailstone had seen and shot many tigers and was not to be intimidated by a growl. He moved forward stealthily and the tiger growled more loudly. Hughie knew the charge would come at any moment.

A little later the tiger charged. It came in great leaping bounds through the dried match-grass. Hailstone waited till he could see the contorted face clearly, till the final spring would land the beast right on top of him. Then he fired. Thus was born the man-eater of Talavadi! Hughie's bullet struck the tiger full in the face. The impact tended to stop it, but the weight of the body behind still pushed it forward, with the result that the tiger somersaulted just a few yards away. Hughie worked the bolt of his rifle rapidly to get in a second shot. The magazine jammed.

He did the right thing after that. He turned and fled.

Evidently the tiger was temporarily blinded or maybe too hurt to follow. It floundered about in the grass, digging great holes in the earth as, in agony, it bit and tore the ground with its claws and teeth.

Hughie dashed into the bungalow to get another rifle, Sweza running after him and asking what had happened. But by the time Hailstone got to the spot again, advancing one step at a time, the tiger had vanished, while splashes of blood and saliva on the ground made it plain he had received a severe wound in the region of the mouth or throat.

It is a common belief among some hunters that a wounded feline should not be followed up immediately. Sufficient time should be allowed to pass in which the animal might possibly bleed to death. At least, the wounds would stiffen to the extent that the beast would be disinclined to move far, or it might even be incapable of movement. But there is another school of thought which advocates following up at once. The theory in this case is that the wounded animal should not be given time to recover from the shock and pain of its wounds and from its immediate fear. The advocates of this theory feel that, with the passage of time and long hours of pain, the wounded beast becomes vicious and bent upon revenge, whereas immediately after being wounded it seeks only to escape. They also argue that on humanitarian grounds it is very cruel to allow an animal to suffer hours of intense agony with a vital organ shot away.

Now I am not going to give my own judgment on these theories, except to say that both are partly right and partly wrong. Each animal has its individual characteristics and special nature and will react in its own way. Hughie was a firm believer in the second theory and lost no time in following up.

The blood trail through the long match-grass was clear. It left Hughie's land and entered the forest, where things became a little more difficult. Hughie had to rely on his own abilities as Sweza, still trailing behind with the other rifle, was no tracker. They followed it across a dry ravine, where the tiger had lain down and then continued, and across flat country the other side. The fact that the tiger had lain down indicated that it was badly wounded, and as Hughie had followed up at once, the animal could not be very far away. Probably it had heard him and Sweza and was taking cover in the undergrowth. The third item of information was that this animal appeared to be a coward; it should have taken advantage of the terrain and plenty of cover in the ravine to ambush the two men.

By now the bleeding had lessened and after crossing the flat stretch for another furlong the trail began to lead downhill, where the ground became increasingly stony. Hughie had to slow down and keep looking about for the next drop or two of blood. Soon even this ceased and he could go no further. On that hard ground no pug-marks were visible.

For some unaccountable reason the tracts of forest in the Mudiyanoor area are entirely devoid of jungle tribes or aboriginal population. It is believed this has been so since the days when Tippoo Sultan, the Muslim ruler of Mysore, invaded the surrounding country, sweeping all before him. So Hughie had no opportunity to return later and follow the tiger, as there was nobody in all that area who knew anything about tracking.

The village of Talaimalai is about two miles south of Mudiyanoor, where Hughie had his farm. It is a small hamlet surrounded by fertile country. Nearly two months later, one of the villagers from this place bought a tract of land from his neighbour, or rather arranged to buy it, for the sale deed pertaining to this transaction had necessarily to be signed and registered in the office of the sub-registrar and the money paid by the purchaser to the seller in the presence of this august individual whose headquarters were at a larger village named Talavadi, situated seven miles north of Mudiyanoor. So the vendor and the prospective purchaser, the latter carrying the money he was going to pay for the land, which came to Rs 400, including the incidental expenses involved in the sale deed, set forth together on foot to cover the nine miles between Talaimalai and Talavadi.

They had covered two-thirds of this distance when they crossed a stream that had a little water in it. Here they stopped under a large tree to eat the curried balls of *ragi* flour they had brought with them as a midday meal. The purchaser then went down to the stream to drink and wash while his companion watched him with sleepy eyes.

Suddenly something huge leaped down upon the drinking man from the opposite bank of the stream and back again across the stream to disappear as abruptly as it had come, except that there was no longer any sign of the unfortunate purchaser. He had disappeared, along with that horrible apparition!

The vendor, now fully awake, leaped to his feet and ran as fast as he could towards Talavadi, covering the three miles to that place in record time. There he gasped out his story before the sub-registrar and the clerks sitting in the office. All this being something out of the ordinary, the sub-registrar sent the man to the police station, where the whole tale was repeated.

In the opinion of the constable in charge there was nothing strange about the story. As he reasoned it out, here we have A reporting that he is selling some land to B for Rs 400. A and B set out to register the sale, B carrying Rs 400. On the way, A says that some strange creature appeared out of the jungle and disappeared again, taking B with it. A reports he was more than half-asleep and cannot describe what this strange something was. But the facts remain that B has vanished, the Rs 400 have vanished with him, and the land still belongs to A.

Without further ado, the head constable arrested the unfortunate vendor and locked him in the police station's solitary cell. Then he wrote a lengthy report, stating why he suspected he had caught a murderer. He did not forget to add that the sub-inspector at Satyamangalam, which was the headquarters of the Police and Forest departments and the place to which the prisoner would have to be sent, might please bear in mind when he read the report that it was the humble prayer of the head constable that promotion was long overdue and this brave and dramatic arrest of a dangerous murderer and thief should forthwith clinch matters and lead to the said promotion without delay. He closed the report by saying that he offered daily prayers for the sub-inspector's continued long life and prosperity.

It was not till a week later that the fourth constable attached to the police station at Talavadi returned from leave. The head constable then felt he could manage with two policemen while he sent the other two on escort duty with the prisoner, and his report, to Satyamangalam, where the sub-inspector resided, forty miles away. They should reach there in three days, for they had to walk the whole distance.

Hailstone happened to be standing at the entrance to the grounds of his farm, which abutted on the track leading from Talavadi to Satyamangalam, when he saw the two policemen coming along with a prisoner handcuffed between them.

Conversationally he inquired what wrong the man had done and where he was being taken. The constables, glad of the respite, said they were escorting a murderer, while the poor vendor burst into tears, sobbing out his innocence and his story afresh.

Hughie pricked up his ears.

'Stop weeping, you idiot,' he said kindly but firmly. 'If you want me to help you, just answer a simple question. What was this strange something that you say carried away your companion? At least, what did it look like?'

'*Dorai,*' the man replied, striving to control himself, 'I saw my friend stoop to drink water. At that instant I must have fallen asleep. I heard nothing, but seemed to see some huge, long body jump down from the jungle across the stream and jump back again. Then only did I notice the man had gone! I woke up and ran all the way to Talavadi. Now these policemen say I have murdered my friend and taken his money.'

Then he started crying once more at the thought of his plight.

Hughie remembered the tiger he had wounded just two months earlier. He had often thought about it and wondered if the animal had died or had recovered from its wound. And if it had recovered, Hughie knew that sooner or later he would hear about the animal again. Could this be it?

'Did it look like a tiger?' he asked abruptly.

The policemen looked at him stupidly, but the man in handcuffs replied quickly, 'Come to think of it, *dorai,* it might have been a tiger. As I said, I was more than half asleep and the whole thing happened so quickly. But it was nothing in human form that carried away my companion, of that I am certain. It was something long and big.'

'Don't take this poor man to Satyamangalam,' Hughie advised the policemen. 'Save yourself the journey, for he is no murderer. I think I know what really happened.'

But the officers of law and order the world over are dogged in their purposes, especially when they have someone in handcuffs. The policemen continued on their way to Satyamangalam with their captive, while Hughie went in his car to Talavadi. To his mortification, he discovered from the head constable that nobody knew exactly where the incident had taken place except the prisoner himself, as nobody had taken the trouble to investigate the story or make an inspection of the spot.

Hailstone considered telling the head constable about the wounded tiger but decided against it. A man of his temperament, with a one-track mind, might do anything. He might even lock Hailstone up! So he left the police station without further ado and set out for Satyamangalam, overtaking the two policemen and their prisoner some ten miles beyond Mudiyanoor. Glad of the lift, the three men piled into the car and in less than ninety minutes the whole party were with the sub-inspector.

The sub-inspector read the head constable's report and then listened to what Hughie had to say.

'And this man wants a promotion' was his comment after Hughie had told him that the head constable had not even troubled to visit the scene of the tragedy. 'I shall see him reverted! Please take me to Talavadi in your car.'

Back they went, all five of them, to give the head constable at Talavadi the nastiest surprise of his life. Then the vendor took them to the place where the would-be purchaser and his money had vanished. The head constable was made to go too.

Over a week had passed, but when they crawled to the top of the bank they found the pug-marks of a tiger at the spot where it had clambered back with its burden, the unlucky would-be purchaser. Casting around, a little distance away but still to be seen in the sand, were the fainter imprints of the tiger before it had launched its attack.

Hughie had not brought his rifle. The sub-inspector inquired nervously if the tiger might still be there. Hailstone said 'no,' and the six men started searching the immediate surrounding for the remains of the victim. Strangely enough, it was the vendor, now no longer in chains, who stumbled upon the gnawed bones. A few rags and the ten-rupee notes that had been scattered by the breeze in a wide circle in the grass and undergrowth, confirmed that the remains were indeed all that was left of the purchaser. There were only a few, as most of the bones had been removed by the vultures, jackals and hyaenas that had visited the carcase after the tiger had finished.

The man-eater struck a second time scarcely a month later. This was at the village of Nagalur, about halfway between Hughie's place and the Moyar river which bounded the Nilgiri district. The third victim was an old man who was walking behind his two sons on the old Sultan's Battery Road, a couple of miles behind Talaimalai village. This killing took place in broad daylight—at noon, as a matter of fact.

The three men had set out together from Talaimalai to Nagalur, where the second victim had been taken. For some distance their way lay along the old road I have named, a relic of the days of that fierce Muslim conqueror who long ago brought terror to this region. They had not gone far when they came to a mighty wild-mango tree. Monkeys had knocked down some of the ripe fruit and the three men stopped to eat. When they started walking again the father had fallen behind, from where he continued to talk to them about the business that was taking them to Nagalur.

He had reminded them that it was getting late and they had all begun to walk faster, when a sudden choking cry made the two sons turn around to see a huge tiger with its jaws firmly in their father's throat, in the act of springing into the undergrowth that closely bordered the road on both sides.

Where the beast had come from they never knew. It had certainly made no sound whatever, not even a growl or snarl, which was rather unusual, for attacking tigers generally roar or make some sort of noise to inflate their own courage before springing. In this case, all they had heard was their father's last gasp. By this time the attacker had disappeared and the two boys took to their heels, running as fast as they could back to Talaimalai.

Consternation spread among the village folk and the man-eater, as if he knew very well that his name had struck terror in the area, increased the number of his attacks as he began to roam over a wider circle. He killed as far north as the high road connecting Satyamangalam with the large town of Chamrajnagar in Mysore state. He killed to the east as far as Dimbum, a hamlet standing on the escarpment of mountains overlooking the Satyamangalam plain. He crossed the Moyar river and went into the Nilgiri district to the south, and on the west he trespassed into the Bandipur area which lies in Mysore state.

Unfortunately, at just about this time Hughie, who had always been a vigorous man, fell ill. It happened suddenly and unexpectedly. I know he felt deeply about all that had taken place and was happening, for he held himself responsible for starting the tiger on its man-eating career by wounding it, and he chafed at the illness that prevented him from going after it, which he would otherwise have assuredly done. So he wrote to me, and that was what took me in my Studebaker to Moyar Valley Ranch.

Sweza met me at the gate and I found Hughie asleep in a canvas chair on his verandah. He had not heard my car.

The change in his appearance since we had last me was almost frightening. A robust man, he had shrunk to half his normal size and looked haggard and very ill. He apologized for dragging me away from home and then, as I sat beside him drinking tea and eating the most delicious mangoes that grew on his land, Hughie told the story as I have told it here, not sparing himself and full of self-recrimination not only for wounding the tiger but for not finishing it off after that.

'These things happen, Hughie,' was all the comfort I could offer. 'You must pull yourself together now and join me in killing it.'

He looked at me wryly and said, 'Kenneth, my hunting days are over. My next *shikar* will be in the happy hunting grounds—if there's such a place!'

Indeed, he never hunted again. Shortly after the end of this episode he went by air to England. He had already bought a house there, a nice place in the country. But he was not to enjoy it, for he had been there only a few days when he slipped and fell down the staircase, injuring himself severely. Soon afterwards he died of a heart attack.

However, we now discussed what should be done. It was clear that it would not be worth my while to visit Nagalur and Talaimalai and other places where the tiger had killed, in order to question the people about the animal's habits and peculiarities. Hughie had already done this before falling ill and told me all he had discovered. To begin with, there was scarcely any doubt that it was the animal he had wounded that had now become a man-eater. The few people who had seen it clearly, particularly the two sons of the old man who had been snatched on the Sultan's Battery Road, affirmed that the glimpse they had got of the tiger's face showed there was something seriously the matter with it. The face had been hideously scarred and contorted. Secondly, the animal's uncanny silence on every

141

occasion when there had been a witness to its attack proved that it was either a very strange animal by nature, or that something was wrong with its vocal chords. Moreover, nobody remembered having ever heard this tiger roar.

Of course, tigers had often roared in the area. This was to be expected, because it was full of tigers. But in no locality where any of the human kills had taken place, or at least not for a few days before or after that killing, had any tiger roared in the forest. For this reason the rumour spread that the man-eater was dumb.

The procedure normally followed in trying to shoot a man-eater is as unexciting as it appears to be self-contradictory. The hunter purchases three or four live baits in the form of buffalo heifers or young bulls and ties them out at pre-selected places where *machans* have already been put up, in the hope that the tiger may kill one of them. The hunter then sits in the *machan* the following night to shoot the tiger when it returns for a second meal.

Having heard that man-eaters eat men, you may wonder why an animal bait is tied out. Would a man-eater want to kill it? The answer is that man-eaters do not confine themselves to a diet of human flesh. They merely prefer the flesh of men to other meat. Perhaps a man is easier to find. He is certainly easier to stalk and kill. Maybe there is something appetizing about human flesh. But anyway, one cannot very well tie out a human being as bait.

With Hughie's influence and Sweza's help I purchased four young bulls at Talaimalai village. The two boys whose father had been killed volunteered to help me in tethering the animals and building *machans,* so I recruited them and two more to assist. With Hughie and Sweza we formed a committee of seven persons when we sat down to deliberate on where to tie our baits. Strangely, it has become customary

to tether a bait as near as possible to the spot where a kill
has already taken place. I do not really know why this is so.
It is certainly wrong reasoning to infer that a man-eater, like
a murderer, may have a guilty conscience and come back to
the scene of his crime. To a man-eater his action is no crime.
It is merely his dinner.

I admit I have fallen into the habit myself, but now I come
to think of it, the practice follows faulty reasoning. As a
matter of fact, a man-eater is more likely to avoid the scene
of one of his former kills rather than go there again, because
he knows of the publicity it occasioned and the number of
people who have visited the spot since the occurrence.

The real thing to do, as I have related in earlier stories,
is to try to work out the line of beat the killer has been
following by studying a map of the locality and marking on
it the places where each human kill occurred and the date
of each event. When the tiger is a man-eater of long standing,
with many crimes to his discredit, such a study reveals that
he has been following a fixed route over and over again,
returning to the same localities (but not the exact spot) in
which he has killed before, once in so many weeks or months
as the case may be. In *shikar* parlance, this habit or practice
is known as the 'man-eater's beat.'

I suppose in a way this answers the question posed earlier
as to why it has become more or less an accepted practice
to tie a bait near the spot where a human kill has already
occurred. One hopes it will be on the tiger's beat and that
he will come again. But this may not happen for many weeks
or even months, for every man-eater does not follow a beat.
Most do, but there are exceptions. And in any case such a
beat can only be worked out with a man-eater of long standing.
The animal I was after had started recently and his killings
so far had been haphazard.

All of which brings me back to the fact that it was difficult for us to decide precisely where to tie out and there was much difference of opinion. The two boys advocated trying the Sultan's Battery Road where their father had been killed. The other two men I had recruited to help me said the track leading from Talaimalai to Talavadi would be best, as tiger pug-marks were seen along it nearly every day. Hughie suggested tying the four baits a mile apart from each other and in a straight line, two to three miles south of Talaimalai, where the ground fell away abruptly to the valley of the Moyar river. Sweza suggested tying up somewhere in Hughie's match-grass, where the tiger was first wounded, because he felt it would return there to eat the spotted deer and wild pig that were still abundant.

Of all these suggestions, I decided the last was the least likely to bring success. The man-eater would never return to a place where it had been so badly hurt. So we ruled it out. All the other suggestions were equally good and it appeared to be a matter of luck where and when the tiger would next show up.

Eventually we decided to tether one of the baits on the Sultan's Battery Road, another on the Talaimalai-Talavadi track, and the third and fourth baits at two of the most likely spots along the ridge south of Talaimalai that overlooked the Moyar river, as suggested by Hughie. I felt that the kill, if and when it took place, would be one of these two baits, as tigers passed to and from the Nilgiri forests to the Talaimalai Reserve across this ridge. However, as there was more than one tiger in the area, we would not know whether the man-eater or some quite innocent tiger had made the kill, and the only course open would be to shoot it in the hope that it turned out to be the man-eater. The selection of the exact spot for each tie-up was to be left to me.

I told my four helpers to return at dawn the next day with another eight men, so that there would be a dozen of them altogether, allowing sufficient men for the task of erecting each of the four *machans* that were to be put up before the baits were tied out.

I have found it wise to erect the *machan* first and only afterwards to tie the bait in a suitable line of fire. Then, when a kill occurs, the hunter is ready to take his place. The other way around much disturbance is caused in tying a *machan* after the bait has been killed, and should the tiger be lying in concealment within hearing he generally fails to return.

The *machan* I favoured using at that time, and still think is best, is an ordinary *charpoy* cot with its four legs cut short. For those of you who don't know what a *charpoy* cot is, I may explain that it consists of a rectangular wooden or bamboo frame of four pieces, about six feet by three. Rope, or wide cotton tape, is laced across this frame, while four legs at each of the four corners complete the cot. Most villagers sleep on the ground, but in certain places unduly infested with snakes and scorpions, *charpoy* cots are the only type that are favoured, for they are made in the villages and cost in the region of five rupees each, including the rope used. Where cotton tape or webbing is employed for more comfort—the price, at the most, is doubled.

My *machan* consisted of a cot of the latter type. Each of the four legs had been shortened to a foot in length, sufficient to provide something by which to tie the cot to the branches of a tree. The cot itself was cut into two and folded on two hinges for convenience of transport. Its advantages are obvious; it provided maximum comfort with minimum weight and noise should I be forced to move about, which, incidentally, is the one thing you should never do in sitting up!

Hughie favoured another type of machan, which was nothing more than a folding canvas chair with a footrest to keep your legs from dangling downwards. Sitting in one of these always gave me a sense of insecurity—a feeling that I would either fall out of it, or that the whole structure would collapse at any moment. Of course, this was only prejudice, as in reality there was no real risk either way and I was grateful when Hughie offered to lend me his canvas chair-*machan* to be used in one of the four places we had selected. This meant that the remaining two *machans* would have to be constructed on the spot with bamboos and wood cut in the jungle.

Work began in earnest next day, when the dozen men arrived carrying their sharp knives. Hughie supplied all the rope we would need, so with four of the men leading the bulls I had purchased to serve as bait, we were soon on the Talaimalai-Talavadi road, where we were to tie the first *machan*.

We had gone scarcely a quarter of a mile along this track when we saw, clearly imprinted on the soft earth, the fresh pug-marks of a tiger that had come down the bed of a small *nullah* that crossed the road. The tiger had passed in the early hours of the morning, which was revealed by the fact that the powdery dust bordering the edges of the track had not yet fallen into the depressions made by the tiger's pads. With the passage of a few hours and the action of the wind, this would certainly have happened were the tracks more than six hours old.

Walking up the *nullah*, both to the left and right of where it crossed the road, we saw several older tracks, indicating that this dry streambed was much used either by the tiger whose tracks we had just seen or by other tigers in the locality. Unfortunately, due to their age, these tracks could not be identified for certain with the fresh ones along the road which undoubtedly had been made by an adult male of rather bigger than average size.

A banyan tree grew on the farther bank of the *nullah* just before it crossed the road, and all agreed that this would be the ideal place for the first *machan*. It was an old tree, and many of the roots that had dropped to the earth from the higher branches had in the course of the years, themselves taken root and grown into the thickness of minor tree-trunks. Within this network of the roots and trunks it would be easy for us to put up an inconspicuous machan, and I decided to save my *charpoy* and Hughie's chair for one of the other places where natural construction might not be so easy. We completed that *machan* in ninety minutes, and after tying the first bait in a convenient position, set out for our second selection, which you will remember was the Sultan's Battery Road.

The sons of the old man who had been killed showed me where the tragedy had taken place, and within a couple of furlongs of this spot and once again where a *nullah* crossed the road, we erected the second *machan*. This again was constructed on the spot, but took much longer to do, so that it was nearly noon before we set out for the ridge, two miles away, overlooking the Moyar Valley and Niligri jungles whence the tigers generally came.

My guides, who had lived in the area all their lives, pointed out first one then a second game trail that led up from the valley to the south of us, down which in the distance flowed the Moyar river, its course easily recognizable by the thick belt of giant trees on its bank. From the height at which we were standing, the Moyar looked like a great green python, writhing its course through the forest.

On convenient trees we tied our remaining *machans*, my *charpoy* first and finally Hughie's canvas chair, while with the tying-up of our fourth unfortunate bull-bait, the work of the day came to an end. The sun was sinking across the jungles of Bandipur to the west when we started on our walk back to Hughie's farm quite five miles away. It had been a long day and we were very tired, but I was very satisfied by the four jobs we had completed. All I had now to do was scour the jungle in other directions by day in the hope of meeting the man-eater accidentally. Meanwhile, I would sleep peacefully at Hughie's place by night till one of my baits was taken.

Little did I know what was going to happen.

The two sons of the old man and the first two men who had volunteered to help me had been instructed to visit the four baits next morning, and every morning thereafter, and to feed and water them, till a kill occurred. They were to begin with the most distant baits, the two animals we had tied on the western ridge, and then work eastwards to the Sultan's Battery Road, and finally to the first bait on the Talaimalai-Talavadi track, which was the closest of the four to Hughie's farm.

It was ten-thirty next morning when I heard them coming up the driveway, talking excitedly, and I knew that a kill had occurred. But the news they brought was surprising—and disconcerting! The last bait we had tied the previous evening—the one under Hughie's canvas-chair *machan*—had been killed and part eaten, and the first animal at the junction of the *nullah* with the Talaimalai-Talavadi road had also been killed and about half devoured.

Two kills on the same night, at points at least five miles apart. This clearly pointed to two tigers. Now which of them was the man-eater and in which of the *machans* should I sit?

Another consultation was held, but this time we were unanimous. The tiger that had killed the first bait—the nearest to the farm—was far more likely to be the man-eater, for its tracks had indicated that it haunted the *nullah*-bed crossing the Talaimalai-Talavadi road on which a human kill had already taken place and which was frequented by human beings. The other kill on the ridge was at a far less frequented spot, where people hardly ever went, but which was used by tigers coming from the Nilgiri district, or returning to it. As such, the tiger that had killed there was in all likelihood not the man-eater. It was therefore decided that I should sit at the *nullah*-crossing that night.

With this settled, the next thing to do was to put in a few hours of sleep.

Hughie called me at one o'clock for a hearty lunch and gave me a parcel of sandwiches for the night, a most acceptable gift. By two-thirty I was on the *machan*, looking down upon the half-eaten young bull as my four assistants removed the branches with which they had covered the carcase that morning to protect it from vultures.

There was silence after their departure and, as was to be expected, no travellers passed along the road, the presence of the man-eater discouraging people, especially towards evening, from using a track on which he had already killed a man. I was surprised, therefore, to hear voices approaching from the Talaimalai village direction some time after five o'clock, and astonished when I recognized the party as my own four attendants, accompanied by Sweza carrying a gun. They came to tell me that the man-eater had killed a woman while she was carrying water from a well near the hamlet of Dimbum, which was seventeen miles away on the Satyamangalam-Chamrajnagar road. Hughie had sent them with the news, as he felt that I might not consider it worthwhile to sit up all night to shoot a tiger which obviously could not be the man-eater. No tiger that had devoured half a bull the previous night would walk a distance of seventeen miles to kill a woman the next morning.

I heartily agreed with the message Hughie had sent and came down from the *machan*. As far as I was concerned the tiger that haunted the *nullah* was welcome to the remaining half of his meal. When I got back, Hughie suggested that I go at once to Dimbum and try to find a place to sit up, either near the well or wherever the woman had been killed. No doubt her family would have removed her remains for cremation, but it was just possible that the man-eater might return to the spot during the night in search of the body of his victim. I agreed and started straight away, taking my four helpers along in case of need.

It was almost dark when we left Talaimalai village and I switched on the headlights of the Studebaker. Just a mile farther on, the road descended steeply to cross the first of several intersecting streams, all dry at this time of the year, and strung out across the road on the opposite bank of this stream, reflecting the beams from my lights, were the eyes of a herd of bison! The herd galloped away, disturbed by the noise when I changed gear to cross the stream—that is, all of them except the herd-bull, which stood squarely in the centre of the road, his head partly lowered and pawning the ground in a attitude obviously nasty and threatening.

Bisons are generally quite harmless animals and run away at the slightest sight or sound of human beings. Here was one of them behaving rather differently. Perhaps he felt I constituted a danger to the herd. More likely he was puzzled by the headlights of the car and never realized that human beings were behind them. In any case, I did not wish to risk the consequences of a charge. It meant shooting the bull—which I had no desire to do—and quickly, for the signs of an impending charge within the next few seconds were unmistakable. If he succeeded, I knew my Studebaker would be a write-off together with some, if not all of us, who were inside. With my own eyes I have seen a loaded trunk overturned by a charging bison on the Tippakadu road in the Nilgiri jungles; the driver had been killed by the truck itself while the bison had disposed of his assistant and the cleaner by goring and trampling them to pulp.

These unpleasant thoughts passed quickly through my mind. There was just one chance left before using my rifle, and I would have to take it at once. That chance lay in the old klaxon horn fixed to the right of me on the wind-shield of the Studebaker. Many an elephant had I scared with this same ancient klaxon! Its blatant, brassy blare had made them flee in abject terror. So I tried it again. I pumped the spring lever of that old horn hard and repeatedly. A ghastly sound rent the jungle silence. The bull raised its lowered head, its eyes dilated by fear of what seemed like all hell let loose, and the next moment it plunged into the bamboo undergrowth and vanished from sight.

After that I saw quite a lot of game, which was rather unusual for so early an hour, and incidentally a 'good omen,' so far as hunting superstition goes. Spotted deer and two sambar crossed individually, a sloth bear was digging by the roadside as my lights disturbed him, and a panther leaped from left to right a furlong after I had passed the Honathetti forest lodge and was negotiating a valley between two hillocks, just seven miles from Dimbum.

We arrived at our destination shortly before 8 p.m., which, all said and done, was excellent going, for the track was not only steep and winding but had been in places completely obliterated by the long grass. Hidden boulders lay in that grass, enough to tear open the bottom of any crankcase or differential that bumped against it. In such spots I had had to slow down to a snail's pace, slowly following two of the men as they walked side by side a few yards ahead to warn me of hidden rocks before one of the front wheels of the car banged against them. Then we would all help to roll them aside, or if they were too big to move I would circumvent them by going off the track.

Dimbum is a hamlet on the main road from Mysore City, past the town of Chamrajnagar, down to another large town in the plains named Satyamangalam, which was the headquarters of the police and forest departments for the area. Fifty miles on lies the city of Coimbatore.

All that Dimbum could boast were a few huts and a tea-shop owned by a Moplah, a descendant of some Arab trader, who centuries earlier had come to the west coast of India for trade but remained to settle down and marry several Hindu Malayalee women. These men have kept their business acumen through the years and there is hardly any trade in which numbers of them do not excel. The teashop at Dimbum was kept open by the Moplah and his three wives throughout the twenty-four hours of the day. Tired lorry drivers ascending the steep ghat-road from Satyamangalam, sixteen miles away, could count on a large mug of steaming tea or coffee at any time of the day or night, together with a hot meal of curry and rice. There was another essential commodity thrown in with the refreshment, and it was free: cool water for their boiling radiators when their trucks arrived in a cloud of steam after that long ascent.

There is a Rest House for travellers, too, and it is beautifully situated upon the edge of the escarpment that overlooks the valley many thousands of feet below. The nearer part of this valley at the base of the escarpment is heavily forested, but the road can be seen winding through the jungle and finally breaking out into the cultivated lands that stretch away to the horizon. In the middle distance is Satyamangalam, while far away on the skyline to the southwest is Coimbatore.

Those jungles at the foot of the hill recall the escapades of the tiger I named 'the mauler of Rajnagara,'* for it was there that I spent some exciting days looking for him without success.

To look upon the plains from this Rest House at nightfall is like looking down into fairyland. The myriad points of electric light, frequently interspersed with coloured lights of every hue, stand out in sharp contrast to the black void. Away to the southwest is an angry glow upon the horizon: the reflection of the lights of Coimbatore, too far away to be seen directly, upon the cloud-layered sky.

I drove to the Moplah's teashop, for that I knew would be the fountainhead of all the information I wanted. Abdulkunni, the ambitious proprietor, knew me well. In fact, I had dropped in for a cup of tea at his place on my way to Hughie's farm and had told him the reason for my visit. He greeted me loudly now and in his high-pitched, excited voice, began pouring out his news.

'Why do you go to Talaimalai looking for your tiger, *sahib*, when it's right here? This morning it killed a woman at the well, just behind this tea shop. A damned nuisance, indeed! We need a great deal of water here, for making tea and for the radiators of the hundred or more lorries that need it every day. This requires many visits to the well and many buckets of water. My three wives have all refused to go there since they heard the news. Disobedient, good-for-nothing bitches, all three of them! I have threatened to kick them out. Even beaten them. But with one accord they told me to go myself. Cannot somebody rid me of these wenches? Now I

---

* See *Man-eaters and Jungle Killers*, Chapter 8.

put it to you, *sahib*. Can I possibly leave the teashop? So I have been compelled to engage a servant on daily wages from today. This costs money and in any case she is a lazy slut! Look *sahib,* as a good Mussulman it is not the custom for me to allow strangers to speak to my womenfolk. But you are a friend, sir. Please talk to my wives and advise them to fetch the water.'

A difficult assignment indeed! Besides, I had better things to do than persuade old Abdulkunni's wives to commit suicide. For that was the fate they would invite by visiting the well with the man-eater about. I could not blame the women for going on strike. Old Abdulkunni thought more of his money than of his wives, but I did not tell him so. It would hurt his feelings.

I said instead, 'I have come to shoot the tiger, Abdulkunni, so if you'll help me, your problem will be solved. Let's not waste time, but tell me exactly how the woman was killed.'

'What is there to say, *sahib*. She went for water. She was returning with it. Then the *shaitan bagh* leapt from the bushes and carried her off into the jungle. She screamed loudly but the tiger only growled. Another woman was going down for water, too, and was but a few yards away when it happened. She heard and saw everything. She ran back to this very place and told us. I had five or six customers here at the time. We bolted and barred the doors and locked ourselves in for nearly two hours. That was another loss of business. It was only when other drivers arrived and banged on the front door that we opened up. Then a large party of us went down to the well. Of the woman there is no sign. Her broken pot remains where it fell from her hands. There is nothing more to tell you.'

'Have there been earlier reports of a tiger in this locality, Abdulkunni? Has anyone else seen it? Did anybody notice anything distinctive about the animal?' I fired the questions rapidly.

But the old man only laughed. 'What can be distinctive about a tiger?' he inquired. 'They all look alike, with a head, four legs and a tail. Besides, why do you ask such silly questions of me? Have I not told you already that nobody except the other woman who was going herself to the well for water saw the tiger? She said it was a huge beast and looked like *shaitan* (the devil) himself.'

One last question I asked, with visions of possibly being able to sit up over the victim's remains of the next day. 'Has, the woman's body been found?'

Abdulkunni's derisive grin widened. 'Who is there to search for it, *sahib*? Do you think we are mad? We are alive now. The woman is dead. If we go in search of her body and the tiger finds us, we too will be dead. And that will not help her!'

How often had I not heard those same words before, spoken in so many different languages, when inquiring if a man-eater's victim or the remains, had been found!

It was evident that the Moplah could give me no further help. I would have to do things for myself and think out some plan. So I ordered two mugs of tea for myself, and a mug each for the men I had brought in the car from Talaimalai, and selecting the cornermost table in the grimy tea shop took out my pipe to smoke while considering the best course of action.

The first thing to do was to get rid of Abdulkunni, who had started talking again. Very frankly I asked him to leave me alone as I wanted to think out a plan.

The old man's behaviour was particularly irritating that day. With a wicked smirk, he remarked, 'If you want the tiger, why not call it?' Then he went to serve the tea.

Four tracks join at Dimbum, almost directly in front of the tea shop. Or rather, two of them are tracks, while the other two consist of the main road that passes through the hamlet, leading northwards towards Mysore and southwards to Satyamangalam. I have intentionally counted this one main road as two because, so far as searching for the tiger went, he might cross it to the north of Dimbum, or go down the ghat road as it fell away to the south towards Satyamangalam,. The third track was the one I had just travelled, leading from Talavadi and Talaimalai, and the fourth track led into the jungle and was hardly noticeable. It began just behind the Rest House and then wound eastwards through the forest for ten miles or more, keeping more or less to the edge of the continuation of the Dimbum escapement that overlooked the plains as far as the watershed of the Cauvery river, fifty miles to the east.

Being the least used of the four, this last track was the one along which most animals were to be seen, especially bison and sambar. Quite a number of bear came up the escarpment and tigers very often crossed it by steep hidden routes on their long trek of more than fifty miles eastwards, through very dense, jungle and mountain terrain, to the Cauvery river. After about ten miles this track dwindled to a mere footpath that threaded through very heavy bamboo jungles, inhabited more by elephants, bison and sambar than by tigers. For the area is infested by tick, and tigers definitely do not like ticks!

It was pitch-dark outside; an ideal night for using a spotlight in searching for animals.

I could motor up the road towards Mysore for about five miles and then return, shining my spotlight and hoping the man-eater might cross by sheer chance. I could then repeat the performance along the ghat road in the opposite direction.

156

I could even motor along the road I had come from Talaimalai. But motoring along the fourth track to the east would not be advisable. Here I would have to walk. For this track was not only in a very bad state, littered with big stones and full of potholes, but it twisted and turned, and was full of sharp gradients. It entailed far too much gear work and consequent noise, which would drive away the man-eater and any other animal that happened to be near, before I had a chance of seeing them.

Where to begin was anybody's choice and I decided to walk along the eastern track first, while I was still fresh and because it would take the longest time.

Finishing my tea, I paid Abdulkunni and told my four men to catch up with as much sleep as they could while I took a walk up the eastern trail. Not being old acquaintances of mine, they thought I was mad. Abdulkunni, who had overheard the conversation and who had known me for quite a long time, remarked: 'You think he's mad, eh? That's no discovery! I've known him to be mad for a long time.'

For some reason the old rascal was annoying me more and more that evening. I checked the torch in the .405 and the spare five-cell torch that I intended using for the actual reconnaissance, as it would be far too tiresome to keep pointing the barrel of the rifle about so as to use its torch. Then I walked to the Rest House, stood on the verandah plinth for a few minutes to admire once more the twinkling lights of Satyamangalam, and finally started along the eastern track that began behind the bungalow. With the first turn, that came within a few yards, I was shut off from the friendly light of the petromax lantern hanging in front of the teashop and from the sounds that came from within.

The man-eater had disappeared with his victim and there was no knowing where he had taken her. Tigers have been known to carry their kills for a distance of half-a-mile and even more, although generally they don't go so far. He had killed the woman that morning and no doubt had eaten part of her. The rest he would have to come back for after dark to make a second meal. It was now a little after 9.30 p.m., and as the habits of tigers generally go, the man-eater should have returned by now for his second meal and be enjoying it at this moment, or very likely he would have finished it by now. After all, there is not much meat in an already half-eaten human carcase!

If he had eaten his fill, he would next seek water, and I knew there were three possible places for him to do that. The closest was at a water hole that was skirted by the very track I was following and lay hardly a furlong ahead. The second was by a regular stream that crossed the road to Mysore about two miles away. The third was another stream that I had already passed in the car that evening and was about three miles from Dimbum on the Talaimalai road. Apart from the water hole I was approaching, the man-eater could drink at any point throughout the course of the two streams, and the chance of meeting him over water was extremely slim.

I was approaching the water hole with these thoughts still in my mind, and the first signs of its nearness were a row of blue-green lights in pairs, that kept jerking up and down as they stared into the bright beam of my torch. Spotted deer! Here was a herd, either on its way to the water hole or returning from it.

I stopped abruptly and put out the light to allow the deer a chance of going away quietly. If any of them caught the human scent behind my light, if would surely voice an alarm cry to warn its companions. That cry would also alert the tiger if it was in the vicinity, and I did not want that to happen.

The night was pitch-dark and not a sound came to me from the spotted deer. The silence was intense. Not even a cricket chirped. I did not like it at all. It was eerie.

I switched on the torch. The bobbing pinpoints of light had gone. The deer had vanished in complete silence. That was good, for they had raised no alarm. I waited a few minutes longer to allow them to get far enough away, so as not to scent me or see my torch-beam. Then I started moving forward silently along the track. The next turn would bring me to the water hole that lay to the left.

That was when I heard the splashing and gurgling and loud swishing noises. An elephant was at the water hole and enjoying a bath. I stopped again. His presence was a nuisance, for elephants, like most human beings, like their bath. Once they start, they not only gurgle and drink and bathe and gambol, but they lie in the water and play in it, even if all alone, sometimes for an hour at a stretch. I could not waste so much time waiting for the creature to go away of its own accord. On the other hand, if I advanced and it saw or scented me, the chances were that it might trumpet in alarm and that, again, would warn the man-eater, should he be within earshot, that something strange was moving through the forest, something unusual enough to disturb an elephant. For me to make a noise to frighten away the elephant would be folly for the same reason.

Then I had an idea. I pointed the beam of the torch high up to the treetops in the direction of the water hole in the hope that it might be seen by the elephant and cause him to move off. Evidently I was too far away at first, because he did not see the light. Then I advanced till I was almost at the bend of the track before trying again. This time I succeeded. All sounds of that most enjoyable bath ceased abruptly.

There came a great squelching as the elephant lifted his big body out of the mud, followed by a rhythmic plop-plop-plop-plop of heavy footsteps as he plodded slowly through the water to the bank. Then followed repeated hissing sounds as of escaping steam. Although disturbed by my light, the elephant did not intend to deny himself the last luxury of a sand-bath, and that was what he was doing at that moment; he was throwing sand over himself.

I allowed him time, while continuing to flash the torch from treetop to treetop to keep him sufficiently disturbed. The hissing stopped eventually. It was followed in a little while by faint crackling sounds as the beast moved its heavy way through the undergrowth bordering the water hole. Once again came silence. The elephant had moved off and just then the sharp crack of a breaking branch told me that he had stopped for feed, but far enough away not to be alarmed at my passing.

I negotiated the turn in the track and came upon the water hole lying limpid and dark before me, a few wisps of vapour already rising from its warmer surface into the rapidly-cooling night air. Hundreds of pin-points of brilliant red light, like tiny rubies scattered over the water, shone in my torchlight, and from the nearer bank bordering the pool came the chorus of frogs. Alarmed by my approach, they had leaped off the bank in great numbers. With vigorous thrusts of their hind legs they propelled themselves into the centre of the pool, where they whirled around to face me, their tiny eyes glistening and reflecting like a thousand rubies.

I had been to such pains to avoid the elephant raising an alarm at my approach only to meet with a singular defeat at the hands of those most insignificant of creatures—the frogs. The tiger heard them, for he happened to be there, and must have seen me and my light simultaneously.

Fortunately for me, he was on the further bank of the pool, where he must have come to drink, and not on the track, or matters may have turned out differently. Under similar circumstances, any normal tiger would have taken himself off quietly and I would never have known of his presence. But this one growled, and continued to growl, the ominous sound rumbling from the darkness at the other end, across the pool and to me as I came to an abrupt and uncertain halt.

The tiny ruby-red eyes of the frogs floating on the surface disappeared altogether, as if some switch had cut off the power, when they dived beneath the surface to escape that awful sound. On the opposite bank of the pool whence the growling arose there was a great disturbance as the myriad frogs that had been resting on the cool sand by the water's edge threw themselves into the pool for safety and with their tiny legs struck out frantically for the centre.

The growling stopped as abruptly as it had begun. The frogs fell into a hushed silence too. I then directed the beam of my torch around the bushes and undergrowth that grew down to the water's edge at the opposite end. Would I see the tiger's eyes glow in the beam? I saw nothing and heard nothing. My light fell only upon the jungle and a deathly silence covered everything.

The tiger had vanished. Had he made off? A normal tiger would do just that, but no normal tiger would have growled at seeing my torchlight. This beast was far from normal. He was angry, and he was unafraid of the approach of man. Was this the man-eater?

I glanced around nervously. My front was safe. To attack from that direction the tiger would have to charge through water and I knew he was very unlikely to do that. Rather, he would come around the pool and attack me from either flank, or from behind. If he chose a flank attack, he would have to charge along the bank or the track, either from the direction I had just come or from the opposite end where the pathway left the pool. More probably he would attack from the rear, where the jungle bordered the edge of the track and not two yards from where I was standing. Then I would have no chance whatever.

There was but one thing to do and I did it very quickly. I scrambled down the sloping bank into the water and, feeling the way before me with each footstep, made for the middle of the pool as fast as I could. I knew it was not very deep and there I would be safe from attack from any direction. No tiger—not even a man-eater, at least not in my experience—would attack across water, and even if it did, the tables would be turned entirely in my favour. I would have the tiger in the open and completely at my mercy, long before he could reach me.

The water had reached a little above my knees when the tiger growled again. This time it was a loud growl, almost a roar. And it came from the jungle bordering the track, from the very direction in which I had expected the attack. Had I not sought the safety of the pool just in time, the tiger would have launched itself upon me. He was growling with fury now at finding me beyond reach.

But was I really beyond reach? The next few moments would answer that question. Of one fact I had no doubt whatever: I was dealing with the man-eater and no ordinary tiger. The hate in its behaviour clearly showed that. Hughie's bullet had turned this animal into a fiend.

I waited in vain. The tiger did not emerge. The growling stopped as unexpectedly as it had started, and once again I was plunged into silence with a sea of darkness around me. I played the beams of my torch in every direction as I turned slowly around, hoping to catch a glimpse of the beast's eyes as they reflected the light, or of the striped body slinking from bush to bush. But I saw and heard nothing.

The myriads of frogs that had experienced such a disturbing night, first with the arrival of the elephant, then myself, and finally the tiger, all went below the surface of the water when I waded into it. But they could not remain submerged for long and had to come up for breath. One by one they came to the surface now, soundlessly, to gulp in air, and soon the nearer edge of the wide circle of light thrown by my torch once more revealed hundreds of pairs of tiny red eyes gazing on me in fear.

A long time seemed to have passed since I left the tea shop, but a quick glance at my watch showed it was only 10.30 p.m. How long would I have to wait for the tiger to move, if he moved at all?

I began to get tired of standing in the water. It grew colder and colder and wreaths of vapour arose from the surface of the pool, obscuring the jungle around its edges and making it difficult for the light of my torch to penetrate. At the same time, I realized that if I got back to the pathway I would be at the mercy of the man-eater should he decide to ambush me at any spot along the track. I felt certain he had not gone away but was biding his time till I came out of the water.

Midnight, and it was biting cold! By now I realized I must not shine my torch continuously, for the five cells would run down and under no circumstances could I risk using up the cells of the other torch, clamped to my rifle, for the accuracy of my shooting depended on them. So I extinguished the light and was plunged abruptly into darkness. That was when I noticed that the night was cloudy, with no stars to be seen.

However, there was no danger so long as I remained in the water. My hearing would warn me of the approach of any animal.

Very soon, that was what happened. An elephant came, perhaps the same one I had disturbed earlier. Probably another. I was standing still and he did not hear or see me. The wind was blowing from him to me, so he could not scent me. I felt I was safe, for in any case his sight was too poor to penetrate the mist that had settled over the whole pool like a thick bank of fog, and he would not be able to see me.

I heard the loud 'fooff-foooff-foooff' as he exhaled air though his trunk, and then the sucking noises as he drew in water and splashed it into his mouth and over his body. He drank and he drank, a seemingly endless number of gallons of water.

At last he decided to have a regular bath and I heard the tremendous plop-plop-plop of his great feet approaching me as he waded through the water towards the centre of the pool. This would never do, I thought. So I shone the torch straight into his face.

That night was for me one in which I seemed fated to meet animals of strange behaviour. According to all the rules of the game, the elephant should have turned tail and bolted from my bright light, but he did nothing of the kind. He trumpeted shrilly, coiled up his trunk, and charged me.

Taken aback, instead of putting the five-cell quickly into its pouch at the left side of my belt, so as to leave both my hands free to handle my rifle, I missed the pouch and dropped the torch into the water. Out it went.

There was no time to retrieve it. The charging elephant was dangerously close. I brought the .405 to my shoulder while pressing the button of the smaller torch that was clamped to its barrel with my left thumb. The beam cut through the darkness as I aimed a foot above the head of the elephant and fired in an attempt to halt that charge.

No rogue elephant had been proclaimed by the Forestry department and so, as far as possible, I should try to avoid killing this animal. I had erred by letting him come too close to me and I should not have shone the torch directly in his face.

As these thoughts rushed through my mind, I awaited the result of that deterring shot. If he still came on, I would be forced to stop him with my next bullet or he would kill me. There was no doubt of that.

Luckily it worked. The great beast braked to a halt by planting all four feet firmly in the mud. The impetus of the rush brought him on, skidding ludicrously in the clay till he ended up sitting on his hindquarters like an elephant at the circus. Encouraged by his failing nerve, I fired a second time, again over his head. The elephant turned and bolted.

When the noise and tumult had died away I felt disgusted, but at the same time relieved. My two shots must have driven away the man-eater. My chance of success was gone. But now I was safe also and could at last get out of the water.

Shivering with the cold, I started my walk back to Dimbum. I knew I had only a short distance to cover, but there was always the danger that the man-eater, driven from the immediate vicinity of the pool by the sound of my shots, might still be lurking somewhere along the pathway and might ambush me.

At last the lights of Satyamangalam, twinkling in the black void of the plains below me, put an end to my tension. I got into the Rest House, took off my wet pants and, as I had brought no change of clothes, went to sleep without them.

A banging on the door awakened me. I had closed all the windows and it was dark inside, but a glance at my watch surprised me. It was 9.30 a.m.

I put on my pants again. They were still wet. The banging on the door was renewed, this time more urgently, and I could hear the murmur of voices on the verandah.

I opened the front door. Confronting me was Abdulkunni himself, his three wives and four or five other people, all in a great state of excitement. Obviously the tea shop had been closed down. Something very serious must have happened.

'Come quickly, *sahib*,' called the excited Moplah. 'The tiger has just carried away the girl we employed to fetch the water.'

Grabbing my rifle and some cartridges, I hastened with the group to the teashop, while he quickly told the story.

Barely thirty minutes earlier the girl had taken a basket of cooking utensils to wash at the well behind the tea shop. She had decided it would be easier that way than carrying a pitcher or more of water to the building for the purpose. One of the wives had been watching her from the back door to ensure she did not linger unduly over the task. The girl, a maiden of about eighteen years, was bending down, absorbed in her work, when a movement behind her had caught the eye of the watching woman. She had glanced in that direction and was horrified to see a tiger, belly to the ground, sneaking stealthily upon the unsuspecting servant girl from behind. The woman had screeched a warning. The girl heard and jumped to her feet. But the tiger drove home his charge. He had leapt upon his victim and, not waiting to kill her, had taken the unfortunate girl in his mouth and leaped back into the cover of the undergrowth. Terrible screams could be heard long after the tiger and victim had disappeared from sight.

Alarmed by his wife's yells and hearing distant wailing, Abdulkunni and the other members of the household had rushed to the rear door to find out the cause of the disturbance. Then they had come in a body to the Rest House. The man-eater had taken another victim at nine in the morning, and exactly where he had killed only a few hours earlier! This was something unheard of in the annals of man-eaters.

Telling everyone to remain indoors, I hastened to the well. The scattered utensils, some washed and the others not, showed that the girl had been taken by surprise while engrossed in her task, and a single sliding pug-mark indicated where the tiger had stopped his rush to seize his victim and had slipped on the wet earth where the girl had been doing her washing. There were no other marks on the surrounding earth, trampled flat as it was by the feet of the many people who came there all day long to draw water, and baked by the sun's rays. The ground was far too hard to carry pug-marks, while the girl had been grabbed so quickly that there was no blood trail of any kind.

The woman who had witnessed the killing, Abdulkunni's second wife, called to me from the doorway, pointing out the direction in which the man-eater had gone with his victim, and I followed it. The clearing in which the well stood ended abruptly in a wall of lantana bushes that fringed the jungle. No tiger, carrying his prey, would dream of forcing himself through this tangled obstruction. It would be impossible for any beast. There must be some other way and I started to look for it. I found it eventually, a game-*path*, close to the ground, tunnelling at a height of not more than four feet through the lower branches of the lantana. It had been made by wild pigs during the rainy season, when they visited the clearing to root and dig in the swamp which would at that season surround the well. In places the tiger had had to crawl along this tunnel, dragging its victim, and I followed suit, crouching low and at times on hands and knees.

Within a few yards I came upon the first evidence of the tragedy. Some torn shreds of a sari and a quantity of blood on the lantana leaves that littered the game-trail. Probably the victim had been struggling to free herself and this was where the tiger had killed her.

167

After that there was a regular blood trail, and more shreds of the sari caught on the lantana. There came a bend in the tunnel and here the remains of the girl's clothing had caught on a thorny bush. The man-eater must have become angry and wrenched his victim free, for the scraps of a sari and a skirt had been torn from her body and were hanging on the thorns. With the removal of all her clothing the blood had fallen directly on the ground and leaves, making a ghastly red trail through the tunnel.

I could not know how far the tiger had carried his victim. Probably the screeching and screaming from the tea shop had made him decide to go to a quieter place before commencing his meal. At least, I hoped so. For if he was anywhere near and attacked me from my rear, I was completely at his mercy in this death-trap of a tunnel.

This thought caused me to stop frequently to listen. He might give himself away by growling. Tigers often do that when followed. Partly in anger, partly as a warning, but more often to strengthen their own courage. For all their lives have been spent in pursuing a fleeing prey and it is an unusual and terrifying experience for any tiger to realize he is the object of pursuit himself. Not a sound did I hear. Complete silence filled that twisting tunnel.

At last the lantana began to give way to jungle proper. The tunnel came to an end and I was able to stand upright. There was a grassy glade through which the blood trail led before it merged into a park-like jungle of *babul* and box-flower shrubs with grass between. I judged that I had not far to go now before meeting the tiger, who must have started his meal. That is, provided the man-eater had not heard me and realized he was being followed. If that had happened, he might take himself off altogether or lie in wait for me at some spot close to his kill. He might even creep forward to intercept me, or ambush me from either side or from the rear.

Then I heard a crow cawing some distance away. I listened carefully, and there was no mistaking that persistent cawing. The crow was watching the tiger with his victim and was excitedly calling reinforcements to be ready to enjoy the feast that was soon to follow.

Sounds and the distances from which they emanate are difficult to locate and estimate correctly in the forest. Air currents, the density of tree growth and the terrain all make difficulties. In flat country conditions are not quite so bad, but in hilly areas like this, sounds and distances are often unjudgable.

I reckoned the crow was about sixty to seventy yards away, and slowly, very stealthily, studying the ground before me so as not to tread upon a dried twig or stone and so betray myself, I advanced step by step. I do not know how far I had gone when I heard the first sounds of the feast. The sharp crack of a bone being broken, followed by crunching and tearing.

The crow was still cawing excitedly. I reckoned that I was within thirty yards now, possibly a good deal less. I stopped and began to think.

The crow offered a greater risk at that moment than the tiger. For he was sitting on a tree and had the advantage of height. I knew that if he saw me he would cease cawing at once. He might even fly away. The man-eater, engrossed in his meal, knew that the crow was watching him but had ignored the bird and his cawing as a matter of no consequence. A sudden end to that cawing and the sudden departure of the crow would tell the tiger at once that something had alarmed the bird, that some danger to himself was approaching. For crows fear no other bird and ignore the presence of wild animals. They fear only the human race.

But I had not yet alarmed the crow. At a snail's pace, with infinite caution, I advanced, crouching low, shuffling forward and halting again, watching the ground in front of me before making any movement, glancing to right and left and even looking behind when the tearing and crunching sounds ceased for a moment. For so long as I could hear those sounds I knew the tiger was in front. When they ceased I could no longer know where he was. There lay the greatest danger, for he might creep upon me from behind. Man-eaters generally snatch their victims that way.

Suddenly an uncanny silence fell over everything. At first I could not account for it. Then I knew the cause. The crow had stopped cawing! Undoubtedly something was afoot. Then I saw the crow, but too late. He had seen me first. With what seemed a tremendous fluttering, he flew to another tree.

And I was right: the man-eater had become suspicious. He had started to move. Was he moving away from me or towards me? Was he trying to escape or attack? As these questions raced through my mind, with the corner of my eye I saw the crow rise again. This time he flew out of sight.

I froze in my tracks. But it was too late. The cunning crow flew back to investigate and perched at almost the same spot as the one where I saw him first. He turned his head sideways for a better view of me, cawed and bobbed. Convinced that I was dangerous, he fluttered his wings and then flew to yet another tree to turn around and watch me.

I stopped watching the crow and stared at the bushes all around. And I turned about to watch the bushes behind me. There was a pricking sensation at the back of my neck. Every cell of my body warned me that I was in great danger. I knew that the man-eater was about to pounce.

But I simply could not see him, stare as I might at the undergrowth all around. The jungle was ominously silent.

Not a twig cracked, not a leaf stirred. The birds and insects were silent, so too were the bushes and the long grass that grew between the trees. I looked in vain for the stirring of a branch or a blade of grass, the bending of a sapling stem that might betray movement below and the passage of a creeping body.

But there was not a movement anywhere, not a sound. I knew that the tiger was employing all his skill to make his last rush a complete surprise.

And then there came to my mind the scene I had witnessed many years before by moonlight, beside a jungle pool in the heart of a deep forest far away. A sambar hind was approaching the water hole cautiously. All was silent. Suddenly, for no reason whatever, she wheeled noisily and rushed away. The ruse worked then, for the tiger patiently lying in wait to ambush her a few yards further on, now lost his head. He thought his prey was about to escape and he bounded after her. But the hind had too much of a start and got away to safely.

Now I did the same thing. But I did not turn and run back, for something warned me that the man-eater was already there. I stamped noisily and ran forward diagonally, but only for four paces. Then I stopped.

As on that moonlit night so many years before, the simple ruse worked again. The man-eater roared and bounded after me from behind. He took two leaps and then halted in crouching amazement as this strange man before him, instead of continuing to run, turned around and fired rapidly.

The tiger knew no more after that, but I know that if I had not heeded that warning of his very close presence behind me, or if I had run backwards instead of forwards, I would not be here to tell this tale.

# Five

# The Killer of the Wynaad

TO THE SOUTHWEST OF THE CITY OF MYSORE LIES THE HEAVILY forested area of the Kakankote jungles, for centuries the home of many herds of wild elephants that are partial to the kind of jungle that grows in this district. The rainfall is heavy and the vegetation is luxurious. Giant bamboos, rank grass and mighty trees grow together in dense profusion, and a passage through the forest, except for the elephants and the large and harmless bison, is almost impossible. Sambar and barking deer are found in the thinner areas, but as one moves farther southwest and the rainfall and the denseness of the jungle increase in direct ratio to each other, the deer become fewer and fewer, leaving the elephants and bison in almost entire possession of what appears from the narrow road to be primeval, virgin jungle.

Still further on is the Kabini river, one of the natural boundaries between Mysore state to the northeast and Kerala state, in the extreme southwest. In my opinion, the state of Kerala, in the extreme southwest of the Indian peninsula, offers a scenery second only in beauty to that of the Himalayas, though very different. It is a land of dense forests, fertile plantations of tea, coffee, cinnamon, rubber and tapioca, and emerald-green fields in the areas bordering the sea; of gently flowing rivers and waterways without number, along which palm-thatched river boats glide among coconut palms laden with huge bunches of green nuts, and a sea coast without parallel, culminating at the southern tip of the peninsula in the famous beach of Cape Comorin.

The town of Manantoddy, on the Kerala side of the border, stands on the Western Ghats, the range of mountains that run down the west coast of India, almost from Bombay to the far south, at an average elevation of about 4,000 feet above sea level. This district is known as the North Wynaad, to differentiate it from the country a few miles further south, which abuts the Nilgiri Mountain and is known as the South, or Nilgiri, Wynaad. Both areas are extremely fertile, enjoy a heavy rainfall, and are the site of many plantations, producing every conceivable crop.

Pleasant as they are in all other respects, these regions abound in leeches throughout the year, and in the rainy season their numbers are enormous. Moreover, that curse of the drier jungles, the tick, thrives in yet greater comfort than it does in the forests of the interior—both the large crab-tick that gives you tick-fever when it bites you in sufficient numbers, and the microscopic jungle, or grass-tick, smaller than a pin's head, that provokes a small sore wherever it has sucked your blood. Since it bites you all over the body, in hundreds of places, you become a very sore creature indeed, covered with sores that last for many months. You scratch and scratch yourself, night and day, into a mental and physical wreck.

Leeches and ticks suck the blood not only of a human being, but of animals as well. Even the bison suffer, while tigers, panthers and deer become covered with them, especially ticks, so that they hang from the softer portions of these animals' bodies, gorged with blood, like bunches of small grapes.

For this reason, the jungles of the Wynaad hold few carnivorous animals or deer. Now and then a stray animal may roam in during the dry summer months to brave the discomforts, but with the advent of the rains they move to the higher ranges of the Western Ghats, or the drier areas of East Kakankote to escape from the leeches and ticks till the monsoon abates with the approach of winter.

Thus it came about that, when a traveller journeying from Kakankote to Manantoddy was taken by a tiger just within a few hundred yards of the outskirts of the latter, it was regarded as a quite unusual event. Tigers had been seen in these parts but were few in number, and no human had been harmed for as long as anybody could remember. The event was soon forgotten and many months passed.

Then, across the border in the state of Mysore, preparations were started for the next *kheddah* operation, in which many wild elephants were to be caught. Coolies were engaged in hundreds to build the mighty wooden stockade into which they would later drive the elephants before the gate was dropped and the bewildered beasts captured. Much preliminary work was required; timber had to be felled, the forest cleared, bamboos gathered and bound together and then moved to the spot selected for the stockade. This required not only hard work but experienced workers. Men from the jungle tribes, the Karumbas and the Sholagas, provided most of the recruits, for they were experienced not only in tree-felling and bamboo-binding, but in the ways of the elephants, in driving them into

174

the stockade, and in roping and shackling them and taming them afterwards.

That was when the tiger struck, a second and a third time, before people realized that a man-eater was amongst them.

Two Karumbas vanished within three days of each other and the half-eaten remains of the first showed he had been devoured by a tiger. The body of the second Karumba, like that of the traveller to Manantoddy, was never seen again.

There is another way of getting to Manantoddy from Mysore city, and that is via Coorg, which was for years an independent state but has recently joined Mysore. It is a more circuitous route, but the scenery is even more picturesque. Like the Kakankote road, this route traverses dense jungle inhabited by elephants and bison, where tigers are practically unknown for the reasons already explained.

The Coorgies are a hardy, lively people. In olden days the British conferred a special honour upon them unknown elsewhere in India. Every Coorgie living within the limits of his state was exempted from possessing an arms licence, no matter how many weapons he possessed. This privilege is, I believe, still maintained by the Indian government. It was a laudable gesture but it had one bad result. The Coorgies never abused their privilege by using their weapons against each other or against other people, but they exercised it against the fauna of their beautiful little state to such an extent that the deer have been practically exterminated.

I know a large number of Coorgie families, most of whom are coffee planters, owning wide estates where the coffee berry flourishes to perfection, with oranges as a profitable secondary crop, and I happened to be a guest of one of these families when news of the man-eater trickled through.

The estate where I was staying was situated about mid-way between the towns of Sidapur and Virajpet, and at a considerable distance from both Manantoddy and Kakankote, where all three killings had occurred. Further, I had not brought my rifle with me from Bangalore, as I knew there was no shooting, at least of the kind in which I was interested, to be had in Coorg. So, when my friend gave me the news one morning over his breakfast table, I listened to it dispassionately, wondering like him as to how a man-eating tiger had found its way into an area so unpropitious, where ordinary tigers and panthers are almost unknown. But my friend waxed enthusiastic and suggested we go after it.

I told him I did not think much of the idea. In my opinion, the animal was not a confirmed man-eater, but was probably a sick or wounded tiger, or perhaps one that had escaped from one of the many miniature circuses that are always touring the country, and had strayed there because of the heavy jungles. I felt that it would either die of its sickness or wounds, or would soon leave these unfavourable haunts and move into normal tiger country, where it could find an abundance of its natural food, when it would stop man-hunting of its own accord. Besides, as I reminded him, I had not brought my rifle.

Timayya, for that was my host's name, offered to bet that I was wrong. The tiger would remain where he was, he affirmed. As for a rifle! He had five, from which I could make my choice.

I reminded my friend that to do so would be illegal. His weapons were unlicensed. It was a part of the stipulation that he, as a Coorgie, was forbidden to lend his unlicensed weapons to a non-Coorgie. And in any case, it was against the rules for anybody, even a licence-holder like myself, to borrow another man's weapon.

Timayya laughed at me, and said, 'What rot!' Then, banteringly, he bet me ten rupees that the tiger would kill again before the week was out. Rather huffed at his words, I took him on.

Timayya won that bet; for on the third day we heard that the tiger had killed again. This time the victim was a woman. She had been washing clothes on the further bank of the Kabini river, just within the limits of Kerala state. And Timayya's free arms permit was not valid in Kerala state.

My friend had set his heart on going after this tiger. I suppose to him, being something unusual, it became a must, and he stated flatly that I was included in the party.

Frankly, I was not keen; but to continue to refuse would have strained our relations. I had known Timayya for a long time, in fact we had been at school together, and stubbornness had always been his failing and his virtue! The estate, when he had bought it cheaply, was considered by the neighbours to be a complete 'write off.' The soil was said to be no good, the variety of coffee that grew there was no good, the shade trees were no good, and so forth! But Timayya was determined to buy. He bought; he worked hard; and he made good.

So I gave in on one condition. I would go back to Bangalore for my .405 and bring along my .450/400 as a spare rifle. He would accompany me. Then we would return to Mysore city from where we would motor directly to Kakankote and the Kerala border. I stressed that I would much rather incur the expense of the additional 240 miles of motoring than be mixed up in arms licence disputes with the police of two states.

Timayya concurred, left his weapons behind and came with me to Bangalore the same night. We spent the next day in buying provisions for a fifteen-day camp in the jungles of the border where we knew no foodstuff, acceptable to our civilized palates, would be available. Timayya bought a jar of some patent cream and a huge tin of D.D.T. as protection against the leeches and ticks. We carried mosquito nets too, along with my small tent, a portable *charpoy machan,* batteries and torches, and my two rifles. Timayya said he did not want to shoot but would rather watch the fun. Knowing him as I did, I realized this was not strictly true.

We arrived at Kakankote on the afternoon of the second day and then drove to the *kheddah* site to try to pick up what information we could about the tiger. As I anticipated, there was little to learn. So many coolies were about, working on the project, that no one appeared to know exactly when and where the tiger had taken his two victims. But rumour and universal fear were rife. The men had just vanished and their absence had not been noticed for two days or so. Even then it was only by mere chance that, being attracted by the stench of putrefying flesh, some travellers had gone to investigate and found some scanty remains.

Many people had theories to account for the presence of a man-eater in that zone, but not one of them had seen the animal. What they had to say boiled down to the belief that an evil spirit was operating in the forest in the guise of a tiger. This instilled an even greater fear into the coolies, so much so that we knew if another of them was killed, the *kheddah* operation would come to a stop. Such a happening, or even a postponement in the date, would be in the nature of a calamity to the local government, which had invited certain V.I.P.s from abroad as guests at the trapping.

Next morning, we motored the short distance to the Kerala border and came to the hamlet on the further bank of the Kabini river from which the latest victim—the woman who had been washing clothes—had been taken. Once more, nobody had seen the tiger. Only its pug-marks on the river bank, the trail of something that had been dragged away, and a few drops of blood on the leaves and earth had revealed a man-eater's visit.

We went on to Manantoddy and made inquiries at that small town regarding the first victim, the traveller who had been coming from Kakankote. Here again nobody knew anything. A forest guard, returning to his quarters near the Forest Range Office, had come across an odd sandal by the roadside. As it was good sandal, and people do not usually throw their footwear away, he stopped to look at it. That was when he noticed the other sandal lying on the sloping bank of a stream that ran parallel to the road. He walked down to see that too, and found a turban entangled in the bracken that grew by the waterside. Then he looked at the ground and saw the pug-marks of a tiger in the mud. They were deeply embedded in the ooze, indicating that the animal had been carrying additional weight, while a few carmine splashes on the fern leaves revealed the truth.

Blood! The tiger had been carrying away the wearer of the sandals and the turban.

We interviewed this guard and heard the story from his own lips. And that brought us to the end of the trail. There was nothing more we could learn, and we did not know where to make a start. Timayya confessed that he was sorry he had urged me to start upon this wild-goose chase.

Manantoddy is a beautiful place and we spent the night at the inspection bungalow which was fortunately vacant. Unlike most of the bungalows in other states, it is fully furnished with comfortable beds and foam mattresses, has neon lights and electric fans, and stands on a hillside opposite the ruins of an old British dwelling house that had its own private cemetery.

This is the land of fireflies. They come out after dark in their thousands, and the twinkling of their little lights are a fitting background to the chorus of the hundreds of small frogs, known as the 'Wynaad' or 'tok-tok' frog, and the hauntingly-sweet, never-to-forgotten aroma of sprays of the 'Rath-ki-Rani,' the 'Queen of the Night' blooms that open only after dark. We lay in armchairs, smoking tranquilly as we listened to the endless 'tok-tok-tok-tok-tok' of the frogs. Now and again a firefly would find its way into the room through the open window, its little light eclipsed by the brilliance of the neon tube that lit the room.

The next morning we made a leisurely start, our intention being to motor by the direct route to Virajpet in Coorg state, and thence to Timayya's plantation, where I would drop him, stay a day myself, and then go on to Mysore city and back to Bangalore.

We had travelled over ten miles from Manantoddy and were negotiating a stretch of dense forest; mostly of bamboo, on the Kerala bank of the Kabini river, when we saw a party of men approaching us, carrying a litter. And this is where my story really begins, for on the litter was a man, his tattered clothing soaked with his blood.

The bearers told us they were bamboo cutters and had been working on contract by the riverside, just over a mile away, when shortly after dawn that morning and without warning, a tiger had suddenly charged upon two of them, in full view of the others, and struck down one, whom it had grabbed by the shoulder and begun to drag away.

But the two men were brothers, and the one the tiger had ignored was very brave. He had run after the beast with the large curved knife he had been using to cut bamboos.

Seeing he was pursued, the man-eater had started to gallop away, still carrying his victim. The pursuer, realizing he had no hope of catching up with the tiger to save his brother, had then hurled his knife at the departing animal in sheer desperation. Luck favoured him, for the heavy weapon struck the carnivore in its flank. Either in pain, or from fright, the man-eater dropped his victim and bounded into the bamboos.

The hero of this episode, who was one of the men carrying the litter, had then assembled the scattered bamboo cutters and mobilized them into a team to help carry his sorely stricken brother to the nearest hospital, which was at Manantoddy.

There was no time to be lost and we acted quickly. Bundling the mauled man, with two others to help him, into the Studebaker, I told Timayya to turn around and drive them as fast as he could to the hospital, where he could leave the wounded man. He would then drive back to the bamboo cutters' camp, directed by the two men who were with him, while I went ahead on foot with the rest to see if we could find the tiger.

While Timayya was still turning the car I started at a jog-trot for the camp, the brave brother, whose name I learned was Yega, running beside me while the rest of the party followed behind. There was not a minute to be lost. In all probability the man-eater was miles away by this time, but there was just the slimmest of chances that he might still be lingering in the vicinity.

We reached the encampment in good time, but did not stop till we came to the place where the tiger had dropped his victim. There was a rank undergrowth of weeds covering the ground that showed no pug-marks, but on the bright green leaves were splashes of red—fresh blood that had not yet had time to dry. Whether the blood came from Yega's brother, who had been dropped here, or from a wound made by the knife in the man-eater's flank, we could not at that moment tell.

At this spot I halted the men who had followed and whispered to them to return to their camp. Yega and I would see this thing through together. The presence of many people would frighten the man-eater away, if it happened to be still nearby.

The bent heads of the undergrowth showed the direction in which the man-eater had run after dropping his victim, and I followed Yega, alert for a surprise attack at any moment and from any direction, particularly our rear. He tiptoed in front with bent head, examining the foliage and such glimpses of the dark 'black cotton-soil' type of earth as he could see between the green stems of the crowded plants.

Yega was looking for his knife. We wanted to make sure if his heavy weapon had actually hurt the tiger or not. If it had really done so, we might expect the animal to act quite differently from what he would have done if the blow from the knife had been a glancing one. Most likely, if injured, the tiger would roar and charge us from a fair distance; but if uninjured the man-eater would either attack only when we came fairly close to him, or slink away.

My part of the business now was to watch the jungle more carefully than ever before, ahead on both sides, and also behind, to protect us against a surprise attack. I could not help Yega in his search.

Then we found the knife. Its edge was clean, with no trace of blood. The tiger had not been hurt and the blood we had passed had come from the wounded man.

We crept forward for some distance and stopped. Then Yega shook his head slowly from side to side. The man-eater had stopped running.

We followed for another furlong, when the trail of our quarry petered out. Here the animal had crossed an area of lemon-grass, which is a scented variety with leaves that are largely used for distilling an essential oil. This grass has long, hard tough stems which had bent with the man-eater's passing and then regained their position, so that no trace now remained of the direction in which he had gone. The earth between the large clumps of this lemon grass was a matted carpet of decaying stems and seedlings, showing not the faintest trace of a pug-mark.

Quickening our pace, we cut directly across the lemon grass area, which extended for perhaps a quarter of a mile, to where the jungle began again. But the tiger's trail could not be found again and we were forced to conclude that we had lost him.

Apart from his courage, perseverance was another quality in which this little bamboo cutter was strong. He refused to admit defeat and urged in a whisper that we should go on and on till we eventually found the tiger. Stimulated by his keenness, I entered into the spirit of the chase and we pressed forward for many miles and most of the remaining hours of that day. We passed two herds of bison and a family of wild elephants and it was past 3 p.m., before we finally turned back for the bamboo cutters' camp. This we reached after dark, at 7.30 p.m. I was covered with leech bites and with ticks, and I was unutterably tired, although glad that we had at last come to grips with the man-eater and had such a stout henchman as Yega to assist.

Timayya had returned in the car many hours earlier and was eagerly awaiting our news. Unfortunately, I had none to give him.

We decided to return to the inspection bungalow at Manantoddy, which was only eleven miles away, for the night and to the bamboo cutters' camp the next morning. The prospect of spending the night with them, lying on the ground, with the mosquitoes and what not, was too terrible to contemplate.

That was where I made a big mistake. For when we did arrive the next morning we found the little camp in terrible confusion and all the bamboo cutters huddled together in a single hut. They swarmed out, led by Yega, to report that the man-eater had returned in the dead of the night. He had crept up and snatched one of them from beneath the walls of a hut!

Now you may wonder how a tiger could do that, but the explanation is simple. The huts which the bamboo cutters had constructed were but temporary shelters in the jungle which they would leave as soon as their work was done. They were built of split bamboos and leaves, and the sides of the structures were never allowed to touch the ground. For if they did, the termites—or white ants, as they are better known—would creep up into the walls in a matter of hours and the whole hut would be destroyed in no time. So a gap was left right round the hut, the ends of such bamboos as had necessarily to be embedded in the ground being first defended by a coating of tar.

The man-eater must indeed have been starving. Perhaps being deprived of his victim the previous day had whetted his appetite. He had returned in the early hours of the morning and, emboldened by the silence that reigned over the slumbering camp, had wandered up to the four huts. There, through the gap below the wall of one of them, he had seen the form of a sleeping man. The rest was easy to the hungry, daring beast. He had crept up to the hut and stretched his paw under the gap, fastening his claws into the sleeping man. The man had screamed for help, but no one had had the presence of mind to do anything and the man-eater had dragged his victim out of the hut, tearing down the lower portion of one of the walls in the process.

Unfortunately for the victim, Yega the one person who might have given help, was not in that hut but in the one furthest away, enabling the tiger to make a clean getaway. The bamboo cutters related in horror that they had had to listen to the poor man's screams for a very long time after the tiger dragged him out of the hut. Strangely, it had not killed him while he yelled and screamed, as man-eaters generally do when their victims make a noise. This animal had carried him away screaming and his comrades had heard his cries grow fainter and fainter as his captor bore him away.

Yega offered to accompany me at once, but the other coolies were utterly demoralized. They remained huddled in a group, calling to God to help them while they rained invectives upon the tiger. There were nine of them, excluding Yega. So I asked Timayya to squeeze them into the Studebaker, even if it came to letting a couple stand on the footboard, and to take them back to Manantoddy and safety without delay. He was then to return to the camp site and wait for me, but while doing so was not to leave the car on any account. In any case, he had my .405/400 with him, so there was no danger of his being unable to protect himself.

Yega and I then took up the trail of the man-eater.

The ground was soft outside the huts and had been cleared of the usual weeds in an effort to keep away the ticks and the leeches. This helped us to find the tiger's footprints, both as he had approached the hut and when he had left, carrying his victim with him. Whatever part of the poor man's anatomy had been grasped by the tiger was clearly not a vital region, for the victim had struggled and kicked the ground, as tell-tale marks revealed. At one place he had grasped the stem of a sapling and must have held on tenaciously. The tiger had literally torn him free, as could be seen by the particles of skin from the palms of the man's hands that still adhered to the stem and the markedly increased quantity of blood on the ground and leaves at that spot. No doubt this had resulted from an enlargement of the wound as the tiger dragged his victim free.

Now we were able to follow the trail with ease. The poor man had bled terribly and splashes of blood on the weeds, grass and leaves marked the way the tiger had passed. A queer sensation of nausea came over me as I pictured that horrible scene at dead of night in the blackness of the jungle, and the victim's realization that he was to be devoured, that nothing and no one could save him, and that he would never see his wife and children again.

At last we reached the spot where the tiger must have felt he had had enough of his victim's cries and struggles. Here he had laid the man on the ground and, releasing his grip, had bitten him again and again till his wails had been stilled for ever.

All this was written in the marks on the ground and the pool of blood that had streamed from those last fierce and fatal bites. After that the man-eater had continued his journey.

We followed for another furlong, and here at last the tiger had decided to begin his meal. He had left the narrow trail and turned into a small hollow in the ground, sheltered by grass, bushes and bracken, where he had set about devouring the unfortunate bamboo cutter. As we had surmised, the beast must have been hungry, for little remained of the man beyond the usual parts: the head, hands and feet, and a small portion of his chest, with rib bones bereft of flesh. The entrails had been torn out and dragged aside. The meat had been removed from the victim's pelvis, exposing the bone, and the thighs had also been devoured, here again leaving the bare bones in evidence of the great feast.

Far less than a quarter of the poor man remained, but this was enough to make the tiger return that night for a second meal, provided we played our cards cunningly enough and did not arouse his suspicions.

Yega and I looked around and at this point we encountered our first setback. There was no tree within at least eighty yards, a range far too great, as I well knew from past experience, to risk a shot by torchlight at night.

To the uninitiated this may seem an exaggeration. Eighty yards in daylight might appear a mere stone's throw. But those who have sat on *machans* in a jungle at night will know what I mean. Bushes, leaves, blades of grass and rocks all cause obstructions at this distance, and to attempt to cut them away, to ensure a better view when the tiger returned, might arouse his suspicions and prevent him from returning at all. Remember, I could not risk wounding him. I had to shoot to kill.

Tigers and panthers, and man-eaters especially, are very cautious when they come back to their kills. They reconnoitre the approaches to the spot for a long time before they show themselves, and if they feel or sense anything suspicious, if they find any cut branches scattered about, any removal of bushes or undergrowth or rocks, or any addition of leaves or branches that may conceal a hidden enemy, they will give the spot a wide berth and never return. Although he lacks a sense of smell, the tiger makes up for this handicap with an uncanny caution and an ability almost to read the hunter's mind and anticipate his every action.

As if to compensate for the distance of the nearest tree from the remains of the woodsman, a dense patch of tiger-grass bordered the bank of the small depression into which the tiger had taken him before beginning his meal, and this patch was barely fifteen feet away.

If I could hide in that grass without the man-eater becoming aware of my presence he would offer a point-blank target. The moon would rise early, and conditions would be in my favour, always provided the tiger did not become aware of my presence. Would this be possible? For if he did find out, the situation could turn into a most unpleasant one for me.

As I well knew, all tigers and especially man-eaters, which appear to be endowed with a fiendish cunningness, exceeding even the natural caution of their kind, have a habit of taking advantage of every vestige of natural cover when returning to the remains of their victims for a second meal. The clump of tiger grass in which I contemplated concealing myself lay in the direct *path* of the man-eater's return and so close to his victim that it was more than likely, if not certain, that he would make use of it to conceal his own approach. And however silent I might be, I knew well enough how silent would be his own coming. Should the man-eater discover me before I discovered him, the bamboo cutter's bones would have those of another to keep them company before many hours had passed. It was a gamble, with a heavy stake, that I would have to take.

In order not to disturb the grass by unnecessary trampling, I walked around it while considering the problem in all its aspects. If I hid in that grass, I would have to keep a careful watch in two opposite directions: over the victim's remains and also in the direction by which the man-eater might be expected to make his approach, which would almost certainly be through this patch of grass. This I could not do; I would have at least to turn my head from side to side, even though I kept my body still. That would mean movement, and movement of any sort would be fatal.

One of two things would happen if the tiger became aware of me: he might take fright and disappear, or he would deliberately stalk and leap upon me before I even suspected his presence. Frankly, I funked that terrible alternative.

At this point, Yega came up with a brilliant idea. He and I would sit back to back in the grass, one of us watching the bamboo cutter's remains while the other listened for the rustle that would herald the man-eater's entrance into that

188

same clump of grass, by which time he would not be more than five or six feet away.

What transpired next would have a lot to do with whether I happened to be the one who was watching the victim's remains or the tiger's approach through the grass. If I were watching the remains and Yega the grass, he would have to warn me with a nudge, and I would have to turn around in a second to be in time to shoot. And I would have to shoot accurately. But if I chose to watch the approach through the grass and left Yega to watch over the kill, and the man-eater crept up to the latter from some other direction, I would have to react similarly, except that the situation would not be nearly so dangerous. At least, the tiger would be more than a mere five or six feet away and I should have a better chance to shoot.

I hated to risk Yega's life. And I hated to risk my own. But this was our only chance and I nodded assent.

Strangely enough, in the Wynaad Forest area vultures are not nearly so numerous as in drier jungles of south India. Nevertheless, we took no chances of them discovering the remains and finishing what little flesh remained on the bones. So Yega cut a few small branches from the tree that grew eighty yards away, and these we placed over the bones and entrails of the man to hide them from any chance vulture hovering in the sky above. Then we returned to the deserted encampment.

It took another fifteen minutes for Timayya to come back in the car from Manantoddy. I told him of our discovery and our plan of action. Then occurred one of those awkward situations that sometimes appear between friends. Timayya stated bluntly that he would sit with me in Yega's stead, armed with my spare rifle, but I was not happy about his decision. I did not wish to risk my friend's life for one thing.

Secondly, quite frankly and I suppose selfishly, considering my own life was also at stake, I doubted his ability to keep watch for the tiger as efficiently as Yega would, with his lifetime of jungle experience. As tactfully as possible I put these points to my friend. Timmy became angry—and rude, too.

'Damn it, I'm a planter,' he said, 'not a bloody town-dweller like you. What the hell do you think? If you don't feel like sitting with me, at least lend me the .405/400 and . . . off back to Manantoddy yourself. I'll do the rest.'

There was a very nasty look in his eye.

I shrugged. 'Okay Timmy, you win,' I said. 'We'll sit together.'

The nasty look faded and a gleam of pleasure and excitement took its place.

When Yega heard the change of plan he was crestfallen. Now it was his turn to look at me reproachfully. I avoided his glance and studied one of the Studebaker's tyres closely.

We returned to Manantoddy for lunch, bringing Yega with us, after which we put in a couple of hours sleep to fortify us for the long, sleepless night vigil ahead. At three o'clock we were ready. Timmy suggested we take tea and sandwiches along with us, to which I assented after reminding him that these refreshments could only be enjoyed the following morning. No sound or movements of the slightest kind could we risk while we awaited the man-eater's return.

We left Yega at Manantoddy, as it would be dangerous for him to accompany us to the spot where we were going to sit and then return alone. Besides, we did not require his services in any way. By half-past three we had reached the woodcutter's deserted encampment. Here we parked the Studebaker close to the huts and before four we were at the patch of tiger-grass.

I removed the small branches with which Yega and I had earlier covered the scattered remains of the bamboo cutter to protect them from vultures, carrying them to a spot quite a distance away. It was a hot and sunny afternoon and what remained of the woodcutter, little enough though it was, had begun to smell, especially the entrails, which the man-eater had dragged to one side. But we dared not remove them for fear of arousing the tiger's suspicions when he returned.

I had already made it a condition with Timmy that I would face the side from which the tiger might be expected to approach through the grass, while he would face in the opposite direction towards the woodcutter's remains. Fortunately, he had not been difficult about this and had acquiesced readily enough. We had brought two of the foam-rubber cushions from the Rest House to sit upon. They would not only provide comfort, but would deaden any sound we might make in movement. Placing these on the ground, we squatted on them back to back and facing in the directions already described. I crossed my legs and settled down to sit in silence, having trained myself to this position after many years of similar experience in the jungle. Timmy whispered that he could not make himself comfortable that way and stretched both his legs out before him. Straightaway a disquieting thought entered my mind: for how long would Timmy be able to sit thus without moving? To me it appeared physically impossible, and I knew he would become fidgety before sundown.

Jungle life in the forests of the Wynaad and the Western Ghats is rather different from that of the drier areas. Animals and reptiles are fewer in number, but bird and insect life is prolific. We quickly became aware of this, for within a few minutes of our arrival and things quietening down, we heard the twittering calls of birds from all directions, accompanied by the chirping of crickets. The cicada of these regions is different from those of the plains: the latter, to which I was accustomed, emits a shrill and continuous high note, but the hill variety, which abounded here, emits a rasping note of fluctuating volume. It almost dies away and then rises to a cadence that jars the nerves, before fading away, only to rise again.

As evening fell, distant junglecocks and spurfowl began to vie with one another in their usual preroosting chorus, to the accompaniment of an occasional, plaintive, brassy cry from a peacock, feeding amidst the fallen seeds of the giant bamboo that grew so prolifically, or grubbing for caterpillars by scratching up the thick carpet of decaying leaves and mould. Around us, from the grass itself came the very faint and indefinable sounds of insects of all kinds on the move: grasshoppers, beetles of countless varieties, and a host of other creatures. A green and slender mantis, that must have been at least eight inches long, appeared just before me, camouflaged so marvellously that I would not have noticed him had he not climbed upon my knee. His body was frail and indefinably delicate, for all the world like a sliver of bamboo and not more than a sixteenth of an inch in thickness, while his wings, of a transparent tissue and veined like leaves, folded across his back to resemble a green sepal of no consequence whatever. So wonderful and impartial is nature's camouflage, that both those that prey upon others by habit, and those that seek to escape from being preyed upon, are equally disguised from one another. This inoffensive-looking mantis, that resembled so closely a slender twig with two green leaves attached, was quite as carnivorous and fierce in its own insect world as the man-eating tiger, whose return we were awaiting, was to the frightened jungle-dwellers.

Darkness came swiftly with the almost instant hushing of the bird-calls. The rustle of activity from the hidden insects in the grass around us increased apace. We felt their movements on all sides, and even upon our bodies. They climbed all over us and got inside our clothing, setting up such an itching that all our self-control was needed to prevent us from moving and scratching ourselves to secure an instant's relief.

I missed my old friends of the jungles of the plains, the nightjars, and thought of them for a few moments. They would be active at this period of twilight, flitting around in their silent, ghost-like fashion, in search of their evening meal, stragglers among the insects of the day that were going to bed late, and early-comers among the insects of the night in search of food.

This diverted my thoughts to the primal instincts of life, the search for food and the urge to procreate that are the two issues that govern all the dwellers of the jungle; to man and his civilization, and the search for wealth, which brings food and power, pleasures and a means of satisfying ourselves in practically any way we desire; and to much similar musing, one idea leading to another. But eventually I pulled myself up with quite a start, discovering that it was now pitch-dark and I had forgotten all about the man-eater and how close to me he might be.

The stench that came to us from the human fragments that had been exposed to the hot sun all day was now quite awful. Myriads of bluebottle flies had settled on them for the night.

The humble bluebottle fly is regarded everywhere as an obnoxious insect, associated only with filth and dirt and carrion. Nevertheless, he can be a great and secret friend to the hunter who watches by night; for the flies in their thousands, when they cover a carcase at night, are alert though resting. Any creature approaching near enough, even if it does not touch the carcase, makes its presence felt to the watchful, restless flies, who rustle in unison. And that rustling can be clearly heard by the watcher in the darkness, provided he is not too far away, is alert enough, has reasonably good hearing, and above all recognizes its significance. The bluebottles were silent now and I was satisfied that neither the tiger, nor anything else for that matter, was anywhere near the carcase.

My friend's back rested against mine tautly, uncomfortably, radiating heat though my sweater. I could sense his nervousness as he strained his eyes into the darkness. This is the most dangerous period for the hunter who risks his life sitting on the ground for a man-eater : the brief fifteen to thirty minutes from twilight till the light of the stars makes itself felt, be it ever so little.

Our greatest danger lay in the direction in which I was facing, the opposite end of the grassy clump in the midst of which we were hiding. If the man-eater approached from there, his keen eyesight, even in that darkness, would enable him to discover our presence while he was yet some distance away. He would not bother to come any closer then. What he would do would depend upon his individual character; he might launch himself from fifteen feet away and be upon us in the fraction of a second, or, if he were a coward, as many man-eaters are, he would just slink noiselessly away.

Then I remembered with considerable trepidation that this tiger could not possibly be called a coward. Barely a few hours ago he had sneaked up to a hut filled with people and dragged a human being away. With tensed nerves and strained ears, I listened for the faintest creak or rustle of grass that might betray the arrival of the man-eater from in front, while hearkening for the buzz of disturbed bluebottles that might herald his advent from behind. There was nothing but complete silence. The immediate danger passed as three things happened almost together. My eyes accustomed themselves to the gloom and I could begin to identify objects around me. The stars came out in their multitude and their gleam seemed to bring back the moments of half-light that had so recently gone. And above all, the fireflies of the Wynaad began their nightly display of living fireworks that would continue till the early hours of the morning, when the mist and the dew would chill the tiny lamp-bearers and force them to seek the shelter of the foliage.

There must have been thousands upon thousands of these little creatures within a few yards of us, winging their way hither and thither in restless flight. The glow of their combined light produced a radiation that dispelled the darkness like a flashlight, then broke again into myriads of individual lights that sparkled through the darkness.

No sounds broke the stillness. The forest seemed strangely devoid of animal life. No friendly calls of sambar or spotted deer could we hear. No cries of the usual birds of the night. There came to us only the undefinable faint movements of the insects in the grass around us. And to the torment caused by the insect marauders on our bodies, the mosquitoes now began to add their torture. They had not worried us unduly until now, perhaps because they had not discovered our presence; but having done so they apparently decided to make the most of their discovery. I did not dare to betray our presence to the tiger which, at that very instant perhaps, might be approaching us. Faintly I could hear Timmy behind me, trying to blow the mosquitoes away.

It was at this instant that there came clearly to my hearing the faint rustling buzz of angry, disturbed bluebottles flies. Something was near the remains of the woodsman. Timmy had heard it too, for I felt him tauten against my back, while he ceased blowing at the mosquitoes. His elbows dug into me in the prearranged signal and remained there as he gripped the .450/400 in his lap.

The flies buzzed again as they rose nervously a few inches above the bones and entrails on which they had been resting.

They hummed a while, they resettled themselves and the buzzing stopped. The intruder, whatever it was, had not yet reached the kill or the flies would never have resettled. It was approaching.

Something made the faintest sound from beyond the remains and there came the distant thud of a stone being turned over. Undoubtedly the man-eater had arrived. He was reconnoitring and would presently approach the remains of his feast.

Or was he creeping upon us?

Casting caution to the winds I whisked around, bringing the Winchester to my shoulder and pressing the torch-button, fitted to the barrel, with my left thumb, almost in one movement. The bright beam cut a swathe of light through the blackness and was reflected by two baleful eyes. But they were rather more reddish-white in colour than a brilliant whitish-red. And they were set rather too closely together.

Sitting on his haunches like a dog, the torchlight caught the panther in the act of licking his lips. We could see the red of his tongue sweep across the slightly opened mouth.

Could the man-eater be a panther after all? I dismissed the thought as soon as it crossed my mind, for I had seen the man-eater's pug-marks on the trail we had followed. They had certainly been those of a tiger. Besides, he had been seen by Yega and some of the other woodcutters. This panther was merely there by chance. In passing by, he had stumbled on the kill. He was sitting there in doubt, wondering how it had all come about and if he could take a chance.

At that moment the panther became aware of the torch-beam that was shining straight into his eyes.

He stood up, snarled, turned and walked away. Disgust was written in his every movement. Clearly he did not wish to involve himself in such a compromising situation. I extinguished the torch as quickly as possible. Was the man-eater nearby? If so, he would certainly have seen my light. That might cause him to run away. Or, having come to know of our presence and whereabouts, he might at that very moment be creeping upon us. But the attitude of the panther soon dispelled this disquietening thought. He seemed absolutely unconcerned. He would hardly be so indifferent if his hereditary and implacable foe, a tiger, were in the vicinity.

The bluebottles settled down and so did we, to a long and uneventful vigil, while the fireflies kept us company to lend enhantment to an otherwise macabre scene. It became cold, and then colder. The insects in the grass around us stopped their restless movements. Perhaps they were feeling the cold too. The mosquitoes grew less active as well and the fireflies began to disappear.

The tiger should have returned long ago. He should have put in an appearance even before the panther. It seemed as if the man-eater did not intend to come back.

Time dragged on. I began to feel sleepy and perhaps I grew a bit careless too. For, although I heard the sound once or twice, it did not register straight away. Then, all of a sudden, I was wide awake and alert.

Something had approached the grass in which we were hiding. Not directly from in front but a little to my left. There had been a faint rustle and then a definite footfall as something heavy had placed its weight upon the grass. There had followed a faint but distinct creaking and cracking of stems.

And that thing, whatever it was, had now stopped.

Had the man-eater discovered our presence, as he must most surely have done? Was he crouching for a final spring? The answer came the very next second when the tiger snarled. He was not more than ten feet away.

I pressed the button of the torch.

The beam lit up a wild scene of violently swaying grass stems. I had a glimpse of something brown that catapulted itself backwards and was gone. Then came a shattering roar from the jungle.

I switched off the torch as the man-eater began to demonstrate by emitting roar after roar. He was very angry; but he was also frightened. I had switched on the torch a fraction too soon. He would otherwise have come on. Perhaps I had done the right thing after all. I might have been too late to stop his charge, once it had been launched.

Timmaya had whisked around and, like me, was facing in the direction from which the tiger was now roaring. The beast began to circle us, snarling and roaring horribly as he did so. It was a war of nerves. Either he was trying to work up enough courage to drive home a charge, or he was trying to scare us away. I felt he was following the second plan.

We waited awhile, hoping he would decide to attack; but this he failed to do. The roars now sank to a series of growls, but they came from different directions as the tiger circled. It seemed he was trying to find out how many human beings were hidden in that grass. Was there only one, whom he could easily overwhelm, or were there many?

This went on for another fifteen minutes. But nothing happened. The tiger would not attack, nor did he go away. It was a game of nerves and I am afraid the tiger won.

I decided to draw him out by precipitating an attack. I whispered to Timmaya to remain where he was, while I got up and started to walk back towards the encampment, which was only a short distance away. The tiger would probably come after me. On the other hand, he might decide that it would be a better proposition to let the hated man-with-the-light depart while he went back for what was left of the kill. This would give Timmy the chance of a shot.

My friend protested vigorously, whispering 'Don't be a fool!'

But, with restraining hand on his shoulder, I got slowly to my feet, stood there a few seconds to restore my circulation, and then started walking deliberately towards the woodcutter's deserted huts, taking care to make the expected amount of sound a man might make in covering such ground.

The effect on the man-eater was instantaneous. He began to roar again; and then he came after me. You must bear in mind that, except for the starlight, it was quite dark. Purposely, I had kept the torch extinguished so as not to frighten the tiger, but the situation had turned into a most unpleasant one.

I had covered about twenty-five yards when the man-eater screwed up enough courage to charge. I remember thinking to myself that it was fortunate he had chosen to be so noisy about it, rather than make a silent and stealthy rush, when I would not have known from which direction he was coming.

There came the all-too-familiar 'Wroof! Wroof! Wroof! as he launched his attack. I whirled around with the rifle to my shoulder, once again pressing the button of the torch with my left thumb. The bright beam of light cut through the darkness to shine upon the angry eyes of the enraged man-eater, coming towards me in an up-and-down motion as he charged.

It was difficult to hold the eyes in my sights as they moved, and while this thought flashed through my mind, something quite unexpected happened. I was blinded by another blaze of light that obscured the tiger, and indeed everything clsc from sight, as it shone fully into my eyes! Timmaya had switched on his torch and was shinning it directly in my face.

Instinctively, I raised my forearm to cover my eyes and jumped backwards to try to get out of the glare.

The next instant everything was plunged into inky darkness. My finger went off the button and my own torch went out while the beam of light from my friend's torch turned away from me.

It cut through the darkness and on to the tiger, which was crouched on the ground hardly four feet away from me in a ludicrous pose. He looked rather foolish with his head bent low, almost to ground level, front paws outstretched, with his rear up in the air behind him, his curving tail upheld and stiff, brought to a halt by Timmy's light.

It was not an instant too soon, for he had been about to spring upon me when Timmy's unexpected light from behind stopped him.

There came an ear-splitting crash and I saw the crouching tiger literally pushed as if by some invisible force, when the bullet from my. 450/400 rifle, fired by Timmy, took him somewhere in the side.

At that instant I stood directly in his *path*, his nearest enemy, and he came for me with all the hate and speed of which he as capable. My own torch-beam must have completely blinded him when I fired directly into his open mouth, followed by a second shot as he crashed at my feet while I jumped aside.

That was when Timmy fired again. His bullet passed over the tiger and hit the ground almost at my feet, raising a spurt of dust. Everything was over when I found myself running backwards at incredible speed to try to get away from the tiger as he rolled on the ground.

It was Timmy who got the man-eater, for apart from his first shot that had struck the tiger's flank and halted the beast at the instant of springing upon me, he had fired a second which had entered the animal squarely behind the left shoulder. This second shot I had never heard in the confusion. My own bullet had blown out the back of the tiger's head, while my second, also striking his head, had struck the ground near me and had been a complete miss.

Timmy was overwhelmed with delight and executed a war dance around the fallen enemy. Although the skin, and particularly the head, would not make much of a trophy, ruined as they were by the bullets from my two powerful rifles, he kept chanting and repeating over and over again that he had never heard of a man-eater being killed under such unusual conditions.

Needless to say although I was not nearly so exuberant, I fully concurred with Timmy's sentiments. I might not object to having the same experience all over again providing I could be in Timmy's place. But not where I had been!

# Six

## The Man-Hater of Talainovu

IN THE KOLLEGAL TALUK OF WHAT WAS FORMERLY COIMBATORE district, part of the Madras Presidency in the days when the British governed India, there is a hamlet called Talainovu. Now the British have gone and with them the Madras Presidency, and Madras state has taken its place; its area is just about half that was covered by the former presidency, for much of the territory has gone to the neighbouring states of Andhra, Mysore and Kerala.

Among these transferred territories is Kollegal taluk, and with it the hamlet of Talainovu. They have now become a part of Mysore state. Cultivation and buildings have spread, and much of the beautiful forest areas that stretched from Talainovu across rugged hills down to the valley of the Cauvery river have been felled ruthlessly, while what is left has been practically denuded of game.

But it will always be easy for me to remember the little village of Talainovu, as I knew it long ago, for two reasons. Firstly, in the Tamil language the word 'talainovu' means 'headache'; secondly, the wily panther that made its abode by the banks of the Cauvery river, in a steep valley some ten miles from the hamlet, gave me a real headache while trying to deal with it.

Man-eating panthers are rare in southern India and have always been so. This panther was never a man-eater in the true sense. Rather, it was a man-hater, filled with deep hostility for the human race, and it treasured this hatred and exacted a toll upon its lifelong enemy until its last day.

To begin at the beginning; a pantheress lived on a forest hilltop, ten miles from the village of Talainovu to the south. Six furlongs away and to the north, lay a deep valley where the hill fell away steeply to the bed of the Cauvery river. To the east the forest stretched for miles upon miles, into and across the boundaries of the Salem district and along the twists and turns of the Cauvery river. But to the west it continued only for about six miles, till it gave way to the low scrub that bordered the main road leading from the town of Kollegal, across a bridge, northwards to Maddur and Bangalore.

This pantheress was a young animal, and when she gave birth to her first cubs, three in number, she was a proud and happy mother, devoted to her offspring and prepared to defend them with her life. According to reports and hearsay, picked up by me at a much later date, some circumstances, we do not know what, induced the pantheress to bring her cubs out of the cave in which they were born much earlier than normal, while they were still too young to move about in safety. Perhaps their father had had designs on their young lives and sought to devour them, as male tigers and panthers

203

frequently do. Perhaps a bear trespassed into their cave. Perhaps food was scarce in that locality.

So the pantheress brought her cubs down the hill and hid them in a bamboo thicket on the banks of the Cauvery river. No doubt this was only a temporary measure till the mother could find a better home for them, perhaps some other cave. But fate decided to be unkind to her that early morning. She had left the cubs in the thicket and had probably been out hunting all the night. The sun had topped the parallel range of hills that marked the course of the big river and was glinting on its tumbling, foaming waters when the pantheress was yet a mile away from the bamboos in which she had concealed her cubs.

And then she stopped in her tracks, for far away she heard a noise, a persistent tap-tap-tap! Humans! And in the very area where she had left her three little cubs unprotected.

The pantheress doubtless broke into a bounding gallop to cover the intervening distance as fast as she could, her only thought for the safety of her offspring. But when she was but a short distance away she must have heard their snarls, and she knew what had happened. The hated humans had discovered her cubs.

The pantheress arrived on the scene to find that half-a-dozen or more almost naked black bodies, glistening with sweat, surrounded her cubs. These were on the ground, back to back, and small as they were they snarled defiance at the intruders. The men jabbered to one another, pointing at the cubs with the sharp, curved knives that they used for cutting the bamboos, an expression of gloating excitement on each countenance, but no sign of pleasure at the three pretty balls of fur that so gamely defied them, nor pity for their helplessness.

Even as she watched, one of the bamboos cutters raised his *koithar* and swiped at the nearest cub. The curved blade bit into the soft body. The cub was flung into the air and fell some feet away, almost cut in two but still living. It groaned faintly as its young blood reddened the grass.

This was the signal for the other bamboo cutters to destroy the remaining two cubs, which they set about doing without further delay. A few slashes of their sharp knives and it was all over. Three mangled scraps of flesh now lay scattered on the ground where previously there had been three living creatures.

Probably an inborn fear of the human to all wild animals, even the worst man-eating tiger and the most ferocious rogue elephant, had held the grief-stricken mother back, but the sight of her dead cubs now drove her crazy. With short, sharp roars, she hurled herself upon the men.

The first man did not know what it was all about for the pantheress tore out his eyes as her raking talons slammed into his face. He fell to the ground, and she leaped over him to bite the second man's chest. He fell, too, his screams joining those of the blinded man who thrashed about on the ground. The remainder, all armed with *koithars,* did not wait. With yells of terror they fled in all directions.

The pantheress made to follow them but then stopped, her attention taken by the two men who writhed upon the ground. With cold fury she set upon the two of them and tore them to shreds.

Then, sniffing at the dead bodies of her three cubs, she picked up the least mangled of them and bore it away in sorrow.

That was how it all began.

When the bamboo cutters returned to their village, they had a harrowing tale to tell of a savage panther of huge dimensions that had attacked them entirely without provocation. They did not mention their part in the incident— at least, not them—and of how they had wantonly destroyed the cubs and infuriated the mother. This admission came later. Naturally, there was a hue and cry. People avoided that part of the jungle where the killings had taken place, or such as had to go there went armed with hatchets and guns, and in groups of as many persons as possible.

The pantheress was not seen or heard of for some weeks after that. People soon forgot the incident, and through apathy or laziness left their weapons behind. The licensed cutters of bamboo and sellers of timber, as well as the poachers, went into the jungle, the former by day to follow their daily routine, and the latter, who lived by stealing and selling the same commodities, renewed their practice of cutting bamboos and wood and floating the stolen material across the river during the bright moonlit nights.

But the vengeful pantheress did not forget. This was her opportunity to strike a second time.

A notorious poacher of sandalwood, whom the people of the forest department and the police knew had been operating for years, but whom they had never succeeded in bringing to book, went into the jungle with his son one moonlit night. They had planned to cut some sandalwood, float it down the river for a mile or so to a spot where the water became calm and there was no undercurrent, and then tow the cut timber across the river to the northern bank which belonged to Mysore state, using the circular coracle made of bamboo and buffalo hide which they kept permanently hidden on the river for this purpose. Once they were on the Mysore side of the river, they knew they would be safe from pursuit by the authorities on the Madras bank and would be asked no awkward questions.

The two thieves began hacking the sandalwood saplings they had marked for this purpose on an earlier visit, and the pantheress heard the hated sound of chopping. As likely as not the noise of wood being cut reminded her, by instinctive association rather than thought, of the day when her cubs had been cut to pieces before her eyes. Hatred must have filled her mind as she started stalking towards the noise with but one thought in her brain—to obliterate those who made it.

The father never knew what happened when the pantheress sprang upon him from behind and fastened her fangs in his throat. He could not even scream for help, but toppled to the ground with the sudden weight upon his back. The son, a lad of eighteen years, saw what was happening, but with thoughts only for his own safety and not for his father's life, dropped his axe and fled precipitately.

It took the pantheress a few seconds to kill the man and that saved the boy from sharing the same fate. Running as fast as he could, he reached the coracle, jumped into it and paddled frantically across the river. When he got back to his hut and burst in upon his mother, it was to tell what had just happened to his father.

The villagers had gone to sleep long ago, but the combined wails of mother and son awoke them. They lit their lights and heard the story, but agreed not to do anything till the next day. After all, everybody knew both father and son were thieves.

The sun was high when a large party of villagers, armed with guns, hatchets, knives and spears and led by the poacher's son, returned to the scene. There they found the old thief lying in a pool of his own blood, his gullet torn out and his whole body badly bitten and lacerated. But it was very noticeable that no flesh had been eaten. The killer could certainly not be called a man-eater. To the men who gazed with horror upon the mangled remains, the attack on the poacher had apparently been for no reason and under no provocation whatever, for at that time few people knew the beginning of the story.

207

Once again there was an uproar and folk went about only in groups and armed to the teeth. The panic lasted for a longer period on this occasion, but once more time and the usual apathy among the people gradually calmed them down. Eventually, the panther was forgotten again and they carried on in their accustomed ways.

Again weeks passed, and again came the moonlit nights, the period when most of the mischief is done in the jungles of India. For it is during this time that the poachers of game sit over water holes and salt licks to shoot the sambar, spotted deer and other animals that come there to quench their thirst or eagerly to lick the salty earth, while the timber thieves, who steal the sandalwood, teakwood, *muthee*, giant bamboo etc., go into the forest to hack down the trees, cut them to convenient lengths and float the timber down the river or take it stealthily away in bullock carts or, when they are daring enough, by lorry loads.

A third kind of thief also takes advantage of the bright moonlight: the poachers of fish. They do not fish with rods or nets, for the catch would be too small and the work too hard and slow. Instead, in the river pools where they know the large fish congregate at nights to sleep or to feed, according to species, these men explode their home-made bombs, made in secrecy from crude gunpowder and fuses. Floating gently downstream in one of the circular coracles made of a bamboo frame covered with buffalo hide, in common use on the rivers of India, these prowlers visit every pool for a distance of about five miles down the river. The fuse is lit and the bomb is then floated on the water.

While the explosion does no general damage, the concussion in the water stuns the large fish and slaughters thousands of the smaller ones and all the fry for yards around. These casualties rise to the surface, where the larger fish are quickly scooped into the coracle with the help of nets attached to poles. The thousands of smaller dead fish, including the fry, are allowed to go to waste and float downstream to rot and be eaten by other fish and by the crocodiles.

And so the operation is repeated from pool to pool. By this time the poachers have gathered almost more fish into the coracle than it can hold, while the wanton destruction of countless thousands of valuable fry and many species of small fish can be imagined.

Generally a number of men share in the operation, employing two coracles, one from which to launch the bombs, and the other for collecting the catch. The second is often almost at sinking point before the poachers feel they have collected enough. Moreover, there is an unwritten law amongst them that they should not trespass upon the domain of the next batch of poachers, which starts where they leave off, for that would provoke a fight and one or other batch would be bound to sneak to the forest department officials or to the police. Everyone is happy, the fish are slaughtered, and the local authorities can do nothing about it. Moreover, to make things absolutely safe, each man receives a basketful after every expedition. Should they prove unlucky and they are discovered by some representative of the law, the poachers have but to present half-a-dozen of the largest fish they have caught to the official and all is well again.

The coracle, loaded with fish, is eventually brought ashore at the end of the five-mile stretch. Here the catch is cleaned and gutted and loaded into gunny sacks that the men have brought with them. Every man shoulders a bag, while two men pick up the coracles and carry them upside down over their shoulders. The light flat paddles are taken by one of the others. Now begins the five-mile walk back to the point from which they started, for it is not possible to propel the clumsy, circular craft upstream against the strong river currents. This is the hardest part of the whole business.

The same procedure is followed through the ensuing moonlit nights until the dark nights come again, when the poachers rest and laze it out for a fortnight till moonlight returns.

In very lonely regions where there are no forest guards or other inconvenient persons to interfere, the bombing of the pools is carried on by daylight, although at the period I am writing about there was some restraint, for the forest departments were controlled by British officers. Alas, that restraint has now gone. With Independence, the poachers no longer work by night.

But to return to our story: the moonlit nights came round again and a party of fish poachers systematically bombed pool after pool and netted the stunned fish, filling them into the second coracle, which was propelled by a single man so as to leave more space. They worked steadily until after midnight, when they decided to take time off to go ashore and eat the snacks they had brought with them.

It so happened that the second coracle, the one filled with the catch and paddled by the single boatman, was nearer the shore when his companions called to him:

'Brother, put ashore. We have worked hard and we've caught much. Let's rest for a while and eat the *shappad* (food) we have brought with us and drink some cold coffee.'

The solitary boatman welcomed the call, for he was lonely. He dug the blade of his paddle into the water, holding the shaft with both hands, first to the right of him and then to the left, with swift, short strokes, to force the clumsy craft across the current which was particularly strong at this place, for not long had passed since the rains had filled the river to overflowing.

Eventually he reached the bank and sprang ashore, carrying in one hand the end of the rope that was attached to the bamboo bottom of the coracle, so as to tie it to the root or trunk of a tree. This he never succeeded in doing. Those of his companions in the other coracle who happened to be watching saw something that looked long and grey spring from behind the *mendhi* (henna) bushes at the water's edge. They heard a rasping roar and saw the black form of their friend go down with a strange grey shape on top of it. They heard his piercing scream and then saw that his coracle, dragging the rope that had fallen from his hands, was rushing downstream on the powerful current.

The boatman who was paddling their craft made a desperate effort to overtake the runaway coracle. But he was at a disadvantage with the load of men in his own boat. The runaway coracle gained speed as the current, spinning it around and around, drew it towards midstream where the water bubbled and foamed in the bright moonlight over a low cataract formed by a reef of rocks.

The pursuing boatman was almost rash enough to drive his craft into those dangerous waters when his companions restrained him. They watched in dismay as the unmanned coracle lurched heavily against the rocks, tossed wildly from side to side and then capsized, throwing the whole of their catch into the river. Then it was that they turned towards the shore to abuse and beat their comrade for being so stupid as to let the rope slip from his grasp. Why, a large coracle such as the one they had just lost would cost a hundred rupees to make and much more to buy, not to mention the value of the fish that had been lost in the river. Idiot that he was they would thrash him soundly!

But on the bank no one was to be seen. Then they remembered the grey shape in the moonlight, and the roaring they had heard, and how their friend seemed to stumble and fall. They had been so concerned to intercept the runaway coracle that they had ignored their companion's plight.

Some of the men ordered the boatman who wanted to go ashore to investigate, not to do so on any account. Perhaps some evil spirit was lurking there. It had got their friend and might get all of them if they ventured too near. For quite a long time nobody thought of the panther. Then somebody remembered, and reminded the rest. They agreed then that the grey form they had seen had been the lurking beast. It had killed their companion and assuredly was devouring him at that moment.

Using the single paddle, the men took turns to propel their weighted craft upstream, as they dared not go ashore. They did this for about half a mile and then found they could go no further. So they made for the river bank, where each man exhorted the other to jump ashore first. Finally they did so in a body, relying on the safety of numbers. So as not to be encumbered by the weighty coracle all the way back to their starting point, they drew it some yards up the bank and made for their village as fast as they could in a group, talking at the top of their voices to keep the panther away.

Next day, when the sun was high, the whole village turned out, the men having armed themselves as best as they could, to discover what had happened to the missing man. They found his remains behind the henna bushes. He had been literally torn to bits, but so far as could be seen, none of his flesh had been eaten.

And so it went on, the pantheress attacking and killing where she could, but never eating her victims. Her handiwork was evident by the manner in which each corpse was bitten and clawed savagely, far beyond what was necessary just to kill the victim. She seemed to be taking savage delight in mangling each body almost beyond recognition.

Now, the stretch of river where these events took place was a favourite spot for catching the great *mahseer*, the king of Indian fishes, in spite of all the poaching. But fishing has never held any attraction for me. I have no patience for it. Yet a great many of my friends are devotees and occasionally I took one or other of them to this river for a couple of days.

These visits had to be few and far between, however, because the rough track from Talainovu, through the jungle to the river, is very steep, with abrupt turns that my Studebaker cannot negotiate. Most of my friends owned English cars, and these were equally unsuitable for the purpose. So our visits were limited to those occasions when we could get someone who owned a jeep to come along with us, or to the lucky occasions when we could borrow or hire such a vehicle.

Well, such an opportunity came our way one day, and this time it seemed to have come to stay. Donald, my son, had bought a jeep! A much-battered vehicle that hailed from Andhra state, painted vivid blue, and with faults in every conceivable part. But Don set to work, and at considerable expense and very great trouble he substituted good parts for bad, so that eventually we possessed a vehicle that would go anywhere.

Then came the day when we set out for the Talainovu fishing grounds, with Donald proudly driving the jeep he had so painstakingly repaired. Next to him sat 'Tiny' Seddon, a great 'mahseer' fisherman, great not only in his fishing potentialities but also in bulk and height. In the back were three of us; an old friend and schoolmate of Donald's, named Merwan Chamar-Baughvala; Thangavelu, who had once been my *shikari* and had found service in our establishment as table-boy, motor-cleaner, the feeder of our domestic creatures and many wild-animal pets, and general jack-of-all-trades, his particular function on this trip being camp cook. Finally, wedged securely and tightly, at an uncomfortable angle that gave little chance to move, was myself.

It is exactly ninety-nine miles from our house in Bangalore to the camping site on the bank of the Cauvery river, some ten miles beyond the village of Talainovu, where we proposed to do our fishing. We left Bangalore rather late, and when the journey ended the sun was setting in flames of red, with a background of orange, vermilion and indigo. We halted a few yards from the river's edge, under the grove of giant *muthee*, tamarind and *jumlum* trees, beneath which we always made our camp.

There were three things to be done at once, and the trained members of the party—Don, Thangavelu and myself—started on them straightaway. Don looked quickly around for fresh elephant tracks, to reassure ourselves that none were in the vicinity to resent our intrusion and come thundering down upon us. Using both feet, I started clearing the ground, in a six or seven yard circle, of all dried leaves, stones and sticks which might shelter scorpions, particularly the small red variety. A sting from such a scorpion is guaranteed to take your mind off all other problems, including the demands of the Income Tax *wallahs*, for the next eight hours or more. Thangavelu hurried to gather dry logs, a task in which Don soon began to help him, for the camp fire that was to be kept blazing all night in case an elephant came our way while we were asleep.

Tiny Seddon jumped on to a rock half-submerged in the water and gazed pensively at the swirling eddies. No doubt he was seeking inspiration as to where to start fishing the next morning. Merwan Chamar-Baughvala threw himself on the ground I had just cleared and remarked how comfortable it was compared with the jeep.

None of us thought of the panther—because up to this moment none of us knew about it!

The moon would not rise till late. We ate Merwan's contribution of chicken biriyani and pork vindaloo, two very delicious but over-rich dishes, and while Thangavelu was preparing the tea, drank water from the river. That is, all of us except Tiny, who was certain the river water contained cholera germs, typhoid germs, and bacteria of every variety. He said he would wait for the tea. Then Thangavelu stroked the camp fire that was to burn all night and we lay back and smoked and told stories, gazing at the starry sky beyond the canopy of leaves above our heads. We counted ourselves fortunate to be able to enjoy such bliss, which so many of our fellow creatures, crowded in stuffy cities all over the world, have never experienced for even a day in all their monotonous lives. And so we fell asleep.

I do not know why it was that I awoke with a start. My watch showed a few minutes past three. The camp fire had died down to a few glowing embers, for Thangavelu, who had undertaken to keep it alive, had long since fallen asleep. Donald, to my left, was snoring loudly. Merwan and Tiny, in that order to my right, had covered their heads with their bedsheets to ward off mosquitoes and the dew, and were sleeping soundlessly.

I wondered what had wakened me so suddenly. Perhaps some jungle noise. Perhaps an elephant breaking branches in order to feed on the higher, more tender leaves. I listened more intently and for a time heard nothing except Don's noisy, rattling snores.

Then I knew what had wakened me, for close at hand I heard a guttural rasping sound: 'Haa-ah! Haa-ah! Haa-ah!' The call of a hungry panther!

Now panthers in the forest are, as a rule, quite harmless animals. Except when they turn man-eaters which is very rarely, or when they are wounded, they are shy, cowardly beasts that avoid the presence of man. No doubt the animal that was now calling, although apparently quite close, had not yet caught sight of the embers of our fire. As soon as it did so, in all probability it would hurry away as fast as it could. Or so I thought as I continued to listen sleepily to the sound.

The call came again, and louder. The hungry panther was certainly quite close. Surely, it must have seen our fire by now? I felt very sleepy indeed and comfortable. Drat the beast, I thought. Why doesn't it let me sleep?

That was when I heard the panther snarl! At last it has seen us, I thought; now it will vanish. But the panther snarled again, long and menacingly.

Strange, I thought, my eyes half-closed with sleep. It is either a very inquisitive or a very angry and daring panther. I mused; but why worry? I was safe in the centre of the party. Tiny was at one end, Don at the other, and Thangavelu by himself not far from the fire.

The panther growled again, low and long, and I sat up abruptly, groping for the torch I had kept near my pillow. Blinking to free myself from sleep, I directed the torch-beam towards the snarling that was growing louder.

It revealed a panther, crouching on the ground a few feet from Thangavelu and evidently preparing to spring upon him. There was no mistaking its posture: I could see its tail lashing to and fro, a sure indication of its malevolent intentions. I felt for my rifle, which I had kept loaded beside me on the ground.

And then Thangavelu ruined everything.

I suppose his jungle instinct was really responsible. It alerted him, but rather late, to the great danger that threatened. He sat up abruptly, and in doing so kicked over the *degchie* containing the water he had boiled for Tiny to drink. Perhaps the clatter it made, or Thangavelu's movement, or more likely my torch-beam, convinced the panther that its presence had been discovered, and before I could do anything with the rifle, handicapped as I was with the torch in my right hand, the brute leaped aside and disappeared behind the nearest bush.

All this time Thangavelu had been blissfully unaware of any danger. Still half asleep, he had not heard or seen the panther. I awoke the others and told them what had happened.

They were surprised at first. Then Don said, 'Dad, you've had a nightmare. Merwan's chicken biriyani and pork vindaloo are the cause of it. I haven't heard a sound all night and I doubt if there's a panther within miles.'

The others laughed and I was a bit huffed. How could Don say he had not heard a sound when he had been snoring all night? I clambered to my feet, still holding the torch and rifle?

'Come and see this,' I invited, shining my torch on the ground and walking towards the spot where the panther had been lying. But the earth there was hard and nothing could be seen.

'See what' asked Don, sarcastically, while Merwan wailed, 'Why did you wake me up for nothing?'

They all went back to their places and fell asleep again, including Thangavelu. Nobody had believed me. But I knew that the danger that had threatened us, and particularly the servant, had been very real and not part of a dream or my imagination.

I rekindled the fire with the wood that Thangavelu had gathered the evening before. Then with my rifle and torch at hand, I remained awake for the rest of the night with my back propped against my bedroll. I was convinced the panther I had seen had been a man-eater and that Thangavelu had been saved in the nick of time. The calls that had awakened me showed that it was hungry. The chances were it might return.

An hour later a sambar started calling on the hillside half a mile away. It called for some time before the spotted deer scented or saw the source of the danger. Then they started calling too. Clearly the panther was retreating across the hillside.

By this time a crescent moon had arisen, outlining the immediate neighbourhood. The water in the river gurgled monotonously as it flowed over the rocks and I felt very sleepy. At last the dawn came, when Tiny was the first to awake. He saw me.

'Don't say you've been sitting up all night?' he asked.

'Wake Thangavelu and tell him to make some tea', was all the reply I gave. Then I went to sleep before the water could boil.

Tiny fished all day. He caught a ten-pound *mahseer*, a couple of seven-pounders and some smaller fish. Don tried his hand, but like me he is impatient and caught nothing. Merwan said he wanted to have a bath, and so as not to disturb the fishing, started to wander downstream with his towel across his shoulders. I thought of the man-eater which no one believed I had seen; and called after him, 'Wait a minute, I'll join you.' Picking up my rifle and swinging a towel, I followed him.

That afternoon we all felt sleepy, particularly myself, and the camp was once again hushed in slumber. But not for long. We heard a series of hollow sounds drawing nearer gradually, 'Boomp! Boomp! Boomp!'

Poachers! They were bombing the river and operating in broad daylight, too, evidently without fear of being caught. Soon, around the bend in the river appeared the usual two coracles, the first loaded with men and the other with fish. Catching sight of our party, they paddled frantically against the current to try to reach the other side.

This move incited us to act though. Don fired a shot into the air. Then he called out, 'Come here, or the next shot will be at you.'

The paddling stopped and the two coracles started drifting downstream. It was evident the men inside were debating whether to surrender or make a dash for it. Then Merwan shouted in English, which of course they did not understand. 'Come here, you bastards, or as sure as eggs we'll sink you.'

Slowly the men started paddling the coracles towards us, but stopped when they were a few yards offshore. From our slightly elevated position on the bank, we could look down on the hundreds of fish lying in the second coracle.

Then began a harangue which was as needless as it was foolish. Don threatened and admonished them alternately, for their wrongful activity. The men replied that they saw nothing wrong in it. The fish belonged to nobody in particular. Then why should the government frame rules or demand fishing licences? And who were we to interfere? And so on, and so on.

Thangavelu, being about the wisest in our party at the time, said, 'Give us a couple of your best and largest fish. Then, go and blow yourselves up for all we care!'

In the midst of all this I asked, 'Look, is there a man-eating panther in these parts?'

There was a hushed silence. Then one of the men replied in a low tone, as if he did not wish to be overheard, 'Indeed, *dorai*, there is. It has killed many, many people. Only a few days ago it killed one of our own comrades, whose name was Balu. That's why we are now catching fish by daylight. Normally, we would only do this on moonlit nights, but not a soul will stir out after sunset now.'

So I was right after all!

219

Don was excited. 'Come here. Come ashore,' he invited. 'Damn the fish. We'll not harm you. I want to know more about this panther. We're *shikaris*. We're interested and will try to shoot it.'

A chord having been established, the fishermen brought their coracles to the bank and tied them with ropes to the roots of trees. Then they stepped ashore and sat around us in a group. Don and I plied them with questions, and from their answers pieced together the story which I have already related. The men admitted the panther was not a man-eater in the strict sense. So far, it had not actually eaten any of its victims, but had contented itself with mauling and mutilating them hideously. Obviously the animal was female, possessed of unusual sagacity and with a quite abnormal memory, for most wild animals generally forget the past very quickly. This pantheress evidently remembered the slaying of her cubs and her feeling of hatred for the human race seemed as fresh now as on that day. After hearing the story, our sympathies were with the aggrieved animal.

Eventually the boatmen asked to take leave of us. The sun would grow hot and the fish could not be bombed so easily, for they would swim into deeper waters. Disgustedly, we told them to get the hell out of it, but not before Thangavelu had remembered to pick out two of the largest and best fish for us.

'So you see, chaps, I was not dreaming after all,' was my first comment as the two coracles began to draw away. Tiny was the only one to think any more about fishing that day. The rest of us, Thangavelu included, went into close conference as to how to shoot this panther. Don and Merwan were particularly keen. For myself, I was of the opinion that the panther had a case.

From the start, the others felt we had a difficult problem in not having a regular man-eater to deal with. Here I disagreed. In my opinion, given the time, this pantheress would be far easier to come to grips with, because, filled with hatred for humans, she would go out of her way to try and attack us. As I saw the situation, we should operate individually in trying to find her. That would give us four chances to one. Correspondingly, the pantheress would most certainly come for any one of us whom she might see alone, although, according to the fishermen, she had not hesitated to attack a whole group of persons. This plan appeared to me to offer a much greater chance of success than the one proposed by Thangavelu, which was to go to Talainovu in the jeep and purchase two young bulls or buffaloes as bait. For these would then have to be driven on foot to the camp site and suitable spots selected before they were tied out. All this I knew would take considerable time and, as matters stood, there was far less chance of the panther attacking either of the baits than one of us.

Fortunately, Don had brought his .423 Mauser rifle along with his .12 bore shotgun, while I had my .405 and my .12 bore too. This made two rifles and two shotguns, enough to arm all four of us.

We decided to have an early lunch, after which Tiny, with my shotgun loaded with lethal shell, would walk downstream along the river bank for two hours or so, and then turn and come back. Merwan would do the same upstream, using Donald's gun. Don and I, armed with our rifles, would search the jungle separately and in different directions. Thangavelu would climb up a tree somewhere close by and await our return, while keeping an eye on the jeep and our camp kit which was lying scattered around. It was agreed that everyone should get back to camp by 5 p.m. at the latest.

We did this and, with parting admonitions to each other to keep a sharp lookout against surprise attack, scattered according to plan each hoping to be the lucky individual to come across the panther. I do not think any one of us quite realized till he was all alone that what he had set out to do, and was doing in fact, was to offer himself for the next four hours or more as a bait to a most dangerous wild animal that had all the advantages of ground and cover in its favour.

I had decided to go in the direction in which I had heard the sambar calling the previous night. Perhaps this led towards some cave and would afford a better chance of success than just roaming aimlessly in the jungle. A few minutes from the river I picked up a game-trail that led up the northeastern slope of the same hill down which the jeep had travelled from Talainovu. It was a well-defined track, used by sambar and other animals in coming to water at the river during the summer months, and recent marks of deer and bear revealed the presence of a fair amount of game, despite the comparative silence of the previous night.

The *path* wound diagonally uphill, skirting boulders and heavy cover at a safe distance, as game-trails made by the members of the deer family usually do, for fear of some carnivore lying in hiding behind a rock or bush. This was in my favour, although I knew that a panther was able to conceal itself behind cover of any sort. My thoughts were uneasy and after a while I became anxious about Don and our other two friends. I hoped they were being as careful as I was.

It was too late and too hot for the birds to be calling, and so I proceeded in uncomfortable silence, keeping a sharp lookout to right and left while studying every bit of cover in front of me before I drew abreast of it. The real danger lay from behind, as I knew, since panthers and nearly all tigers for that matter, even when they have made a practice of

THE MAN-HATER OF TALAINOVU

attacking human beings, never completely lose their fear of man and in most cases spring upon their victims from behind.

And so I halted frequently to look behind me, trying to catch the least movement of leaf or blade of grass that might betray the pantheress as she prepared to pounce. As was to be expected, there were a number of false alarms. My searching eyes detected a twig shaking suspiciously, or a blade of grass springing suddenly upright from where it had been held down by the weight of some hidden presence. Sometimes I heard a rustle, or the distinct crack of a dried twig, often behind me and many times in other directions. Then I froze, half raised the .405, and stared intently towards the sound, expecting at any moment to see the spotted form come hurtling down upon me. Nothing happened. The rustling or the snapping of the twig was not repeated, and the forest remained uncannily silent. Or the twig that shook did so again, or the blade of grass continued to wave in the breeze. Then tension died within me, the hair at the back of my neck relaxed, and I realized there was nothing to fear. Thus I proceeded for some distance till some other movement frightened me once more.

This sort of thing went on for some time, till I realized my nerves were playing havoc with me and that I was behaving like a greenhorn. As likely as not, the pantheress was miles away. As I walked along, thinking my own thoughts, fits of alertness alternated with periods of carelessness and indifference. Time passed uneventfully, and I began to feel things were not as bad as they had been painted by the poachers. No doubt, like all villagers, they had exaggerated the matter grossly.

I reached the shoulder of the hill and began to descend the other side into a lush valley of heavy bamboos. A faint rustle and swish of leaves, then the sharp crack of a frond betokened only one thing. An elephant!

I stopped and gazed at the spot whence the sound had come. Much depended upon whether it was a solitary animal or one of a herd. If solitary, I might expect trouble should I go too close. If I had stumbled upon a herd, it was almost certain that, upon discovering my presence, they would take themselves off. The game-trail I was following led directly towards the origin of the sound. If I now abandoned the trail to avoid the elephant, I knew I would not be able to go far, for very soon I would be foundering in thickets of bamboo and thorn, no place in which to meet an angry panther or an equally angry elephant. So I made up my mind to stick to the trail.

The breeze blew strongly from behind and there were no further sounds from among the bamboos in front. I waited awhile, but the silence continued. This indicated that the elephant had become aware of my presence, having scented me. Either he had moved away, or he was waiting for me to come closer.

No, had he moved away I would in all probability have heard him, for although these giant creatures can walk almost soundlessly, in that heavy undergrowth there would have been at least some faint sounds of his passage. I therefore concluded that he was waiting for me to approach. I delayed for another ten minutes, hoping the elephant would change his mind and avoid an encounter. He did not move. Perhaps he was thinking the same thing.

I should have waited longer, but I became impatient and decided to oust the beast. It was a wrong move, and one that nearly ended disastrously.

Thinking that a nonchalant approach on my part would frighten him off, I began to whistle loudly and advanced boldly along the game-trail. The result was immediate. The elephant charged. He screamed in the way of all elephants when attacking, partly to inflate their own courage and partly to strike terror into their victims, and came crashing through the bamboos straight towards me. The green undergrowth parted violently to reveal a monstrous head with gleaming tusks, a trunk coiled inwards between them, and ears laid tightly back against the skull.

I thought quickly. No rogue elephant had been proclaimed in this area. Therefore, to shoot this monster would mean endless trouble for me with the people of the Forest department. To run away would invite being chased and caught within a short distance. To try to stop him by wounding him, in the knee if possible, would be cruel and cause him endless suffering.

There was but one possibility. A very slight one, but I took it. Shouting loudly, I aimed the rifle over his head and fired a round into the air. If this did not stop him, I knew the next round would have to be at the elephant, if I intended to remain alive.

It worked! The giant animal braked hard by planting all four feet into the ground. There was a cloud of dust and fallen leaves as he slithered to a halt. Knowing his courage had failed him, I seized the advantage by running three or four steps forward and firing a second round into the air.

The huge beast turned about. The note of anger had died out of his scream when he trumpeted shrilly again, this time with a note of fear as he swayed in indecision and then bolted; the short tail which had been stuck out behind in the manner of all charging elephants was now between his hind legs like that of a whipped cur. The noise of his departure died away and I sat down disconsolately upon a nearby stone.

I was glad I had not been compelled to fire at the elephant, but I was disgusted at myself for not having exercised more patience by sitting it out rather than by advancing and so precipitating a charge. For my rifle shots, among those hills, had made a terrific racket. The hope I had entertained of the pantheress showing herself, or attacking me, was now gone. Only half-an-hour had passed since leaving camp. Would it be worth my while to carry on along the track I had been following for the remaining ninety minutes before turning back to the river as arranged?

A few moments' thought made me realize the futility of crying over spilt milk. So I stood up and continued along the trail. There was little danger from the pantheress for the next ten minutes or so. The noise of the rifle shots would have frightened her. The elephant, and any others like him, would now be far away. I made rapid progress through the bamboos, which eventually thinned out as the ground rose gradually higher from the basin of the Cauvery river. The vegetation changed slightly and I came upon a parkland of *babul, boram* and dwarf tamarind trees interspersed with areas of long grass, and here the friendly game-trail I had been following all the way from the big river gave out. Rather, it became lost among innumerable other *paths* that crisscrossed this parkland, which was obviously a favourite grazing ground for deer.

Little pellets of dung lay everywhere, the larger ones made by sambar and the smaller by spotted deer. To my right was quite a mound of tiny pellets underneath a fig tree, now laden with a rich red harvest fruit. Thousands of these figs had fallen to the ground, knocked down by monkeys and all manner of birds by day, and the huge fruit-bats, called 'flying fox' in India, by night. The maker of the large heap of tiny dung-pellets was a jungle-sheep, which we call 'kakar' or 'muntjac.'

These pretty animals, which reach the height of a small sheep and are coloured a uniform reddishbrown, are very gracefully shaped, the males having short, bifurcated horns. They love figs and other wild fruit. The stags, particularly, have the habit of coming all the way back to a chosen spot to pass their dung on alternate days. All hunters, human and animal, know this habit, and so all they have to do when they come across such a spot is to conceal themselves adequately and wait long enough for the return.

Carnivores are well versed in the habits and movements of the deer family and all the lesser animals that form their prey. They have to be, if they would eat. So this lovely parkland, filled as it was with deer, would be a very likely place in which to come across the pantheress and I redoubled my efforts to look for her.

I had gone some distance when, from a direction a little to the right and before me, I heard a series of bird-like calls. The cries grew louder as they approached rapidly. Wild dogs! A pack of them was hunting down a quarry and the chase was coming in my direction. I stepped quickly behind the sheltering trunk of a nearby tamarind tree.

The wild dog of the Indian forest is the cleverest of all hunters and the implacable foe of every living creature. Once a pack of these creatures scents or sees a deer and gives chase, its fate is sealed. They hunt it down mercilessly and intelligently. The main body of dogs run behind their quarry, giving voice to a hunting cry that resembles the high-pitched call of a bird more than anything else, while a few dogs gallop ahead at terrific speed and on both flanks of the quarry. These flankers then ambush the victim and worry it, if they are unable to bring it down themselves, till the main body catches up and completes the job. I have seen a sambar doe, worried by these flankers, cross a dry riverbed with her entrails trailing in the sand for yards behind her, both eyes bitten out, and dogs hanging by their teeth to her throat and flanks.

I heard the clashing sound of horns against wood and a splendid sambar stag appeared. Foam flecked his mouth and sprayed backwards to his neck and shoulders, and his eyes were wide with terror as he galloped in headlong flight. The next instant there was a terrific roar and a mighty striped form launched itself through the air and directly on to the sambar' back.

My earlier thoughts had proved correct. A tiger had been patrolling the parkland in search of a meal. He had heard the wild dogs approach and knew they were pursuing a quarry that was coming his way. Ordinarily, tigers avoid wild dogs and fear them for their reckless bravery, their intelligence and their numbers. Probably this tiger would have avoided them too but for the chance that the hunted animal and his pursuers happened to be coming in his direction. So before he quite realized what he should do about it, he took the decisive step.

For this same reason, the tiger had not discovered my own approach from behind him. His keener hearing had appraised him of the wild dog's hunting cries before I had heard them and he had been listening intently in that direction and had not caught the faint sounds I may have made.

The sambar's back bent to the sudden weight of the tiger and he let out a hoarse bellow of terror. Their tightly entangled bodies sank from view into the long grass. I heard the sharp crack of bone as the vertebral column was broken skilfully by the tiger, and the drumming of the stag's hooves upon the earth as the twitching muscles and nerves of his four legs continued to respond to the last message to flee. Upon this scene, the next instant, burst the pack of baying snarling wild dogs!

Recovering from their momentary surprise at seeing themselves forestalled, they quickly rallied. In a flash they surrounded the tiger and the body of the quarry they regarded as their own. I counted nine of them.

The bird-like hunting call that had been coming from the pack only a moment earlier changed abruptly to a series of long and plaintive notes. I had heard these cries on an earlier occasion, many years before, in the far-distant jungles of the Chamala Valley. There a pack of wild dogs had been chasing a tiger and this queer new cry was the same those dogs had made on that occasion. They were summoning reinforcements. Every wild dog within miles would hasten to their aid. It appeared to be an unwritten law of the species that no member dared disobey.

The tiger rose to his feet threateningly and I could see him clearly. His body turned slowly to enable him to see how many enemies beset him. His face, was contorted hideously as he snarled and roared with all the strength of his lungs, and his tail twitched from side to side spasmodically, a visible indication of nervous tension, rage, doubt and an unaccountable fear of these unruffled, implacable and cruelly clever foes.

The circle of dogs stood fast, legs firmly yet slightly outspread, each member of the pack now making that loud, shrill summons for help. The roars of the tiger and the yelping call of the nine wild dogs were pandemonium. The jungle echoed and re-echoed with the din.

The tiger realized that every second lost now counted in favour of his foes. In two bounds he charged the dog directly in his *path*. The dog skipped nimbly aside, while those behind leaped forward to attack from the rear. The tiger sensed this and whirled around, flaying wildly to right and left with his two forepaws. The dogs within reach of those mighty paws fell back helter-skelter, but one was too slow. The raking talons struck the dog's hindquarters, his body was thrown into the air with one leg almost torn off, and the dogs behind the tiger leaped forward to bite off chunks of flesh from his sides. Once more the tiger whirled around, once again his enemies scattered before him, while those at the back and on both sides raced forward to bite him where they could.

The tiger feinted and made a double-turn and the dogs from behind him that had rushed forward could not turn back. They met the full force of his powerful forelegs with their widely extended talons. Two quick blows and two more dogs were torn asunder. One of them tried to drag itself away, but its nearness to the tiger tempted him to make a false move that immediately offset the advantage he had just gained by his clever double-turn. He pounced upon the disembowelled wild dog and buried his fangs in its body.

The dogs from behind and both sides now fell upon him and covered his body, tearing out scraps of the living flesh. The tiger roared and roared again, but now there was a note of fear in each roar.

The huddle of tearing rending beasts disintegrated and the tiger had freed himself for the moment. There were now but six dogs around him and some of them were injured. But the tiger was bleeding profusely from the many wounds he had received. He gasped for breath. The dogs would not relax. From all sides they renewed the attack, yelping and snapping. The tiger roared again, but not nearly so loudly. The will to continue the fight was ebbing. He was definitely afraid.

Just then quite another sound could be heard above the pandemonium: the distant cries of answering wild dogs, not from one direction, but from several, all at once. Reinforcements.

The harassed tiger heard them too, and the fight went out of him. He turned tail and raced away with the six dogs, despite their wounds and exhaustion, after him.

Within a minute the reinforcements began to arrive. First three dogs, then another, and yet another. They halted a moment at the scene of battle and sniffed the blood-tainted grass and the three mangled dogs. This roused them to a fury and they growled and snarled. Then they raced in the wake of the fleeing tiger and his six pursuers.

Soon a larger pack of about a dozen dogs arrived on the scene. In a few seconds they had taken stock of the situation and followed the five that had preceded them. The fate of that tiger was sealed, for by now there were two dozen wild dogs on his trail. They would not relax their pursuit till they had caught him and torn him to shreds.

The sounds of the chase died away in the distance as I stepped from behind the tamarind tree to look at the three dead dogs and the scene of battle. The sambar stag that the tiger had slain lay untouched a few feet away. After disposing off the tiger, no doubt the surviving dogs would return and eat their fill.

Tiny had returned by the time I arrived and Merwan showed up soon after. Neither of them had seen or heard anything. It was quite late when Donald returned. He had met the tracks of a panther and not long after had passed a cave. Associating the two, Donald had thrown stones into the cave, expecting and hoping the panther would emerge. Instead, a sloth bear had dashed forth with two cubs riding on her back. She was greatly annoyed at being disturbed and Donald would have been compelled to shoot her in self-defence, had she seen him. Fortunately, this did not happen. The bear rushed blindly forward into the jungle, and that was the end of that. No panther could have shared a cave with a family of bears, and so Donald passed on.

Strangely enough, none of the party had heard the shots I had fired to frighten off the elephant and everyone was greatly interested in my account of the fight between the tiger and the wild dogs.

This time we all helped in gathering wood for the camp fire and arranged to take watch-turns of two hours, each. Then came an early dinner, followed by a smoke and a chat. Eventually the conversation began to die as, one by one, we became sleepy. It was only nine o'clock but time to turn in. We had chosen Thangavelu to be on watch for the first two hours. We did this deliberately, for later on he was bound to fall asleep anyhow. Merwan came next, followed by myself, Donald and Tiny. Merwan had tried hard to exchange turns with Tiny, but the big man was too clever for him.

As I fell asleep, a tiger began to roar somewhere over the hill, where I had been that day. I thought to myself that it must be the mate of the animal that the wild dogs had pursued and surely slain.

When Thangavelu called Merwan at eleven o'clock, he would not wake and the ensuing argument disturbed me. I told Thangavelu to throw cold water over him, but the former felt that such conduct by a servant might be misunderstood. So I had to get up and throw the water myself. Merwan sat up with a jerk and was very annoyed, but he took his revenge at 1 a.m., when the time came to wake me, for he did so with cold water. Merwan is like that!

He told me that he had heard a panther sawing a few minutes after midnight, apparently on the hill behind us and pretty far away. Then he told me something that was very important indeed. Only a few minutes before he woke me, a bird, which he thought must have been a jungle fowl, had clucked a noisy alarm and flapped away heavily. This had been quite close. Merwan remarked that he had almost forgotten to mention the incident; he thought it was a matter of no consequence anyhow!

I said nothing in reply as he covered himself up before falling asleep, but I knew the matter was of great consequence indeed. Why should a jungle fowl be so alarmed that it had cried out and left the secure place where it had sat to roost the evening before, to risk changing its perch and a flight in darkness? They don't do that unless some potential danger has passed very close. Perhaps it was a python searching for food. Perhaps a wildcat or a tree-civet. Perhaps even a panther.

The more I thought about it, the more I felt that here was the animal we were seeking, that it had returned to our camp with the deliberate intention of stalking and killing one or more of us. I arranged another log on the fire to make more light to see by. Then I changed my position so that I sat with my back to the nearest *muthee* tree, that grew a few feet from the water. This enabled me to face the jungle, with my companions a little before me and to the right, while I was safe from an attack from the rear. Then I settled down to listen and watch intently.

Nothing happened till after two o'clock. The gurgling sound of the river as it cascaded over the rocks prevented me from hearing the more subtle noises of the forest. A fish plopped loudly in the water, followed by a yet greater splash, perhaps a bigger fish, or even a crocodile in pursuit of the first fish. On the opposite bank of the river a night heron raised a wailing, plaintive cry, and a dark shadow caught my eye against the lighter hue of the star-studded sky: a giant horned-owl, a species confined to the forests and feeding on the smaller mammals, including rabbits.

Just then I heard a faint hissing, rasping sound. I could scarcely distinguish it because of the murmur of the rushing water. It stopped and then was repeated, quite close at hand, from near a clump of bushes a little beyond my sleeping companions, where the jungle grew thickest and was pitch-black. I had heard that sound before and recognized it at once.

I knew then that the pantheress was hiding in the thicket that was closest to the spot where Don and the others were sleeping, and that she was working up her courage for an attack. In a few seconds she would reach the point of springing upon them.

I could not see her. Only the blackness of the thicket. If I shone my torch on that blackness now, it might reveal the pantheress or it might not—according to whether or not she was sheltering behind some bush or shrub. Should the latter be the case, I knew full well she would disappear as soon as she saw the light. So I decided to wait a little longer.

But the pantheress decided to wait no more. She acted. Voicing the short, sharp roars made by her kind when they charge, she sprang clear of the thicket to land a few feet from the sleeping men. With the next bound she would be amongst them.

I was waiting for this and it was fortunate that I had the rifle to my shoulder with my thumb on the light switch.

The torch-beam cut through the darkness like a knife and reflected the blazing eyes of the pantheress. She hesitated a second, taken completely by surprise and dazzled by the light. I was about to press the trigger when there was a shattering explosion, followed quickly by a second shot.

'Beat you to it, dad!' yelled Don, as he sprang to his feet, having wakened and fired his two shots while still lying on the ground.

Then the other sleepers awoke, and their surprise was indeed comical. Thangavelu just yelled. Tiny sat bolt upright and remarked, half asleep, 'Mother dear!' But Merwan surpassed them; he rolled about as if he'd been shot himself.

Then they saw the dead pantheress, or almost dead, I should say. For she was gasping and twitching still, while life faded slowly from eyes that were held in my torch-beam. They died to a cold, watery blue and became still. Then I knew that the pantheress was dead.

We gathered around and examined her. A fine specimen of a female. Truly my heart had not been in that night's work and I regretted every part I played in hunting her from the time we heard her story. I consoled myself with the thought that what had to be done had been done, and I left it at that, but my congratulations to Don on his prowess were more heartfelt than he ever suspected.

Seven

# Sher Khan and the Bettamugalam Man-Eater*

MANY YEARS AGO A RETIRED BRITISH ADMINISTRATOR, POPULARLY known as the Collector in those days, had acquired for himself 300 acres of jungle land on the northern slopes of the Gutherayan range of hills in the district of Salem, where he built an incredible bungalow. He built it all of stone and to the pattern of a castle.

This man loved the jungle and he preserved it at a tremendous expense to himself by engaging an army of coolies to hack away the thorny undergrowth and the lantana plants which, in those years, were just beginning to envelop the forests of southern India.

---

* For map, see Chapter 1.

Since then the lantana has grown apace and now covers thousands of acres of Reserved Forest land. Various government departments, including the forest department, have tried and are trying in vain to eradicate this scourge. Spraying with a poisonous solution can obviously be done only on a very limited scale. A white bug has been found which multiplies in millions; it covers the lantana bushes, blackens the stem, branches, all leaves, and kills all the lantana in perhaps an acre or two of land. Then something happens to the bugs themselves: they die within a few days, from some poison absorbed from the lantana itself, which thus gains the ultimate victory.

Jungle fires rage periodically, particularly during the hot weather. The lantana is burnt to the ground, only to spring up again and flourish with the coming of the rains, fertilized by its own ashes.

Incidentally, the juice from a few freshlycrushed leaves of this plant, rubbed upon a scratch or an abrasion on the skin, will assist the wound to heal completely. It is as effective as tincture of iodine, with the added advantage that it does not irritate.

But to return to the British Collector and his 300 acres: he called his place Bettamugalam Estate, after the name given to the local sub-taluk area, and his stone house he called 'Jungly Castle.' Cleaned of the strangling lantana, the natural forest grew apace. The grass that flourished in the glades between the trees attracted bison and deer, which in their turn brought their natural foes, tigers, panthers, and the still more voracious wild dogs.

Conditions then began to change. The British Collector died and Bettamugalam Estate, with Jungly Castle, was bought by an Anglo-Indian who did not have the means to keep the place up to the standard of the former owner. Once more the lantana started to encroach upon the grassy glades, and as a consequence the bison and deer decreased in numbers. But the carnivores remained and they grew hungry.

Then the Anglo-Indian died in his turn, and no legal owner came forward. Jungly Castle fell into disrepair. Villagers came on moonlit nights in bullock carts and stole the cut granite blocks, pulling down the walls to get them. For these stones, especially when they could be obtained free, offered first-class material with which to construct the walls of their own huts.

The bison had by this time vanished, and the herds or deer had almost disappeared. The tigers, panthers and wild dogs that congregated to eat the deer followed them. Only the jungle fowl, spurfowl and peafowl remained to increase in numbers, for the heavy undergrowth of lantana gave ideal cover. Otherwise, the whole area assumed a forlorn appearance. Now and again an odd tiger or panther would pass that way, hoping but generally in vain, for a stray spotted deer or jungle-sheep to break his fast. He was generally very hungry but there was nothing to be got.

Now, in the village of Aiyur, a little over four miles away, lived a man of about twenty-five years, whose name was Gurappa. Gurappa had married very late in life for one of his caste and status, the usual age being around seventeen to eighteen years for a boy and thirteen to fourteen years for a girl. But Gurappa's father could not get his son married earlier, for they were a poor family, and the parents of every prospective bride turned down the marriage of their daughter to a mere yokel, the son moreover of such a poor father. But a girl was found at last. I was told that she was very deaf and had walked with a limp from birth. Very likely these impediments had caused her parents to agree to the marriage with Gurappa, who was so poor.

Now another problem presented itself. The bridegroom had no house. His father had sold the hut the family had lived in. Not even in India can a bridegroom bring his bride home on their wedding day to no house!

So Gurappa decided to build one in a hurry. True, he had no money, but fortunately a good number of stones still remained of Jungly Castle, although the best and largest of them had already been pilfered.

Scorning to wait for a moonlight night, the would-be bridegroom begged the village headman to lend him his cart. With a long-term policy in view of extracting free labour from Gurappa in return when the harvest came around, the village *patel* consented.

It is safer if there are no witnesses when one sets out to commit a felony. Gurappa knew this, so he set out alone after his midday meal, intending to collect the stones and be back by sundown. Working single-handed is invariably a back-breaking job, as he soon found out. To lever the stones out of the crumbling walls with the short crowbar he had brought for the purpose, and to carry each stone and load it on to the bullock cart, took much energy and time, calling for a fair number of resting periods. The sun had dipped behind the hills to the west and the nightjars were already calling from the sandy track along which the cart had come, when Gurappa decided to call it a day and bring away the first load. Tomorrow he would borrow somebody else's cart and fetch a second load.

So he beat the bony bulls with a piece of broken bamboo. They started to walk dejectedly homewards, for this strange man, who was not their owner, had not bothered to feed or water them all day. Gurappa followed behind leisurely, his mind at peace for the moment. Up to now there had been nothing to disturb the bridegroom. No sound had he heard to cause him any uneasiness.

The waiting tiger that had seen him must have been very hungry indeed, if not on the verge of starvation, to act as he did. Perhaps he was sick or wounded and had been disabled from hunting his natural prey. Certainly he was not a regular man-eater, for nobody had been killed in this area by a tiger for quite a time.

The bulls hauled the cart past a *babul* tree, the lower half of which was smothered in lantana. The tiger must have been hiding within that lantana, for that was where he sprang from. When I came to the spot with a Forest Range Officer, several guards, the sub-inspector of police and a constable, just twenty-four hours later, some of the stems still bent down by the weight of the animal as he had lain in wait for Gurappa.

Probably Gurappa had never known what happened till he found himself being carried away by a tiger. Then he must have struggled and screamed loudly, for the bulls took fright and bolted, hauling the heavily laden cart behind them. They did not get very far, for there was a curve in the track ahead, where it skirted some lower ground. In turning, the cart went off the track and down the *khud*, taking the bullocks with it.

Miracles often happen, even with bullock carts. While the vehicle was considerably damaged, there was no injury to either bull. Freed from the restraining yoke, they found their way back to Aiyur, terrified but unhurt, long after the sun had set.

Adjacent to the village of Aiyur is a Forestry department school where officials already working in the department, along with students who have passed the required examination, undergo practical instruction in field forestry. A Range Officer is stationed at the school, along with two or three senior foresters and a number of guards and watchers, who look after the nurseries and departmental buildings.

The headman, alarmed by the fact that his bulls had returned without the cart, assumed that an elephant had attacked and smashed it, and had accounted for Gurappa in the process. With half the village trailing behind him, he sought the cooperation of the Range Officer for permission to send out a search party into the jungle. Permission was readily given, but there was a marked lack of enthusiasm among the villagers to volunteer. Finally four of five persons were persuaded to offer their services, but by this time darkness had already fallen. Even in broad daylight a wild elephant that has killed a man is something no villager will face. In pitch-darkness an encounter of this nature is not to be thought of. So the search was postponed till the next morning. The headman must have spent a sleepless night thinking of his cart, while cursing Gurappa for being the cause of his misfortune.

Early next day the search party set out. It did not take them long to find the cart at the bottom of the *khud*, but of Gurappa there was no sign. The tracks of the cart wheels and the bullocks, made in the soft sand, showed that the animals had taken the corner at a gallop; hence the accident. What had caused them to do that?

Still suspecting that an elephant was to blame, the villagers backtracked and soon found the real cause. The whole story was written in the dry, soft sand of the track. There was blood, the pug-marks of a tiger, and a distinct drag-mark, left by some part of the victim that had trailed along the ground. Fear fell upon them then. It was dangerous enough to encounter a possible rogue elephant. But they were many in number and an elephant might be expected to hesitate before attacking such a large party. Not a man-eating tiger. He might reappear at any moment, from anywhere, with disastrous results.

241

Without further delay the group returned to Aiyur. Gurappa was dead beyond doubt. What could be gained by searching for him?

By chance, I happened to be camping at Sivanipalli that day. This little village lies about five miles to the west of Aiyur. It is a favourite spot of mine, and being just over fifty miles from Bangalore, I often go there at weekends. Incidentally, it marks the scene of the shooting of the only black panther that has ever been known in this region, the details of which adventure have been related in another story.*

The forest guard of Sivanipalli, who had gone to Aiyur to meet his superior, the Range Officer, returned at about noon to tell me what had happened to the unfortunate bridegroom, Gurappa. Carrying a torch and my sweater, with a pocketful of dry biscuits and a flask of tea for dinner in case I was delayed, I set out for Aiyur within fifteen minutes of hearing the news.

A report had already been made to the Forest department headquarters at Denkanikota, a small town eight miles to the north, by the Range Officer, so that shortly after my arrival the sub-inspector of police turned up on his motorcycle, with a constable on the pillion seat. Thus it came about that the two police officials, the Range Officer, a retinue of guards and myself came to the lantana thicket at the foot of the *babul* tree from which the tiger had sprung, almost twenty-four hours earlier, upon the unfortunate Gurappa as he had walked behind the bullock cart that was laden with stolen stones. The prologue of this story, as I have told it, had already been pieced together by me from scraps of conversation with the two officers and their assistants. The sub-inspector of police, who was a Brahman and a fatalist, remarked more than once

---

* See *The Black Panther of Sivanipalli*.

on the connection in the web spun by fate between the old British Collector, long dead and gone, who had owned Bettamugalam Estate and Jungly Castle, and the modern bridegroom, Gurappa, who had no house at all and had been striving to build one. Not quite seeing the point, I quipped that there might also be something in the thought that fate may have taken a dim view of the general situation and decided to punish someone who was in the act of robbing the dead. I meant this as a joke, but was surprised at the manner in which my suggestion caught on. The superstitious Brahman and the somewhat nervous Range Officer accepted my point completely.

Nobody was keen on looking for what was left of Gurappa.

As I have said, I found the spot in the lantana where the tiger had been hiding before it sprang upon its victim. The drag-mark was still faintly visible, although much of it had been obliterated during the night by the action of the wind upon the sand, grass and leaves, and the movements of ants and other insects.

However, we were able to follow for a hundred yards or so when, quite unexpectedly, our search ended. An 'aeroplane' tree was growing here—known thus by the local Tamil inhabitants because it sheds its seeds by a wonderfully clever and novel device. Each seed is situated at the junction of two three-inch-long leaf-like blades exactly resembling in miniature the twin propellers of an aeroplane. These blades fall from the parent tree and are spun and carried by the breeze, along with the seed, to incredible distances before they tumble to the ground. In the shade of this tree the grass was still green, and protruding from this grass, as if beckoning to us, was a human arm and hand, the five fingers spread and pointing upwards.

We had found Gurappa at last—what was left of him!

Peculiarly enough, the upper parts of his body, from breast to head, had been untouched. While one arm stretched upwards, the fingers of the other hand were stuffed into the mouth as if to stifle a scream. The eye sockets were empty, because the black ants had already eaten away the eyeballs. Then red ants had come, and these now swarmed over the face and skin. In many places the black outer skin had been devoured, exposing patches of white and red flesh, now rotting underneath. The reason why hyaenas and jackals had up to now not touched these toothsome portions was simple to guess. Red ants are notorious for their aggressive nature and painful stings.

But there was hardly anything left of Gurappa's body below his chest. The tiger had eaten his fill, while the scavengers of the night had removed the rest.

The foliage of the 'aeroplane' tree had hidden from the vultures what the tiger and the others had left, for had these birds arrived before us, nothing at all would have remained.

The stench of death and putrefaction hung heavily in the still evening air. Flies squatted in myriads on the stems of the surrounding grass, prevented from settling on the rotting flesh by the army of red ants that had already driven away their cousins. A terrific battle appeared to have been waged between the two species, as large numbers of dead, of both varieties, strewed the ground for a yard around Gurappa's head and arms. Now and again a sorely-wounded member of one of the opposing armies tried to drag itself away.

The tiger would certainly not return to eat the little that remained. Why he had left it in the first place was unaccountable; but he would anyway give the red ants a wide berth.

The sub-inspector ordered his underling to arrange for the removal of the remains. Then he wrote an unnecessarily verbose statement which I was asked to sign as a witness. It was getting dark when we returned to the Forest Rest House at Aiyur. The Range Officer offered me accommodation at his bungalow for the night, but the thought of the dry biscuits in my pocket made me decide to return to my camp at Sivanipalli and the corned meat that awaited me there. I had my torch, and after all the tiger might not be a confirmed man-eater.

So I started out to the dismay of the two officers, who shouted a warning behind me that I might never reach Sivanipalli. The path wound downhill mostly, between lantana, scrub and scattered *babul* saplings till, as a lower level was reached, the trees became loftier and clumps of heavy bamboo grew in among them. The darkness became intense, through which the beam from my torch cut only a narrow pencil of light.

Suddenly a feeling of great uneasiness came over me—rather, a feeling of mortal fear. Why, I could not imagine. I had heard no sound, nor had I caught any audible cries of alarm from the deer and other creatures in the jungle to warn me of danger. Complete silence reigned on every side. There was only the soft crunch of my own rubber-soled boots on the ground, and the occasional crack of a twig or crackle of a leaf as I trod upon it.

I halted abruptly and spun around, fully expecting to see the tiger stalking me from behind. But there was nothing to be seen, not even the glimmer of a firefly. There was nothing to be heard; not even the chirping of a friendly cricket.

Then I knew why I was so afraid: it was the idea of absolute loneliness. There was no living creature nearby to witness what happened to me. Nothing, and nobody to help. And, although I could not see him in the gloom, or hear him, even in that absolute silence, I was as certain of the presence of the tiger there as I was of my own.

I have found that at times of great peril in the jungle, the human reflexes act in one of two ways. The trumpeting scream of a charging rogue elephant, or the guttural roar of an attacking tiger or panther, sometimes galvanizes the victim into precipitate flight, or else he is so paralysed by fear that he is rooted to the spot and quite incapable of movement. It is rare, indeed, that the victim can think at all, much less think clearly, of what he should, or rather could, do in the circumstance. There is no time for thinking.

But in this case there was no screaming elephant before me, nor a roaring tiger for that matter. Only silence, and the certain knowledge that the man-eater was there. And the reflex that came to me was to run, and to run fast, as fast as I could, away from that dreadful spot. I had the greatest difficulty in restraining myself, for I knew that if I started to run it would be just what the tiger would like me to do. For then he would attack. All tigers, including man-eaters, know that every other creature is afraid of them. They are accustomed to striking terror into the hearts and minds of their prey, and with that knowledge comes the greater confidence that enables them to hunt so successfully.

I knew at that moment that the only thing that could save me from the tiger would be to act otherwise. He was lurking somewhere, watching and waiting for me. Perhaps he was behind, perhaps ahead, or may be to one side or the other, waiting and watching for an opportunity to spring upon me. He would have done so long before had it not been for my torch and the bright beam of light that was cutting through the darkness. This had worried him. If I wanted him to attack, all I had to do was extinguish the torch and start running. Then he would come.

I thought quickly. And I kept on walking at a measured pace, flashing the torch behind me, to both sides and then in front. The *path* was narrow, not more than six feet wide at the most.

The track turned a corner and ahead of me the light revealed a rock, standing to the left and about a hundred yards away. It was a sloping rock and appeared to be about six to eight feet high. I felt that I could run up and on to it without difficulty, provided I had a sufficiently long start. For I had had an idea. Here was a suitable place at which to try to tempt the man-eater to show himself.

As I turned the idea over in my mind, I continued to walk forward. Those hundred yards were far too long to risk a show-down. The speed of a charging tiger is something fantastic and has to be seen to be believed. But when the rock was fifty yards away, I decided to take the chance.

Making certain my rifle was cocked, and fixing the location of the rock clearly in my mind, I suddenly extinguished the torch and ran as fast and as hard as I could.

The darkness, when the torch went out, was intense. I could not see a thing. That was why I had taken care to face the rock and fix its location before putting out the torch and starting to run.

It took quite a few seconds for the tiger to gather his wits and realize that his victim had actually done what he had been waiting for. As I ran, I was just beginning to think that perhaps there was no tiger at all and that my nerves had made a fool of me, when there was a shattering roar from behind and the man-eater launched his attack. I heard that roar, but I could run no faster anyway.

I was only a few feet ahead of the tiger when I reached the rock and ran up the slope. Then I whirled around, raised the rifle to my shoulder and pressed the torch-switch with my left thumb all simultaneously. The man-eater had reached the base of the rock and was crouched for the spring that would carry him to the top when the rifle went off, almost at point-blank range. With the crash of the explosion he somersaulted backwards while I worked the underlever of the .405 to place the second round in the breach. Then I pressed the trigger.

Nothing happened.

A moment later, with a loud snarl the tiger leaped to its left and disappeared into the long grass that grew there. Working the underlever again, I ejected the cartridge that had misfired and fired the next round at the spot where the tiger had just vanished.

I had been too frightened when I fired the first shot, but I distinctly remember hearing the echo of the second one reverberating against the slopes of Gulhatti hill, which I could not see in the darkness but which is within a mile of the rock I stood upon.

The growling had ceased. Had my second bullet found its mark? Had the tiger collapsed from the effect of my first shot? Perhaps both had taken effect. Or had I missed entirely? Worse still, perhaps I had only wounded the brute.

With the torch still shining upon the bushes where the tiger had vanished, I sat down on the rock to collect my scattered wits and control my breathing. Mostly, to try to think. Only then did I realize how narrow an escape I had had. Had the tiger been closer behind me, or to either side or ahead, he might have cut me off before I could reach the rock. Moreover, had the cartridge that had misfired been one ahead in the magazine of my rifle, it would have failed at the crucial moment and the man-eater would certainly have completed his spring.

When I grew a little calmer I began to wonder what had happened to the man-eater. It seemed inconceivable that I could have missed him at point-blank range. Then I remembered I had been running fast and had rushed up the rock at the last moment. Fear, excitement and exertion had made me breathe hard and this had evidently caused me to press the trigger unconsciously, causing me to miss entirely or perhaps just wound the beast.

It was impossible for me to follow up in that darkness. If I had missed him, he would have been scared away entirely. If he was wounded, it was very unlikely that the man-eater would resume the pursuit if I continued on my way to Sivanipalli. So after a few moments I decided to do that and return the next morning to take up the trail.

I reached Sivanipalli without event and lay down in my little tent, still thinking of what should be done the next day. Then the dried biscuits in my pocket reminded me that I was hungry and I got up to make tea and open the tin of meat that had been the cause of the whole incident.

There are no poojarees or aboriginal trackers at Sivanipalli, but there was Sher Khan, a character who had led a colourful existence and must at the time have been about forty years old. He was a Muslim, a poacher of game, a timber thief, and the suspected author of several dacoities on a minor scale, when bullock carts carrying sacks of grain to the villages of Denkanikota and Anchetty had been held up and robbed at night. The method of dacoity had been as simple as it had been effective.

The carts used to travel by night in order to save time. Generally, half-a-dozen of them would move, one behind the other for company and for protection from wild animals, particularly elephants, and of course the evil spirits that are said to be everywhere. Highway robbery, up to that time, was unheard of.

The first case reported to the police was by five cartmen who had been behind one another from Anchetty to

Denkanikota. They were on the ghat road when it had happened, nine miles from their destination. The time was 1 a.m. and the bulls strained at their loads on the steep gradient. Each driver sat in his cart, more than half asleep. Suddenly a voice hailed them from the darkness of the roadside. It was harsh and loud. They saw no man, but the voice said that a gang of dacoits was hiding by the wayside. They had loaded muskets and all would be well if they followed orders. Then followed the orders. They were very simple.

'Get down from your carts, all five of you, and walk back for a full mile. When you reach the tenth milestone, you may sit dawn. Light a fire and wait there till morning. When daylight comes, you may return to your carts. Remember, some of us will follow and keep a watch over you till dawn. If any one of you dares to disobey, he will be shot without further warning. Remember also that we promise we shall not harm your carts or animals. You are poor men and we do not want to hurt you. It is the rich men's belongings, carried in your carts, that we want.'

The cartmen obeyed. They were thankful they had been spared. Early next morning they found their carts, standing where they had been left. Some of the foodstuff had been stolen, but not all if it. Only the more valuable items. The gang could not have been a very large one after all, or they would have taken everything.

This happened two or three times more, on other roads and tracks leading to Denkanikota and Anchetty, before the carts stopped moving at night and police patrols took their place. Several suspects were rounded up, including Sher Khan. They were beaten and locked up. But all of them always affirmed complete innocence and all of them had alibis.

That was how I first met Sher Khan. He was returning to Sivanipalli after one such beating and complained aloud of the injustice that was rampant in this world. But there was a mischievous twinkle of insincerity in his eye as he spoke.

As I said, he was a Muslim, and the literal translation of his name is 'Chief among Tigers'. He was a ruffian, but a very likeable one, and that is how he became my friend. I would never fail, when at Sivanipalli, to visit his little house and drink tea with him, and he would never fail to return my call.

So I went to Sher Khan early in the morning after my adventure, and asked him to assist me. For I was confident that I had not missed the tiger when I had fired at point-blank range. I knew I must have hit it. That meant following up a wounded tiger in the jungle, and to do that there must be two persons. Following a blood trail through bushes, over leaves and on hard and stony ground requires concentration of eyesight and mind. One must look here, there and everywhere, for a speck of blood or a mere smear of the underside of a leaf, or against a stem or rock. While you are engaged in so looking, the wounded tiger might be just ahead, waiting for you, or he may be lying to the right or the left, concealed behind a tuft of grass, a clump of bamboo, a tree-trunk or a termite-hill, waiting till you come within springing distance. There is a third possibility, and that is he may be stalking you from behind even while you are looking for him. But you are blissfully unaware of his presence, because your attention is concentrated on the ground, following his trail. On the other hand, if you try to keep an effective lookout for the wounded beast, you will soon find you have lost the trail. You just cannot do both jobs effectively, and so a second person is essential. One of you concentrates on following the tiger's bloodspoor and tracks, while the other keeps a sharp lookout ahead, to the right, left and also behind. In the hands of this second person lies not only his own life, but the life of his companion.

Sher Khan volunteered to help without hesitation, but insisted that I drink the customary cup of tea with him before we set out. A clap of his hands and one of his four wives responded. He told her to make: 'Attcha-cha-first class!' for the *sahib*.

Being a Muslim, he was allowed to have four legal wives—and he had them. Most of us find it a problem to manage one, but he managed all four with ease! And this is how he did it.

Sher Khan showed no preference towards any one of his four spouses—either to the youngest or the most recent or the prettiest. They were all kept strictly *gosha*—that is to say, they were compelled to cover their faces with a *bourkha* when they went out in public. No man was allowed to look upon them. I, as a very particular friend, had the privilege of seeing their faces, and even of speaking to them—but very sparingly, mind you—when I visited his house.

Sher Khan made it a practice to divide the household duties among his four wives on a weekly-roster basis. For a week one of them would be responsible for the cooking of all the food, with a second to assist her; the third would be responsible for washing all the utensils; the fourth for the household work such as sweeping, mending, washing of clothes, etc. The following week, the roster would change, and so on week by week thereby dividing all the work very equitably among all four. Sher Khan himself would not lift a finger to do any household work. He did the marketing—if his rather nefarious activities could be so described—and brought home the earning, or the money, whichever you my prefer to call it. The wife who did the hardest work for that particular week, namely the cook, he would sleep with two days in the week, the remaining three women one day each. Fridays and Sundays were 'off days' from that sort of thing. 'Days of rest' as he called them.

They were a poor family, but disciplined, happy and contented. The women never quarrelled with him and hardly ever among themselves. For if they did, a beating would be administered; fairly, equitably and impartially, each recalcitrant wife receiving an equal number of blows or cuffs according to the nature of the offence. And in spite of the often undeniably pressing demands made upon him, he had no children.

As soon as we had drunk our tea we were off. Sher Khan announced that he had no gun and brought a rusty sword with him instead. He remarked that it had belonged to his father, and to his father's father's father's father, who was a soldier serving under the great Tipu Sultan, the tiger of Mysore. The mathematics involved in the problem of checking whether this man's great-great-grandfather could have lived in Tipu's lifetime are rather too involved for me. In the meanwhile, we had walked out of earshot of all his wives and I raised an impersonal question, addressed perhaps to the air: 'A voice comes out of the darkness and threatens to shoot many cartmen. Yet there is no gun. How can that be, Sher Khan?'

The silence for a moment is complete. Then he replied. 'You may call me a liar if you wish, *sahib*. But that is exactly what happened. There was no gun at that time, nor any other. I never possessed one and still don't have a gun. And the gang consisted of myself and three of the wives, *sahib*. The fourth is too old. But she had the brains, and it was all her idea.'

And, I believed him.

We were nearly at our destination. There stood the sloping rock from which I had fired at the man-eater the previous night. This time it was to my right. We approached in silence and looked at the ground. No blood was to be seen and the earth was too dry and hard for tracks. Without speaking, I pointed to the bushes bordering the *path* where the tiger disappeared from view.

I took the lead for the moment, with my Muslim friend directly behind. In spite of the prevailing dryness all around, it was evident that a heavy body had recently passed through. A couple of broken stems hung loosely, still joined to their parent-branch by the outer skins. A yard or two further and we saw it almost simultaneously: blood!

There was a splash of bright red on the carpet of dry, brown leaves that covered the ground. I touched it with my forefinger and rubbed it against my thumb. It was thick and coagulated, and by that I knew that my bullet of the night before had inflicted more than a mere surface wound. It had penetrated deeply.

We changed places now, and I put Sher Khan ahead of me. He would concentrate all his attention on following the blood trail, while I would cover him and myself in all four directions.

The Muslim was no born tracker, but what he lacked in ability as an aborigine he made up for in intelligence. He fussed and fumbled around, taking far more time than would a member of any of the jungle tribes in following such a trail, but he found one blood spot after another. The tiger had bled far more freely now. The exertions caused by his wounds had no doubt opened the wound. Splashes and pools of blood lay all along the trail, making it easy to follow.

I caught sight of a slight movement ahead and lightly touched Sher Khan with my hand. He halted at the prearranged signal and froze. With rifle to shoulder, I watched the spot from whence the movement came. I also watched on both sides and even glanced behind us. For wounded tigers are notoriously clever in lying in ambush or in creeping upon their enemies from behind.

The movement came again. A small branch swayed ominously a few feet ahead of us. I prepared for the attack.

Stretching out my hand, I gripped Sher Khan by the shoulder and pulled him unceremoniously behind me.

The branch swayed again. I stared at it for a minute. And then I relaxed. A false alarm. I noticed the leaves on the swaying branch were all upside down. That is because it had been broken by an elephant and was hanging suspended to the place from which it was broken by the stems of some creepers that were strong enough to bear its weight.

There must be no talking whatever in a situation like the present, so I reached backwards, gripped Sher Khan, and once again placed him in the lead. Then I nodded my head as a signal for him to press on. We proceeded slowly and passed the suspended branch.

Under a bush we noticed that the dried grass had been dyed deeply with blood. It seemed to be all over the place, on the leaves and stems of the bush as well. The tiger must have lain down here. Perhaps he rolled on the ground. Perhaps he covered his injured face with his paws and got them all covered with gore too. That would account for the blood, spread so widely under the bush before us.

I touched Sher Khan again to halt him, and we listened for a full five minutes. But we heard not a sound. As carefully and silently as we were moving the two of us would necessarily have made some noise in the undergrowth over that dry terrain. If the tiger was nearby, he must surely have heard us. Then he would either growl in warning, attack, or slink away silently. But nothing of the kind happened.

The blood trail now unexpectedly veered to the left and we knew that the tiger was making for a small stream that skirted the foothills. The wound must have been taking effect, and thirst had driven him there for water. At that time of the year the stream was dry except for a few isolated pools here and there. The tiger was making for one of these pools and the chances were that when he reached it he would lie up in the vicinity till he recovered from his wound or died of it, a lingering, starving, horrible death.

I hate wounding an animal and spare no pains, when I have done so, to follow it up and put it out of its misery. From the amount and nature of the blood lost by the tiger it looked as if my bullet had inflicted a severe wound from which there was little chance of recovery. Once more I thought of the dreadful lingering death that was in store for this animal unless I succeeded in finding it.

I stopped Sher Khan and we conferred in whispers for a few minutes. I knew of a pool on the riverbed which I judged to be at least two miles away, but Sher Khan said there was a closer one, smaller but which held water throughout the year, higher up the stream and less than a mile from where we now stood. So we continued to follow the blood trail, and as the Muslim predicted, after a short distance it veered to the left and made for the smaller pool, now directly ahead.

The ground sloped as we approached the streambed and I was made aware of its nearness by the repeated cries of jungle fowl that sheltered in the thick belt of trees and undergrowth that lined both banks, sustained in summertime by the water that was hidden from sight but still flowed beneath the dry sand. In a few minutes the short dry grass, withered by the sun, was replaced by long green stems, the heat and sight of the sun was shut out by a canopy of trees, and I knew we had reached the rivulet.

The blood trail went straight ahead; we were in sight of the dry sands of the streambed, stretching to right and left. I can imagine the agony of the wounded beast that came here last night or in the early hours of this morning in search of water to allay its burning thirst, only to be confronted by this waterless stretch.

But Sher Khan whispered that the pool was just around the corner to our left, now a stone's throw away, and unerringly the trail led in that direction. Once again I changed places with my friend and took the lead. Tracking was unnecessary now, as clearly the wounded tiger was making for the pool and I felt we would find it there. We turned a corner but I could see no pool. I stopped in silent perplexity, when Sher Khan came up from behind to point to an outcrop of flat rock which could just be seen above the sand of the stream and within a few feet of the further bank.

A plover rose into the air from the rock, crying 'Did-you-do-it! Did-you-do-it! Did-you-do-it!', and I knew that water lay hidden from my view in a hollow of that rock. The stream had narrowed there and both banks had come very close to each other. The undergrowth was dense, and the forest loomed menacingly around and above us from the ground that dipped down to the bed of the rivulet.

We halted again. There was silence and no indication of the tiger's presence. I looked down and could see no blood trail. Evidently it did not approach across the sandy bed, but kept to the cover of the undergrowth bordering the banks.

Forward we went once more. We were there at last, and what a sad story revealed itself in the water of the tiny pool and the sloping rock that led down to it! For the water was red with blood, and the rock was sticky with it, where the tiger had evidently lain in agony with his head in the water to assuage his thirst and to lessen the pain of his wound. His pug-marks were visible on the rock in several places, steeped in his own blood. Finally he had gone to the shelter of the bank and I knew that was where I would find him; laying in the cool of the undergrowth like all stricken animals, he would await his end with patience.

Then I remembered that this animal had been responsible for killing a human being, as far as could be made out for no apparent reason. If not brought to book, he would no doubt in time have became a confirmed man-eater. Motioning to Sher Khan to stay where he was, I advanced to meet him and finish him off.

I heard a slight sound behind me and looked around. Sher Khan was following. Perhaps he wanted to be present to witness the last scene in this drama. Perhaps he was just nervous at being left alone. We advanced into the dense undergrowth beneath the canopy of trees and were lost to sight.

The silence that had reigned all this while was then broken by a shattering roar that seemed to come from the very ground at my feet, and things began to happen very fast. Momentarily the undergrowth was agitated violently and then a mighty form launched itself past, and almost over me, on to Sher Khan who was not two feet behind.

The Muslim yelled and swiped wildly his rusty sword. The blunt edge met the bulk of the springing tiger and the impetus of both objects caused the blade to bite into the flank of the animal. Sher Khan went down, still screaming, and the tiger fell on top him.

Fortunately, Sher Khan had the presence of mind to cover his head and face with his two arms as the tiger sought to bite him. Leaning forward, I placed the rifle behind its neck, ensuring the bullet would not endanger my friend, and pressed the trigger.

I fired once again while Sher Khan scrambled to his feet and leaped out of range of the dying creature's claws. Then the drama was over.

Strangely enough, my friend was practically unhurt except for a few scratches, and the reason was that my bullet of the night before had gone into his upper palate and come out above his nose. The whole frontal or nasal bone hung loosely by the flesh, a truly ghastly wound from which the poor beast could never have recovered.

It was fortunate that the blow my friend aimed at the tiger with his ancestor's rusty sword had met its mark for I was directly in line with it. Had he missed, Tipu, the Tiger of Mysore and his henchman of long ago, Sher Khan's ancestor, would have claimed one more victim! I would have been decapitated by the force of that blow.

Sher Khan laughed afterwards when I told him this. He said I had my own revenge when my bullet, fired into the tiger's neck, had passed but a few inches above his head. He asked me if he might have the skin of the animal as a memento of our encounter and I gladly gave it to him. For, despite his many faults and his rascality, Sher Khan is a brave man and a most likeable fellow. Above all, I admire the way in which he manages his four wives. Long may they be spared to him, and he to them.

We sat by the camp fire before I left him and swapped yarns. He told me some of his adventures while I smoked my pipe and listened. Beyond the leaves all was lost in the darkness of the jungle night. Now and again a burst of sparks soared skywards as one of us threw a fresh log on to the fire to keep it brightly burning.

From behind his hut came suddenly the jungle chorus of the jackal pack: 'Oooo-ooo-oooh; Ooo-where? Ooo-where? Here! Here! Heere! Hee-yeah! Heeee-yeah! Yah! Yah! Yah!'

After that there was an abrupt hush. A heavy, all-pervading silence. You can hear it, you feel it, you know it. It is the silence that heralds the unexpected. As complete as if a switch had been turned.

Then, far away across the hill the second came rolling down to us, permeating the jungle and riding across the tops of the trees in the valley below.

'Oo-o-o-n-o-o-n! A-oongh - gah! A-oongh - gah! Oo—ugh! Oo - Ugh!'

A tiger roaring.